With his mouth against hers, he whispered, 'You want me. Say it.'

'Yes,' she breathed, trembling and breathless, sliding her arms round his neck to draw him closer, all her senses becoming limited. 'I want you. Though I may be damned tomorrow, I do not want you to leave me tonight.'

Helen Dickson was born and still lives in South Yorkshire, with her husband, on a busy arable farm where she combines writing with keeping a chaotic farmhouse. An incurable romantic, she writes for pleasure, owing much of her inspiration to the beauty of the surrounding countryside. She enjoys reading and music. History has always captivated her, and she likes travel and visiting ancient buildings.

Recent novels by the same author:

JEWEL OF THE NIGHT
HIGHWAYMAN HUSBAND
THE PIRATE'S DAUGHTER
BELHAVEN BRIDE
THE EARL AND THE PICKPOCKET
HIS REBEL BRIDE
THE DEFIANT DEBUTANTE
ROGUE'S WIDOW, GENTLEMAN'S WIFE

TRAITOR
OR TEMPTRESS

Helen Dickson

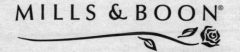

First published in Great Britain 2007
Harlequin Mills & Boon Limited,
Eton House, 18-24 Paradise Road, Richmond, Surrey TW9 1SR

© Helen Dickson 2007

ISBN-13: 978 0 263 85175 5
ISBN-10:   0 263 85175 3

Set in Times Roman 10½ on 12¼ pt.
04-0507-93964

Printed and bound in Spain
by Litografia Rosés S.A., Barcelona

TRAITOR
OR TEMPTRESS

Prologue

Far up in a green glen to the north-west of Loch Lomond the mighty solid limestone rocks rise perpendicular and saw toothed on either side of the burn that tumbles with great velocity to the loch below, throwing foam and spray high into the air. Hidden by a rocky shelf is a low and narrow opening giving access to a small cave, a cave the natives of the area call the giant's cave. Many centuries ago, so legend has it, a voracious giant had dwelt in the dark chamber, where he could guard the entrance to the glen through which marauding bands of Fingalians would come from the north to rob and burn the villages of Kinlochalen and Drumgow, along the north and south banks of Loch Alen.

It is said that an old woman who lived in Kinlochalen long ago and had the reputation of a witch, under constant threat of raids from the wild northern highlanders, had used all her powers of sorcery to install the giant in the cave. The creature would roar and breathe forth wrath at thieves who came to enrich themselves at the expense of the people of the villages, and, too afraid to confront and defy this dreadful giant, they would tremble and go home again.

The giant was never seen, but the fear of him lay on all the country round about. It was said that on the night the old witch died, a mighty wind had risen and blown the giant off the rock, toppling him into the burn below, and the rushing water had carried him off to the deeper waters of the loch. But his spirit still resided in the glen.

It was no more than was expected for highland clans to fight among themselves and steal each other's cattle and sheep, and there was no giant to deter the hundred or so raiders who came with stealth under cover of darkness on a night in the autumn of 1691, to plunder the sweet fertile lands around the loch. But the people of Kinlochalen and Drumgow had been warned and took the initiative, and were prepared to hit the hostile raiders before they themselves were set upon.

Looking mighty fearsome and swinging their claymore swords and yelling their battle slogans, they chased the raiders back up the glen to the bleak, flat moor above, a no man's land, where unfriendly desolation had been successfully fashioned by Mother Nature. The encounter, fought between men gigantic of mould and mighty of strength amidst labyrinths of peat bogs and stagnant pools and squelching morasses, was brief yet bloody, and when the men of Kinlochalen and Drumgow had slain those who had stayed to fight, they took off over the moor in pursuit of those who ran.

On the south side of Loch Alen, which was five miles long and stretched from east to west, stood Drumgow Castle, jutting out into the loch with all the assurance of long association. This sixteenth-century tower house and its entire demesne belonged to the Laird of Drumgow, Edgar McBryde. Here his eleven-year-old daughter Lorne lived with her two older brothers, James and Robert.

When Lorne learned of the night's happenings she left the castle. Thin wisps of mist still clung to the surface of the water as she rowed, with unwavering tenacity, the half-mile across the loch to Kinlochalen, which spread along the north shore.

Meeting up with her friends, Duncan and Rory Galbraith, talking excitedly about the events of the night, the three of them left the village, where women and children huddled in doorways, waiting anxiously for their menfolk to return. Several already had, some wounded, bringing with them detailed accounts of fierce combat up on the moor. Ascending the steep road up the glen, young Rory was unable to keep up with his garrulous older brother's long stride and Lorne's agile steps.

'Keep up,' Duncan told his brother crossly, having just told Lorne that his older brothers' parting words had been that they would hunt the thieves down, and when they were caught they would string them up and leave their carcasses to rot and the birds to peck out their eyes.

'My legs are tired,' Rory complained sullenly, hating Duncan's tale of blood and gore.

Lorne paused and, looking back, smiled at him. Rory was a quiet boy with a gentle, sensitive nature, unlike Duncan, who was imperious and strutted about Kinlochalen as though he owned it. He constantly bullied Rory, which drew severe reproach from Lorne. She was fond of Rory and always ready to defend him with a smile and a kind word, which earned her his unquestioning devotion.

'We won't go all the way up to the moor, Rory. I have no wish to see where our fathers and brothers have played out their foolish charades either. We'll sit on the rocks halfway up and wait for them to come back.'

'No, we won't,' Duncan objected stubbornly. 'I want to see where the fighting took place.'

'I'll go if you want me to,' Rory said bravely, but his eyes fell and he clenched his small jaw tightly to keep it from trembling.

'You go if you must, Duncan,' Lorne retorted. 'Rory and I will sit and wait by the burn.'

Torn between going up on to the moor and staying with Rory and Lorne, when they reached an elbow in the burn, Duncan grudgingly sat beside them on a large boulder, folding his arms across his chest and scowling down at the rushing water.

Suddenly, from the mist that still clung to the bottom of the rising hills, something drew their attention. Lorne blinked until she recognised it as a human form almost hidden in a clump of bracken. Quickly all three left their perch. Lorne was there first and fell to her knees beside the inert form, noticing that blood soaked the ground where the man lay on his side. Her hand trembled as she reached out and gently pulled him on to his back, gasping on seeing a youth of no more than fourteen or fifteen.

Her heart almost ceased to beat as she gazed down at his face with a passionate intensity, never having seen a face so fair or so perfect in every feature. Indeed he was as beautiful as the Archangel himself. But his handsome face was white and pinched with pain. She noted that he wore tartan trews and plaid, instead of the simple, loose, flowing kilted plaid the common folk wore in the Highlands, and she could see no point of sword or dirk beneath the tartan. His eyes flickered open, the blue orbs rolling upwards, as if the effort proved too much. Realising the danger and what this youth's fate would be if he were to fall into the hands of the returning angry men, Lorne looked at her companions, her soft voice holding an urgency when she spoke.

'We have to move him. We can't leave him here.'

'Is he going to die?' whispered Rory, his dark eyes wide and apprehensive with fear.

'No. We're not going to let him,' Lorne answered fiercely. 'We're going to look after him—but we'll have to get him away from here before anyone sees him.'

Observing the way Lorne was looking at the youth, jealousy, fierce, hot and raw, smote Duncan's heart. 'No, Lorne. We can't. He's one of the raiders. My father and brothers won't like it if we hide him.'

'Aye!' she flared scornfully. 'I know your brothers—and we both know what they would do to him when their tempers are hot from battle. They'll hurt him cruel. He'll hang for sure.' She cast her eyes up over the surrounding rocks, her eyes lighting on the rocky ledge concealing the entrance to the giant's cave. 'We'll hide him in the cave. No one ever goes there.'

Rory's eyes opened wide. 'But what about the giant?' he gasped.

'There is no giant, silly,' Duncan said with scathing impatience. 'That's nothing but a stupid fairy tale.'

Lorne glared at Duncan through narrowed eyes, which softened when she turned her gaze on Rory. There was no place on earth like the Scottish Highlands where superstition and magic were mixed into everyday life. The drama and fairy tales gave Lorne an immunity from a genuine fear of the Highlands—unlike Rory, who was more fearful than a rabbit of some of the mysterious creatures of folklore.

'Don't be afraid, Rory. We were all brought up on fairy tales—of giants and brownies and witches—and if there was a giant living in the cave he's long since gone.'

'He'll be telling us he believes in magic and miracles next,' Duncan muttered scornfully.

'Why? It can't hurt. Why can't there be giants or miracles? If you believe in magic, anything might happen,' Lorne said defensively, having prayed for a miracle to happen to her all her life that would spirit her away from this inhospitable place and her cold and lonely existence at Drumgow Castle and her father's and brothers' barbaric ways.

Gently she shook the youth's shoulder. 'Come on—you can't stay here. You must get up. I'm sure you can manage if we help you.'

Their strength nearly spent, it was all they could do to haul him on to the flat rock at the mouth of the dark chamber and drag him inside. Lorne fell to her knees beside him, peering into his pale face.

'How badly are you hurt?'

The youth licked his lips. 'My side,' he gasped, speaking in Gaelic. 'I—I stopped a sword—I think. I wasn't with the raiding party. My companions and I were travelling from Oban when we were set upon by the men from Kinlochalen, believing us to be with the raiders. I—I don't know what happened to my horse or to my friends. They rode back up the glen on to the moor. My brother is riding to meet me on the road from the south. Try and get word to him—please—and tell him what has befallen me. My—my name is David and my brother's name is Iain.' Finding it difficult to speak, he closed his eyes. 'Iain Monroe—of Norwood—south of Stirling.'

Lorne stared down at the youth, unable to believe what he said—that he was a Lowlander. The McBrydes' and the Galbraiths' grievances and prejudices against the powerful English-speaking Lowlanders by whatever name they came were old and unhealed. But Lorne was capable of feeling the softer emotions that make living worth while.

'I'll do my best,' she promised, trying hard not to look at Duncan, knowing full well the fury and hatred that must be burning in his breast on finding he had just helped a detested Lowlander.

'If he wasn't with the raiders, then he'll have nothing to fear,' Duncan said haughtily to Lorne, his resentment of the youth having more to do with the way Lorne was gazing down at him than finding he was a Lowlander.

Lorne looked to where Duncan stood, a slender, pale-eyed figure of hostility. 'Yes, he does,' she retorted crossly. Duncan was being as rude and ill mannered as his brothers were. 'Your brothers wouldn't believe him. They would cut him down without questions asked.' She fixed her gaze on the youth once more, her eyes tender. 'Were you, a Lowlander, not afraid to pass through Kinlochalen? You must know that any man from there is not welcome here.'

'I pass through as friend, not enemy, and I know that in the Highlands, should it be requested, food and shelter will always be given—even to the most bitter of enemies.'

'That is true. Highland people pride themselves on their hospitality to those who are admitted to their homes. But it's a hazardous journey at the best of times, and at night—with Highland rebels and outlaws roaming the hills—it is doubly so.'

'That I know—and the longer route to Stirling would have been safer. But my brother sent word telling me that my father is dying—which is why I return home by the shorter route and why I travel at night.'

It was not until Lorne had made the youth as comfortable as she was able that she followed Duncan and Rory back down to the glen.

'No one must know he's here. It's going to be our secret.' Her green eyes blazed when she met Duncan's belligerent expression. 'If you tell anyone about him, Duncan Galbraith, I'll never speak to you again. As God is my witness, I swear I won't.' She looked at Rory's petrified face. 'You won't tell, will you, Rory?'

'No, Lorne. You know I won't.'

Later, after obtaining medicaments from Widow Purdy in the village, and food and blankets, Lorne and Rory returned to the cave. Duncan refused to go with them. Lorne glowered back to see him morosely throw himself down on to a boulder to await his father's return.

In the small cave David lay with his eyes closed, breathing heavily with sharp gasping sounds. He was trembling, his face shiny with sweat. Lorne's youth and inexperience exasperated her, for she did not know how to deal with anything as serious as the exposed and blackened suppurating puncture wound. Dread shivered through her with a coldness that was oppressive when she thought that he might die because of her ignorance, but it was a thought she angrily pushed away as she resolutely set about tending the ravaged flesh as best she could.

'Why is he shaking, Lorne?' Rory whispered when they had finished.

'Because he's weak and cold, I think,' Lorne replied, covering the youth with the blanket and tucking it securely around him, wishing she could do more. 'You go now, Rory. I'd like to stay with him a bit longer.' She tried to smile reassuringly as she nestled close to the unconscious youth in an attempt to warm him with her own body heat.

Lorne was not aware of falling asleep, but suddenly she jerked, lifting her head and looking at David. She was lying beside him with her arm flung across his waist, and even through the thickness of the blanket she could feel the heat of him. Scrambling to her knees, she could see his skin had no relieving moisture. Now it was stretched dry and fiery with heat. The dim light seemed to accentuate the hollows of his face, and when his eyes flickered open she could see they were fixed and staring, with no sign of recognition. He had the fever, and she was not too young or ignorant to know the reason for this was because the wound must be poisoned and that he could die.

With fear in her heart, immediately she got to her feet and

left the cave, knowing David's only hope of survival lay in his brother reaching Kinlochalen in time. She would wait for Iain Monroe on the road past the village and direct him to the cave when he arrived. On reaching the glen, she felt her heart sink when she saw Duncan's father, Ewan Galbraith, and two of his older brothers, Fergus and Lachlan, riding towards her. Duncan had been hoisted up behind Fergus and Rory sat behind Lachlan, his short arms clinging to his brother's stout waist. Their father led a horse with the body of Donald, the oldest of all the Galbraith brothers, draped over its back.

With his flame-red hair and imposing stature, Ewan Galbraith was perhaps the most fearsome man Lorne had ever seen. All the Galbraiths were hot blooded and quarrelsome, and it was plain to Lorne that they had been roused to a black fury at being deprived of one of their own kin.

Wearing the kilted plaid and a blue bonnet on his head, an eagle's feather kept in place by the silver badge of the Galbraiths, Ewan scowled down at the young girl. 'What are you doing, wandering in the glen when your father and brothers have ridden down from the moor just minutes ago?' He growled deep in his throat, taking note of her nervousness and that her eyes darted from Rory to Duncan. 'Did you not see them?'

'Yes,' she lied, knowing her voice sounded high and nervous, 'but I was too far away. I—if I run I'll catch them.'

When Lorne turned and fled, Ewan Galbraith did not urge his horse to ride on. Instead he looked at Duncan and followed his gaze, raising his eyes and focusing on what he could just make out to be a red plaid dangling over the edge of the rock concealing the cave. He looked at it long and hard before dismounting and indicating for Fergus and Lachlan to do the same, his questioning gaze coming to rest on Duncan once more.

'The McBryde lassie has been up to something. Do you know what it is, Duncan?'

Unable to lie to his father even if he wanted to, Duncan stuck out his chest boldly. 'Aye. She found a wounded man—one of the raiders—in the glen and hid him in the cave.'

'Then we'd best take care of him ourselves, eh?'

When they were alone Rory turned angry, accusing eyes on his brother. 'He isn't a raider and you said you wouldn't tell,' he said fiercely, close to tears. 'You promised Lorne. You promised,' he cried wretchedly, wanting to pound his brother with his bare fists.

Duncan jumped down from the horse, glaring at Rory. 'I promised no such thing. You did.' Haughtily he strutted up the hill after his father and brothers, trying to look bold, but unable quell the feeling of unease of having betrayed Lorne's trust quivering inside him.

Unbeknown to Ewan Galbraith or Lorne McBryde, who was running along the road to the south to await the arrival of David's brother, hidden in a thicket high up across the glen crouched the lone figure of John Ferguson. With his eight companions murdered by the men of Kinlochalen and Drumgow, he had come down from the moor to search for the injured David.

John was no stranger to these parts, having been born and raised not far from Drumgow before going south. He knew Ewan Galbraith and Edgar McBryde, lairds of Kinlochalen and Drumgow respectively. Two of the most troublesome, incorrigible families in the Highlands, they were of a warring nature. Having been kept apart from the rest of the world within the Grampian mountains for centuries, these men considered themselves to be true Highlanders—the original possessors of Scotland—and harboured a smouldering resentment for all Lowlanders.

The Galbraiths and the McBrydes were a curse. Their

names were frequently brought before the Privy Council in Edinburgh, on charges of robbery and fire raising, and they were ordered to appear before the Justices, but the order—when someone was brave enough to convey it to them—was always ignored. What might appear as criminal behaviour to the more civilised men in Edinburgh and the Lowlands, was, to the Highlanders, who were reluctant to acknowledge any authority but their own, the settlement of an affair of honour.

John had observed Lorne McBryde emerge from the small cave and scramble down the steep incline. Her bright golden hair shining like a beacon in the night made it easy to identify her. He had watched her speak to Ewan Galbraith and when she had gone that same man had immediately climbed up to the cave with his sons and dragged David down the glen to Kinlochalen. Unable to help the youth, John silently cursed Lorne McBryde, fully believing that she had betrayed David's hiding place to the Galbraiths.

Darkness was creeping over the hills when Lorne tore her gaze away from the road to the south and dejectedly made her way back to David Monroe. She was disappointed and saddened that his brother had failed to appear and didn't know what she could do to help the injured youth. The glen was quiet, uneasily so. With a dart of terror she climbed up to the cave. David wasn't there. With an awful constriction of her heart Lorne knew her trust in Duncan had brought about this horror. That was the moment she began to hate him.

As she scrambled back down to the glen she saw nothing, heard nothing. Running with every nerve at full stretch, her heart and soul in her feet, she approached the village, one picture of what the Galbraiths and her own kin would do to David—might already have done to him—burnt on her brain in agony. Death stalked the quiet streets of Kinlochalen. She was too late.

A burning curiosity to see the prisoner who had been brought down from the glen had induced the citizens out of doors. They were silent, huddled in groups, but Lorne saw only David's wretched corpse where it lay in the square by the Mercat Cross, a place where witches and adulterers were scourged. His face was upturned to the sky, as fair and perfect in death as it had been in life.

There was silence in Kinlochalen for a small space of time as the people and her father and brothers watched the small girl fall to her knees beside the youth and tenderly place her hand on his frozen cheek, her heart seized by a terrible anguish. Tears of hopelessness traced their way down her face, which she raised, fastening her accusing eyes on her father and brothers, noticing that none of the Galbraiths were present.

'Daughter—get up off your knees,' Edgar McBryde demanded, looking at her with bitterness and contempt.

Lorne saw the murderous gleam in his eyes, clearly angry at the compassion she showed so unashamedly for this Lowlander, but it did not frighten her. She had gone beyond that. Her small chin jutted courageously upwards and her flashing eyes met his.

'Why? Why did you do this?' she cried. 'He was not one of the raiders.'

'The lad was dead when Ewan brought him down from the glen,' her brother James told her gently, having sensed from what Ewan had said before going home to mourn his son that Lorne had tried to befriend the youth. Once young Rory had told them the young man's name, a name familiar to them all, they knew that as a consequence of his death, they could expect no mercy from the powerful Monroes in the south.

Galloping hooves broke the silence. Lorne scrambled to her feet and stood back when a party of about twenty men rode into the square. They stopped, their contemptuous gazes passing over the band of tough, unpolished warriors before finally coming to rest on David. Slowly the man at the head of the rest—a man accustomed to instant attention—rode forward and dismounted, going down on one knee and bowing his head over the dead youth, remaining silent for a moment as in prayer.

Without looking at those around him, he lifted the boy up into his arms and carried him to his horse. No one attempted to stop him. The implacable authority in Iain Monroe's manner and bearing caused the Highlanders to fall back. Assisted by one of his friends, he gently placed his brother over his horse's back and swung himself up into the saddle behind him.

Lorne moved forward, a small, slight figure in the midst of so many men. Averting her eyes from the youth whose life she had so valiantly and ardently tried to save, she looked into the face of his brother, Iain Monroe. At twenty years old, with his towering build and well-muscled chest, his hair and beard as black as jet, his brilliant silver eyes blazing with hellfire and damnation, some might say he had the face of Satan himself. Yet Lorne refused to lower her eyes or step away. It was important to her that this man should know she had meant his brother no harm and that she had tried to help him.

'Please—wait,' she begged him, unconsciously speaking in English and moving to the side of his horse. Her emerald eyes were awash with tears, her gaze riveted on the glittering violence in his own.

Looking down, Iain saw a child. His eyes raked her stricken face. Without taking his eyes off her he listened as one of his companions—John Ferguson, who had met him on the road and directed him to the village—leaned towards him and said something in his ear. But recalling John's description of the girl who had revealed his brother's hiding place to

Ewan Galbraith, the gold of her hair had already told Iain who she was. Lorne watched in agony as his eyes, refusing to relinquish their hold on her own, registered his hatred, a hatred so intense that all the muscles in his face tightened in a mask.

To Iain Monroe, these Highlanders were a different species from his own, whose force of nature threatened the law-abiding civilisation of Scotland. In their tribal ignorance they conformed to no patterns of behaviour but their own. Their disdain of the rest of the world, their habits and manners, prejudices and superstitions, made them peculiar, and Iain cursed the whole lot of them to eternal damnation. But he would not be beaten by the likes of Edgar McBryde and Ewan Galbraith, Highlanders who would stick their murderous knives in your back as soon as look at you, men he vowed to see hanging from a rope's end before he was done.

'Stay where you are,' he ordered, speaking with a cultured English accent, his words halting Lorne's steps, his teeth, when he spoke, showing white and even in the midst of his black beard. He inspected her as if she were some repulsive creature crawling in the dirt.

'I curse you, Lorne McBryde—I curse you all,' he shouted, letting his cold eyes sweep the frozen faces of the onlookers, dwelling at length on Edgar McBryde, probing deep into his eyes, as if seeking something to weigh and to judge. His voice was awful and piercing deep, clutching the heart of every man, woman and child. Even the mighty Edgar McBryde and his sons bristled and stepped back before his icy wrath. 'I shall make you pay for this day's work, McBryde. You—and yours—will pay dearly. You slew my brother out of hand, unarmed as he was. Waging war on a defenceless lad is the work of mindless savages.'

Iain was right. Edgar McBryde and the men gathered around him did resemble savages. Some had thrown off their plaids and stood half-naked, bristling with arms, a wildness in their eyes, their hands and bodies bloodied from the affray up on the moor.

'We were not to know he was not one of the raiders. He should have had more sense than to ride down the glen at such an hour. It was impossible for the men of Kinlochalen to distinguish between them in the dark.'

Omnipotent and contemptuous of his unworthy enemy, Ian's voice was scornful. 'Those men were under your control, McBryde—yours and Galbraith's. Not even the plaid you disgrace can hide the fact that murder is your true vocation. You resemble a tribe of uncivilised, marauding barbarians, enmeshed in your blood-feuds and indiscriminate murder and content to remain there. The world is changing—Scotland is changing— and it will not be long before the lot of you are broken men and humbled. I—for one—am impatient to see that day.'

The square was filled with tension and a dangerous hostility in the face of Iain Monroe's contempt and bitter condemnation for the Highlanders' way of life. Every fibre of Lorne's body was vibrating with her need to have him know the truth about how she had tried to save his brother. In desperation she moved to go after him when he turned his horse about, but James's hands grabbed her, jerking her back.

'No—stay, Lorne. It's over. Let him go.'

She struggled in James's grip, freeing herself and running after Iain Monroe, reaching up and grasping his bridle, her short legs moving quickly in an attempt to match the horse's stride. 'Please wait,' she cried, almost choking on her sobs, so distraught was she. Halting his horse, he glared down at her and the expression in his eyes made her want to die. 'You must listen to me. Please—I didn't hurt him—'

'Remove your hands from my horse,' he seethed.

When she refused to do as he ordered, he grasped her hand

and forcibly uncurled each of her small fingers, one by one, from the bridle and thrust her from him. Like a broken doll she fell to the ground, where she lay and watched him ride away, the feeling of wretchedness and defeat lying on her young heart surpassing anything she'd ever felt before.

Not until they were gone did James approach her and gently lift her up, his warrior's heart strangely touched by her silent weeping. His sister had a tender heart moulded by every impression, a natural curiosity and a memory so retentive that whatever took place or affected or interested her was engraved on her mind for all time. He knew the impression made on her by this unhappy occurrence would remain with her for ever.

Iain Monroe remained true to his word. When the Privy Council in Edinburgh heard what had occurred in Kinlochalen they ordered the arrest of Edgar McBryde and Ewan Galbraith, intent on ridding the Highlands of these two rebellious men. Edgar escaped to Ireland and then to France, but Ewan Galbraith took to the hills and it was two years before anyone could put a rope round his neck. He was caught and taken to Inveraray, the seat of the Crown's authority in the Western Highlands. Shackled and thrown into the Tollbooth, he was eventually hanged on Gallows Hill from the great tree.

Chapter One

⁓⦾⦿⦾⁓

1698

Astley Priory was situated in one of the most delightful settings that could be found north of York. Once a priory of the Augustinian order until the dissolution of the monasteries by Henry VIII, it was now the home of Lady Sarah Barton, Lorne McBryde's maternal grandmother. Her father had sent her to live with her grandmother following the affray in Kinlochalen, and Lorne now considered Astley Priory to be her home where, in the care of her grandmother, she enjoyed a free and protected life.

One bright but cold morning, Lorne left the house with her cousin Agnes to take some exercise in the gardens. Since her father had been killed fighting for King William at the Battle of the Boyne in Ireland in 1690, Agnes and her mother, Lorne's Aunt Pauline—her mother's sister—had lived at Astley Priory. To ward off the chill, long cloaks covered their pretty dresses. With arms linked and spirits soaring, smiling broadly, they were in frivolous mood as they excitedly discussed their forthcoming visit to London. Ever since their grandmother had told them she was to take them to the capital for their nineteenth birthdays, after weeks of waiting, the time for them to leave had finally arrived.

Devoted to each other, Agnes had been just what Lorne had needed to shake her out of the sullens when she had come south, where everything was so very different from her life in Scotland. Despite her father's and brothers' constant blusterings and their barbarous way of life, she had missed them terribly at first. For a long time, what had occurred in Kinlochalen had been a private nightmare, painful memories that came to her in the dark like unloved friends with hostile faces and ugly smiles.

'Perhaps we can persuade Grandmother to take a London residence,' Lorne said gaily, feeling absurdly happy and an odd burst of pleasure at the thought of going to London, 'then we could go there more often.'

'She won't. You know how she detests crowds and that awful smog, which she says makes her wheeze and her head ache. She much prefers the country.'

'But we cannot remain in the country for ever. Perhaps if Lord and Lady Billington didn't make us so welcome whenever we go to London, she might be persuaded. Oh, Agnes—London is going to be so exciting,' Lorne enthused. 'People only wake up after midnight—so I'm told. It's a shame that when we were there before we were considered too young to be allowed out after dark.'

'Fifteen, as I recall.'

'I know, but this time it will be different. There will be theatres to attend, and balls where we can dance the night away and wear our best gowns.'

'And handsome young men all vying with each other to dance with us,' Agnes giggled, her eyes sparkling as she became caught up in the excitement of the occasion. 'Let's just hope that Rupert Ogleby won't be in town—his military duties should be keeping him occupied elsewhere,' she said, looking worriedly at Lorne, knowing the effect this particular young man's name always had on her cousin.

The name sent a blaze of animosity jolting through Lorne's entire body. 'I sincerely hope he is not there,' she replied vehemently. 'You know what my feelings are for that particular gentleman.'

'I do. He treated you most shamefully, and if he knows what's good for him he won't come within a three-mile radius of you. He almost ruined your reputation.'

'Afraid that Robert might order me back to Scotland, Grandmother never did inform him of the incident. Still,' Lorne murmured quietly, giving Agnes a brief, distracted glance, before shifting her gaze and resting it sightlessly on the trees ahead of them, her eyes hard and remote with an expression of sadness, regret, and something else mingled with memory when she thought of her brother, 'I don't think Robert would have given it much attention anyway. He would have been too busy fighting one of his clan wars to worry himself over what his sister was doing.'

Thrusting back the dark images that were trying to worm their way into her mind, Lorne laughed and linked her arm through her cousin's once more. The happiness they felt about their forthcoming visit to London barely concealed beneath the brim of their bonnets, the two of them strolled through the park, unaware that their grandmother was watching them from a window of the second-floor drawing room.

Lady Barton's face was white. In her hand she held the opened letter that had just been delivered from Scotland. It bore the bold writing and elaborate seal of her grandson, Robert McBryde. When his father had been outlawed back in '91, feeling deeply the disgrace and dishonour of the sentence issued by the Privy Council in Edinburgh against his father, Robert had followed him to France, leaving Drumgow under James. There he took part in the war that broke out against the Protestant powers in Europe. After the recently declared peace, he had returned to Scotland in disgust, angered that the French King, Louis XIV, had humbled his pride and abandoned King James VII of Scotland and II of England, and recognised the Protestant William III as King of England and Scotland.

After all these years—years in which Lady Barton had deluded herself into thinking Robert and James, and even Lorne's father, had forgotten about Lorne—Robert had sent for her. He demanded that she leave for Scotland to be married to a Highland Laird, Duncan Galbraith, without delay. One thing Lady Barton had learned when her daughter had married Edgar McBryde was that the McBrydes were inflexible and obeyed no law but their own. It would cost her dear to return her darling granddaughter to her brothers, but with her father outlawed and in France, Robert was Lorne's legal guardian, and as such would exercise his right.

Lorne felt the blood draining from her face as she tried to assimilate what her grandmother had told her. She stared at the older woman in confused shock, her long fingers clutching the back of a chair as the room began to spin with sickening speed. She was to go back to Scotland, to Drumgow—a place she never wanted to set eyes on again—to marry Duncan Galbraith. She shivered, yet she was not cold. It was a physical reaction to what was expected of her.

Closing her eyes against the scalding tears that stung her eyes, she shook her head, a blaze of animosity and shock erupting through her entire body. 'Never. It's impossible. I cannot—will not—wed Duncan Galbraith. He is the last man in the entire world I could ever marry.'

'Robert writes that there will be no discussion on the matter,' Lady Barton said quietly. 'Since the death of the two older Galbraith brothers—both he and James have decided that this match is for the good of both families.'

'My brothers do not know what they ask of me.'

'Oh, my dear, I'm so dreadfully sorry. If I could, I would defy Robert and James and keep you with me—but I cannot. Robert is your legal guardian whose wishes must be regarded as law.'

Lorne stared at her. 'Then I am lost,' she whispered.

'I learned long ago, my dear, that it is best to live for the present and to leave the future in the lap of the gods.'

Lorne raised her head, a spark of resistance igniting in her emerald eyes. 'Nothing my brothers can say or do will induce me to marry Duncan Galbraith.'

Lady Barton shook her head sadly. There was about her granddaughter the same gentle qualities her mother had possessed, but there was also the implacable stubbornness and steely determination of the McBrydes.

In a matter of days, and after tearful goodbyes, with a heavy heart Lorne departed for Scotland in her grandmother's big travelling coach. The coachman and two grooms perched on top were heavily armed, for highwaymen did constitute a major hazard. Her grandmother had placed her in the care of a single maidservant, Mrs Shelly, who had been at Astley Priory for as long as she could remember. They were to travel to Edinburgh, almost two hundred miles away, where James would be waiting to meet her. There she would leave Mrs Shelly, who would return to Astley when she had delivered her charge safely into her brother's care.

Because of the frustrations of inland travel in Scotland,

when it could take up to a week to travel fifty miles with a horse and cart, Lorne and James would journey the hundred or so miles on the cattle-droving roads to Drumgow on horseback. Roads were few; with the ever-constant danger of being attacked by wild beasts in the forests—and wild clansmen—James would have a party of men with him.

The coach travelled slowly north, stopping occasionally to take refreshment and to rest the horses. The quality of the service offered at the coaching inns was highly variable. Some were comfortable and welcoming, others less so, and their frequency and comfort deteriorated when they crossed the border at Berwick.

The gentle hills of the Lowlands were spangled with crimson and gold, the trees already shedding their autumn foliage. When they were just twenty-four hours from Edinburgh, Lorne was swamped with gloom and foreboding. Not in the least tired after finishing her meal at the inn in which they were to spend the last night of their journey, she rose from her seat at the corner table in the crowded wainscoted room.

'Excuse me, Mrs Shelly,' she said. 'I find it rather stuffy in here and would like some air before I settle down for the night.'

'If you must, but just for a minute, dear—and don't wander away from the inn. All manner of wild men and beasts could be lurking in the darkness.'

Lorne suppressed a smile. Mrs Shelly was a lovable, fussy old thing with an overactive imagination, who was convinced that Scotland was inhabited by wild savages and had fancied certain death awaited them when they crossed the border.

Stepping outside, she was disappointed to find the inn yard still busy with ostlers and stable boys going about their work. Ignoring Mrs Shelly's warning, she stepped into the road and left the inn, glad of the quiet and solitude as she allowed her thoughts to concentrate on her future. The road was illuminated by a half-moon and the cold air nipped her face under the voluminous hood, but Lorne was too unhappy to notice. The closer she got to Drumgow, the more she thought of what awaited her.

She would appeal to Robert and James and make them understand that she couldn't possibly marry Duncan. With a sigh, she peered into the darkness of the trees on either side of the road. Somehow the thought of being eaten by a wolf seemed a better prospect than that. James, who had shown her gentleness and kindness when she had last been at Drumgow, might be persuaded, but Robert, whom she remembered as being a tough, forceful man, with the same proud arrogance and indomitable will that had marked all the McBryde men, was a different matter entirely.

A gentle rustling and a hint of movement among the trees caught her eye and she paused, suddenly uneasy, having wandered further away from the inn than she had intended. When the rustling continued, she hurriedly began to retrace her steps, totally unprepared when two phantom figures lunged out of the darkness, slamming into her. Knocked off balance, she started to fall, her cry broken as she hit the ground. In no time at all she found herself gagged, tied, swung into the air and unceremoniously flung over a horse. One of her assailants then climbed up behind her.

She found herself in total suffocating blackness, chafed and extremely uncomfortable as she was bounced along over the saddlebow of the galloping horse with her bottom facing heavenwards; the waves of fear and hysteria crashing through her were palpable. Unable to know why this was happening to her and who these men could be, she had the impression that she was caught up in some strange dream, but the discomfort she was being forced to endure told her that it was all happening, all unmistakably real. One thing was plain. She was being kidnapped. But by whom? And to what end?

Without respite they rode on. Lorne lost all track of time, her torture—both physical and spiritual—increasing with each passing mile. Just when she thought she would faint away, mercifully her assailant slowed his horse to a walk and fell into conversation with his companion. Their voices sounded muffled through the sacking that covered her head, but on hearing the occasional English word she assumed they must be Lowlanders.

Anger and revolt were already brewing in her spirit when the horse clattered over a cobbled yard and finally halted. After being dragged roughly from its back and flung over someone's shoulder, she was carried inside a building. On hearing more male voices, she was aware that they were no longer alone.

'So, John, ye're back then,' Lorne heard someone say. 'What happened to ye and Andrew? One minute ye were with the hunt and the next ye'd disappeared. Rode after quarry of yer own, I see.' The man laughed, which was accompanied by his hand slapping Lorne's rump. Hidden from view, she seethed with the indignity of it.

'Aye—of the two-legged kind,' someone else guffawed. 'What ye got there, John? Come—let's see what ye have. Something to eat, is it?'

'Nay, but what I've got is lively enough—and makes up for our lost time.'

Without more ado John dropped Lorne's wriggling form on to the hard floor, removing the sacking and loosening her bonds before taking the gag from her mouth. Shrouded by her cloak and quivering with fury, Lorne struggled to sit up, her body stiff and sore from the rough treatment she had received.

Making a brief sweep of her surroundings, she saw she was in the hall of some ancient castle, although it had a distinct air of dereliction about it. Ancient timbers supported the high ceiling and the walls were bare but for festoons of spiders' webs. It smelt stale and musty and damp. A combination of firelight and candlelight illuminated the features of a large number of men seated around the room, drinking from flasks being passed round. Some were dressed in kilts, their tartans in a variety of colours, their plaids slung across their chests.

Lorne suspected they were a hunting party a long way from home and staying the night in this ruined castle. No doubt they would resume their sport at first light. In a huge open hearth where a fire was sustained by one massive burning log, meat was being cooked on a griddle, and something bubbled and steamed in an all-purpose three-legged black pot, the appetising aroma pervading even the darkest corners of the hall. Someone said something that Lorne could not understand, and the laughter that ensued was coarse and loud, adding fuel to her rage.

'Brute, swine—savage,' she cried, spluttering with fury as she glared at the man standing over her, who was grinning broadly down at his prize, his eyes filled with something akin to triumph. Beneath the short brown beard bristling fiercely from cheek and jaw, she could see it was a face not handsome or ugly, a face used to living with the harshness of the land. 'You will pay for this insolence—this outrage. My brothers will make you pay dearly for this—this insult.'

'So—scratch the wee lassie and she shows her claws,' her abductor, John Ferguson, chuckled throatily, a strong Scottish brogue marking his speech. He was amused by her anger. She looked like some well-bred, high-sprung horse ready to bolt. 'Let me introduce ye ta my friends. They'll not be laughing so heartily when they learn yer identity.'

Reaching out, he snatched away the hood covering Lorne's head so that the golden treasure of her hair—the thick tresses coiled close to her head—was revealed. It gleamed softly in the golden light. A heavy silence fell inside the room as everyone gazed at it, and Lorne felt their hostility creeping around her. The men who were sitting got to their feet and moved closer, closing ranks around her.

An edge of fear caught at Lorne. The atmosphere had become ugly, the circle of faces masks of hate. Living for many years in her grandmother's world, Lorne had never had reason to despise anyone, but crouching dishevelled and filthy before this crowd of hostile men who wished her nothing but ill, filled her with a humiliation and hatred she could not even have imagined. Clenching her teeth, she held on to her fury—it was the only thing she had to combat her fear.

'Behold, Lorne McBryde, me friends,' John proclaimed. 'The beautiful spawn of Edgar McBryde—scourge of the Highlands, murderer, arsonist and thief—is reputed to have the most magnificent hair in the whole of Scotland—and I'll be damned if this isn't it.'

'You'll be damned anyway,' Lorne spat. 'My brothers are strong and you would be wise to fear them,' she threatened, as if the mere mention of her brothers would send a shiver of fear through the stoutest of hearts. 'When they learn you have taken me, they will slit your throats while you sleep.'

John bent over, thrusting his face close to hers, a snarl turning his mouth. 'Aye—like rats stealing grain in the dark. I thumb me nose at this carrion ye speak of,' he scoffed. 'And where me manners are concerned, I agree they are somewhat lacking—but compared with the brothers McBryde, they are impeccable.'

Lorne was aware of another person entering from outside, but she vented all her anger on her abductor. Her defences manifested themselves in the most unexpected way. Somewhere deep within, a reserve of strength propelled her to her feet and she lunged at him, pushing him hard and sending him staggering before falling on his backside.

Stepping into the fray, Iain caught her arm as, incensed with fury, she was about to inflict further damage on his friend. Instinctively Lorne administered a mighty kick to Iain's shin and sank her teeth into his hand, relieved when it relinquished its iron hold on her arm.

'Enough!' Iain roared, his voice reverberating off the walls of the cavernous hall, experiencing a sharp pain in his leg and hand, where her sharp teeth had punctured his flesh and drawn blood.

Lorne's whole attention was strained to the sound of the male voice, a voice that sent shivers down her spine. It brought her head jerking up.

Iain was momentarily stunned. He saw a woman with hair the colour of sunlight, and found himself meeting eyes of emerald green set in a face of incredible beauty. After a rewarding and exhausting day with the hunt, he allowed himself a moment to look his fill. A faint smile of admiration tugged at his lips. The sight of her infused passion into his blood and loins. Her skin was creamy white, her lips rosy and moist, and her angular cheekbones gave her dark fringed eyes an attractive slant. She was perfect. She was—

Then he recognised her and he drew himself up, his face convulsed in a spasm of violent rage and disbelief. 'God help me!' he uttered, his voice quivering with a murderous fury. 'What have we here?'

Lorne was struck dumb to find her dream of meeting Iain Monroe again made flesh. His eyes were on her face, evaluating her with a light so intense it sapped her strength. Looking up to meet his incredible silver gaze, she saw he was exactly as she remembered. His features were stamped with implacable authority and granite determination, and there was a dark arrogance about him. His blue-black hair was rough and tousled, and the features not covered by his short beard were sharply defined, his mouth having acquired a bitter line.

'The lassie's name is Lorne McBryde, Iain,' John told him. 'Ye canna have forgotten the wee girl who betrayed ye brother's whereabouts to the Galbraiths of Kinlochalen.'

Only the collective breathing of the men in the room and the crackle of the fire could be heard above the silence the memory of that day evoked in each and every one of them—in Lorne, too. It was all around her and inside her, still alive, not quiet as it had been when she had lived at Astley Priory. She saw Iain's body stiffen as he pinned his rapier gaze on her face. She met his hard, discerning stare and forced herself to return his assessment with a measuring look of her own, but he emanated a wrath so forceful that she felt fear begin to uncurl inside her.

'I know who she is,' Iain hissed. 'Get her out of my sight.'

John was always ready to do Iain's bidding, but this was one order he would not obey. 'Nay, not when Andrew an' me have gone to the trouble of bringing her here. We've waited too long to let an opportunity to entrap Edgar McBryde slip by.'

Astounded, Iain glared at his friend. 'Are you mad? You abducted her?'

John nodded, unperturbed by Iain's anger. 'How else do ye think she got here? When we stopped to sup at the inn on the Edinburgh road, I couldn't believe me good fortune when I saw the McBryde lassie come in. Seven years may have gone by, but I wouldna mistake that face—or that hair.'

'Was she alone?' Iain asked sharply, his eyes alert.

'Aye—more's the pity—apart from a maidservant and the coach driver and a couple o' grooms, that is.'

'Who did you expect might be travelling with me?' Lorne snapped, speaking for the first time since Iain Monroe had entered the room.

'Yer father—Edgar McBryde,' John growled.

Lorne stared at him in bewilderment. 'But—my father is in France.'

'Not any longer. 'Tis a known fact that he's returned to Scotland—to organise a network o' Jacobite sympathisers in the Highlands, I suspect,' he told her, his lips twisting with scorn.

Lorne's eyes shifted to Iain. 'Is this true?'

'It's true,' he clarified coldly.

Lorne paled. When her father had escaped to France seven years ago, the wrench of leaving his beloved Highlands had been almost too painful for him to bear. She had always known he would not remain in exile and that one day he would return, despite the shadow of the noose hanging over him. And now he had, endangering his own life and others. She was longing to plead her own cause, to tell Iain Monroe, who was looking at her with cold contempt, of all the suffocating horror she had endured since that day in Kinlochalen—if only he would listen.

But he refused to listen. Even now, after seven years, any words she said would not pierce through the armour he had built around himself. As she started to speak, he held up his hand in warning, his expression stern and unyielding. 'Be quiet. I want no pretty speeches from a McBryde,' he hissed fiercely through clenched teeth, the glitter in his eyes as hard and cold as steel as they imprisoned hers.

Now Iain hated the flaunting abundance of her golden hair, the beautiful face, and in particular those green eyes that looked at him with an urgent pleading. They disturbed him, evoking an unreasoned disorder of distant anger and pain. Someone else had looked at him like this long ago, a child who had begged him to listen to her, a child he had shoved away as he would now she was a woman grown. He recalled how she had clung on to his reins, and how brutal he had been when he had prised her small fingers off the leather straps, his huge hands capable of snapping each one of them in two. His jaw hardened and he coldly rejected the memory.

'I know, remember? I know I had a brother I adored, a brother your people slaughtered as they would an animal on a butcher's slab. I saw what those savages did to him.'

'I know,' Lorne whispered brokenly. 'I saw him, too.'

These simple words, innocently spoken, were enough to bring Iain's wrath to boiling point. Grasping her shoulders, he brought her close, thrusting his rage-filled face close to hers until only a hand's-breadth distance separated their noses.

'Then I pray his image never leaves you—that you never forget the part you played in bringing about his death, Lorne McBryde. What did you see?' Iain demanded, his eyes burning with the fever of unspeakable agony. 'Tell me.'

'Please,' Lorne breathed, uttering the word as she would a plea for absolution, raised out of a vast sea of despair that threatened to drown her every time she revived the memory of that day.

Iain's fingers bit cruelly into her flesh and he went on, ignoring her plea. 'Did you see how those butchers dragged him down the glen so that his youthful body was torn and bleeding, before thrusting a dagger into his heart to finish him off? Did you?'

Scalding tears rose to Lorne's eyes. 'No—you don't understand. It wasn't like that. David—'

'Silence,' Iain roared, flinging her away from him with such force that she fell to the floor.

Shocked by his violent outburst, Lorne stared at him.

'Please—will you at least listen to me before you condemn me and cast me out?'

Iain's face tightened as he glared down at her, his eyes pinned on hers. Her whole heart and soul seemed to scream at him through those eyes, which gazed hard into his, but he felt no weakening. When he spoke his voice was ominously soft. 'If you ever speak his name to me again, just one more time, I will make your life hell. I could strangle you for your treachery—and if you hadn't been a child at the time, I would have done it then.'

Looking into those glacial, murderous eyes that showed no mercy, Lorne fully believed he would carry out his threat. She realised it was useless trying to explain what had really happened. What did it matter anyway? David Monroe was dead and nothing she could say would bring him back. His brother's hatred and contempt and the injustice of it all gave her back some of her courage. Clearly everything about her and her family infuriated him, making vengeance blaze inside him every time he was reminded of that day. Propping herself up on her hand, she glared up at him.

'Or condemned me to the gallows—as you did my father.'

'My only regret is that he didn't hang beside Galbraith.' Stepping back, he looked at John. 'Take her back to the inn,' he bit out. 'The very sight of her sickens me. I don't want her here.'

'Yes,' Lorne said, getting to her feet and brushing herself down. 'I demand you return me to my maidservant at once. Nothing can be achieved by keeping me here. If you refuse, you will be called upon by the Privy Council to answer for abducting me. You can count on that.'

'Nay,' John said, stepping forward. That Iain would release her stirred his anger. 'I say she stays—and so does every man here. The McBrydes and the Galbraiths have cost us and our neighbours dear in the past. Think, Iain,' he said fiercely, fired up by old grievances he would not let die. 'Take yer mind back to when the Highland Host came sweeping down to the Lowlands like scourings from a dung heap, called up by the King's Ministers in the hope that their wild and arrogant presence would persuade us to accept Episcopacy with all its religious obligations—when authority seemed to sanction thieving and blackmail.'

'For God's sake, John—that was twenty years ago.'

'Aye—and no' forgotten—and I'll *never* allow myself ta forget. Nor is it forgotten that it was the Galbraiths and the McBrydes who descended on Norwood when they were returning to the hills like a swarm o' locusts—terrorising women and children and stealing everything they could carry and any stock they could drive. Do I have to remind ye that I was born in the Highlands and it was the McBrydes and the Galbraiths who wiped out my entire kin folk?' John went on bitterly, 'I welcome any punitive measure, however savage, that can be used against them.

'Edgar McBryde has yet to pay for that crime—and now we have the bait we need to trap him. Give me one good reason why we shouldna? The Government knows he's back in Scotland and seem to be in no hurry to send in the redcoats to hunt him down. It's unlikely he'll calmly surrender himself in return for his daughter's release, but of one thing ye can be sure. When he learns she's our prisoner, not wishing any harm to befall his lassie, he'll come looking for her all right.'

Lorne stared at John Ferguson in stupefaction. Her heart had constricted painfully as she had listened to the crimes listed against her family, but she could not believe that they intended to use her in their retaliation.

'You're mad. My father will never yield to a bunch of thieving kidnappers. What you are doing is criminal. By abducting me you have stepped outside the law, and it is almost certain that it is the law my brothers will use against you.'

'No, they won't,' Iain said coldly. 'You forget that the Highlanders recognise no law but their own. Must I remind you that your father is outlawed and adrift in a hostile land? John's right. His pride will be well seared by us taking you prisoner. He'll come—bringing a large contingent of Highlanders with him. He will try and rescue you with force, which is his way of doing things.'

'Then I advise you to be wary. He may have a trick or two up his sleeve that might surprise even you, Iain Monroe,' Lorne taunted, too furious to quail before the contempt tightening his face.

Iain lifted his black brows in glacial challenge. 'We are a match for the McBrydes. There isn't a man in this room who didn't lose a friend or a brother that night on the moor above Kinlochalen and swore an oath—an oath that has brought you here tonight. Nine men and my brother set out from Oban— only John survived, which may explain to you his hatred for the McBrydes. When I buried my murdered brother I swore an oath of my own. Edgar McBryde may have escaped the justices once, but now he is back in Scotland he will not do so again. I shall have my vengeance upon the McBrydes. I swear it before God.'

Holding herself proudly erect, Lorne looked at the men surrounding her, gentlemen and servants alike, refusing to cower before them. Tension stretched taut in the room. Never had she witnessed so much hostility at first hand. These men were as hungry for vengeance as Iain Monroe, and they would not be satisfied until they had her father's blood—and her own, perhaps, if the hatred gleaming unpleasantly in their eyes was an indication of how they felt.

'Well—now you've captured me, why don't you dispose

of me to save you the trouble of keeping me?' she suggested steadily to Iain, her eyes challenging his own, realising that she had been insane to try appealing to this heartless, arrogant beast. 'It would be better than your injustice. All I ask is that you get it over with quickly. So what is it to be? Will you shoot me or would you rather take me outside and hang me from the highest tree?'

'None of those things,' Iain replied, feeling a reluctant admiration for this headstrong young woman, who faced him fearlessly and with more courage than most men. The force of her personality blazed through her eyes. It leapt out at him like a warrior band of Highlanders brandishing swords. 'As for hanging you from the highest tree, I lack the appetite for harming women. In any case, you are more valuable to me alive than dead. While my friends might well enjoy the sight, it wouldn't please the authorities quite so much. I've no wish to have a regiment of redcoats descending on my home.'

'They will do that anyway when you release me and I issue a complaint against you to the authorities. What do you propose to do with me in the meantime?' Lorne asked, her head coming up in an arrogant pose.

Iain's gaze raked her before meeting the open contempt in the green eyes staring defiantly into his. 'I don't know yet,' he replied in answer to her question. 'I'll sleep on it.'

At that moment a tall fair-haired man with a good-humoured face entered the hall and came to stand beside Iain. His eyes were a brilliant, lucent blue, and he stared at Lorne with undisguised amazement, completely transfixed. ''Struth! Who is this bonny wee lass? And what's she doing here?'

'Allow me to introduce you to Lorne McBryde, Hugh,' Iain muttered angrily to his friend, Sir Hugh Glover of Dunlivet Castle, where the hunting party had spent the previous night enjoying his hospitality. 'As to what she's doing here, you must ask John. I'm going to bed.' He turned to his young man-servant who, unlike the rest, was gazing at Lorne with undis-guised admiration. Iain gave him a sardonic look, but did not rebuke the youth. 'Make our guest comfortable, Archie. I'll bed down with the horses.' He turned back to Lorne. 'Is there anything you need?' Immediately he regretted asking when she plunked her hands on her small waist and cast an imperi-ous eye round the room, wrinkling her pert nose with distaste.

'A brush and shovel, perhaps—or a mop and bucket and a basin to wash in and a bed to sleep on would not go amiss. And some privacy,' she retorted, glaring at the circle of hostile faces.

Iain's firm lips, almost hidden behind his black beard, twisted with a wry smirk. 'Don't be concerned. You have a pretty face and may have a body to rival that of Venus hidden beneath the layers of petticoats and skirts, but there isn't a man in this room who would touch you as he would a lover, Lorne McBryde. I assure you that the emotions you stir in every one of us are of a different kind. I apologise if the ac-commodation is not to your liking, but it is only temporary. Most of the men will bed down in here, but there's a chamber through there…' he indicated '…that will offer privacy.' Turning abruptly, he walked towards the door where he paused, looking back. 'Providing you don't try to escape, no harm will come to you. Sleep well. You will have plenty of time to reflect on your predicament.'

Lorne gave him a scalding glare that could have melted an iceberg. 'And you would do well to consider yours,' she mocked sarcastically. 'As your prisoner, I will lead you such a merry dance that you will rue the day you met me.'

He raked her with one last contemptuous glance. 'You have given me reason to do so already.'

His voice, devoid of hope, was as cold and unyielding as her prison.

Chapter Two

Archie showed Lorne into the small chamber where she was to sleep, bringing her a candle, a blanket and a straw mattress to sleep on. When she rejected his offer of a bowl of game stew he left her, feeling the warmth of her smile when she thanked him for his kindness. Despite knowing who she was, he considered her to be the fairest maid he had ever seen—and the bravest, for anyone who had the courage to withstand his master—whose presence on the field of battle struck terror into the hearts of his enemies—was brave indeed.

When Archie had left her, and feeling the cold, Lorne took to the mattress and wrapped her cloak about her beneath the blanket, curling her body into a tight ball. The men were in good spirits now she had left them, and as she listened to the low rumble of their laughter penetrating the thick stone walls of her chamber, never had she felt so isolated, miserable and alone. Would her brothers come to her rescue when they learned what had befallen her? Mrs. Shelly would be out of her mind with worry, wondering what had become of her. No doubt she would go on to Edinburgh to meet James tomorrow when she didn't appear.

Chafed and bruised and exhausted by fear and rage, she closed her eyes tight, recovering from the physical effects of her abduction, but not from the shock of it. In a fairly uneventful life at Astley Priory, no one had purposely hurt her, and tonight's events made her feel ill and frightened. When she had mentioned David Monroe, his brother had looked close into her eyes, and just for a moment something had stirred in their silver depths. It was gone in the blink of an eye, but she did not want to see it again.

Iain was preparing to bed down with his horse when Hugh came striding across the moonlit, cobbled yard in search of him. The two men were close friends, and there was a buoyant, sprightly manner between them that was the result of long association. Their families had always been close. Like the Monroes, the Glovers were ardent Protestants and had acquired army distinction at home and abroad on behalf of governments of their own religious persuasion.

'You've talked to John?'

Hugh could see his friend was greatly troubled. He nodded gravely. 'I would no more interfere in your business than you would in mine, Iain. But there isn't a man or woman in these parts who doesn't remember what happened to your brother and those men escorting him from Oban that night, and it is clear to me that the men in there,' he said, indicating the castle with a jerk of his head, 'in particular those who lost friends and kin, want appeasement. I don't envy you, my friend. But you should return Mistress McBryde to her brothers. Whatever grievance you have with her father, it is inevitable that you will be brought to account for abducting her.'

Iain's sigh was one of profound frustration. 'I know that, Hugh. That's what worries me. But as much as I would like to,

I can't let her go. If I release her, I'll have a full-scale insurrection on my hands—especially from my own servants, who remember David well and had a fondness for him. They're good and loyal men. I can't let them down. Nor do I forget that John Ferguson—my own mother's cousin—has a creditable knowledge of Highland robbers and murderers. When he was a lad, his entire family was wiped out in one night when the Galbraiths and the McBrydes made a raid on his village to collect old debts. Make no mistake, Hugh, John will go to any lengths to lure Edgar McBryde out of his lair, and if it takes holding his daughter hostage to do it—then so be it.'

'Then have a care. Do not be over-confident,' Hugh advised. 'I have heard of Edgar McBryde, and it is said that he is a difficult man. You must recognise this—and I urge caution.'

'I'm hoping that when he learns we hold his daughter, he will surrender without a struggle. The last thing I want is for blood to be shed over this.'

'Then with any luck the redcoats will get to him first.' Suddenly Hugh grinned, lightening the moment. 'Still—the wench is a beauty and extremely desirable and no mistake. On reaching Norwood, I don't reckon much to your chances with so much temptation lodged beneath your roof.'

Hugh laughed in the face of his friend's glower. 'Unless you lock her away out of sight, I'll wager that within one week you become so tormented by insatiable desire that it won't matter a damn to you who sired her,' he taunted good humouredly before going off to seek his own bed, little knowing that his words, spoken glibly, would come home to roost. Nor did he realise that for a hot-blooded male like Iain Monroe, with the legendary Monroe charm evident in every one of his lazy smiles, and whose handsome looks and blatant virility compelled the attentions of women, it would take less than twenty-four hours.

* * *

Looking up at the stars through the hole in the stable roof, his hands behind his head and covered by a single blanket, Iain considered the unexpected turn of events and the disruptive influence the presence of Lorne McBryde would be sure to have on his men.

Like Robert McBryde, Iain had fought in the war against Louis XIV, but whereas Robert had served France, Iain had served William III. He had returned to Scotland on the restoration of peace, and now he was content to indulge in the simple pleasures of hunting and fishing and running his vast estate of Norwood. He was a battle-hardened warrior who thought he was up to dealing with most things life threw at him, but nothing had prepared him for Lorne McBryde.

When he awoke, his rest had done much to soothe and cool his ire. The presence of the aforesaid young woman was very much on his mind. He had an undeniable curiosity to see his hostage in the morning light—to see if she looked as lovely as when he'd first set eyes on her last night, before realising who she was. Her comeliness had been a vision worth remembering.

Was her hair really as shining and golden as it had looked in the candles' glow? he mused, trying to imagine how it would look unbound, how it would feel to run his fingers through the thick tresses. And were her eyes really that captivating shade of green that made him think of dew-soaked grass? He remembered how soft and creamy her skin was, how angular her cheekbones, which gave her eyes an attractive, feline slant. In contrast to these delicate features her nose was small and pert, and there was a stubborn thrust to her round chin.

His lips broke in a wicked grin, for Lorne McBryde had attributes enough to pleasure a man into eternity. Pity, though, who she was, he thought with a certain amount of regret. Whistling softly, he jauntily made his way to the burn to wash, feeling a strong desire to feast his eyes on his captive once more.

With a thin watery light filtering through the tiny window—a window which was too small and narrow for the object of Iain's musings to climb through, otherwise she would have attempted to escape—Lorne awoke shortly after dawn. It took a moment for her to convince herself that she wasn't trapped in some terrible dream, but gradually memories of the previous night's happenings emerged from the mists of sleep.

Archie appeared in the doorway, feeling shy and a little awkward in the presence of Lorne McBryde, and sorry that she had been subjected to a lack of respect on what had probably been the most fearful night of her life.

'John has instructed me to ask you if you would like to refresh yourself. There's a burn close by and enough seclusion to offer you some privacy.'

Gratefully, with a warm smile, she thanked him. With frank, earnest eyes, rust-coloured short-cropped hair and a smattering of freckles over his nose, Archie seemed a pleasant youth—he was also the only one in the party who had shown her kindness. Lorne followed him into the main hall. In jovial spirits, those present fell silent when she appeared. In daylight they looked a rumpled and unkempt lot with grizzled countenances as they sat about eating bannocks and porridge and supping draughts of ale. Their eyes followed her across the hall. Muttered comments were made, and knowing they were anything but complimentary, Lorne raised her head imperiously and met their stares with a cold defiance. Some instinct deep within her drove her to defy these men and she found comfort in this. John was standing by the door.

'Keep a close eye on her, Archie. Don't try to escape,' he said to Lorne.

She glared at him. 'Are you threatening me?'

'No. Just don't make me have ta come looking for ye.'

Head held high, Lorne followed Archie outside. She had never been afraid of any man—not even her father—and she refused to be intimidated by these Lowlanders. She was greatly relieved to find there was no sign of her tormentor of the night before among the men milling about in the court-yard. Already a number of the gentlemen and servants and falconers were assembled, saddling their handsome steeds, and several were leaving to begin the day's hunt.

The chief huntsman holding the hunting horn sat his mount apart, and leashed, lithe and graceful deerhounds strained against their collars in excitement, smelling the air for their quarry, alert and impatient to be off. It was a scene Lorne had become accustomed to during her time at Drumgow, when her father and brothers would often disappear for days on end into the Highlands to hunt the red deer.

Taking stock of her surroundings as she walked beside Archie, she saw the castle was a small, squat drum tower covered in ivy, supported by a complex arrangement of crumbling walls.

'The castle used to belong to Sir Donald Ramsay until the Civil War,' Archie told her in answer to her enquiring gaze.

'What happened?' she asked, relieved to speak to someone who wasn't hostile towards her.

'It suffered the same fate as others whose owners supported the King. You might say it's just another of Cromwell's legacies,' he grinned. 'Impoverished by the war, the family couldn't afford the expense of rebuilding, so they moved to Stirling. Now the castle is used as a resting place for drovers and hunting parties who venture far away from home during the deer-stalking season.'

'I see. This seems to be a large party.'

'Sir Hugh's party makes up the largest part. After partaking of his hospitality at his home two nights ago, he joined us on the hunt. Ours is just a small selected party of gentlemen and servants from Norwood.'

'When do you intend returning to Norwood?'

'That depends. Probably tomorrow. The weather has been good and we are on our way to getting a good quota of stags. Come—and please watch your footing,' he said, following a path down a steep incline. 'The burn is this way.'

Breathing deep of the tingling fresh morning air, Lorne gazed at the still and peaceful gently rolling landscape. Low mist lay in the valley bottom, which on this autumn morning had not had time to disperse. The burn was deep and fast flowing. It gurgled over protruding rocks, plunging and roistering in the pools, before disappearing round a bend in the hill to follow a hidden course.

Archie stood guard behind a tangled screen of willows and bushes to wait for Lorne to complete her ablutions.

Removing the pins securing her hair, she combed out the long thick tresses with her fingers, wishing she had a comb to do it properly. Kneeling by the side of the burn, she shivered when the ice cold water touched her face and neck, but it was invigorating, and when she dried herself she felt refreshed in spite of her situation. Sleep and the crystal-clear water had revived her spirit and imbued her with a reckless determination to escape her captors at the first opportunity. She would find a way. She must.

Having completed her ablutions and calling to Archie that she was almost done, daringly she walked along the green sward, hoping against hope as she clambered over a group of rocks that it might provide her with a way of escape.

It didn't. Instead it led her into a situation she would rather have avoided.

With his breeches rolled up to his knees, Iain was washing himself in the burn. Surprise widened her eyes and her mouth formed a little circle as she sucked in her breath sharply. There was no escaping the fact that Iain Monroe was a magnificent, virile male—things she'd been too young and naïve to take in before. He strode out of the water, the lean, hard muscles of his thighs flexing beneath the tight-fitting breeches. His thick, curling hair was damp and shining, and prisms of water trickled down over his skin and the mat of black curling hair on his imposing chest, which swelled magnificently, narrowing to his flat, muscled belly. His taut muscles rippled as he reached for the towel and dried himself, before slipping his arms into his shirt and shrugging it across his broad shoulders.

Cautiously taking a step back, Lorne silently cursed when she startled a cock pheasant in the tall reeds. Irate at being disturbed, the splendid bird rose from its cover with a ferocious flapping of wings and flew off, squawking its complaint. The noise brought Iain's head jerking up and round. Seeing Lorne watching him, he came towards her with the swiftness of an animal, like a stalking wolf, graceful as a gentleman should be. With dark brows raised in question, he propped his shoulder casually against a tree and crossed his arms over his chest, watching her in insolent silence.

'Well?' he enquired at length. 'Have you had an edifying look, Mistress McBryde?'

Trying to ignore the treacherous leap her heart gave at the sight of his bare chest exposed beneath his unfastened shirt, feeling trapped like a rabbit in its own snare, Lorne gazed helplessly into those inscrutable eyes—silver or dove grey, she couldn't decide which. Wishing she could hide her pink cheeks she said hastily, 'I—I was just—'

'Running away?' Iain caught the spark that ignited in her

eyes and the temper behind them. She looked so young, innocent and wild. An inexplicable, lazy smile swept his face as he surveyed her from head to foot. The wind ruffled her hair, which he saw really was as gold as a sunburst, and her slanting emerald eyes were fringed with absurdly long and curling black lashes. Without her cloak her gown revealed an alluring womanly form with ripened curves in all the right places. The bodice of her dress was low cut, which afforded him a glimpse of the thrusting fullness of her breasts pressed tightly against the fabric. He looked down at her dewy skin—tinted with roses after its brush with the cold water—and soft mouth, feeling a hunger he had not felt in a long time.

The intimate smile that appeared on his firm lips during the silent, searching interval caused Lorne's flush to deepen and her eyes to flash indignantly. 'Can you blame me for wanting to escape my father's enemies?'

He shrugged. 'I suppose not. Do you defend him?'

'He is my father.'

'Don't equivocate. That was not what I asked.' His eyes became probing, questioning. 'I asked if you defend a murderer—a man who considers the lifting of his neighbours' cattle and the burning of their cottages to be an ancient and honourable Highland profession. Have you no pride when it comes to the truth of the matter? Doesn't what he did flaw his character in your mind? Does he not shame you to the core?'

A sudden coldness crept up Lorne's spine and her stomach churned. In fury she faced away, unable to look at him lest he saw the truth. No, she did not defend her father, but she would not betray any of her kin by saying so to this stranger— her father's enemy. But Iain Monroe was right, she was ashamed—deeply so—and since that day when his brother had been murdered, she had been like a ship adrift on a storm-tossed sea, having no security wherever she was, but having no escape from it either.

'I am not obliged to discuss my family with you, Iain Monroe. You can go to hell,' she snapped.

Iain's laugh was low and scornful and infuriating. 'Nay, Lorne McBryde. That particular abode is reserved for the devil and those he spawns—men of your father's ilk.'

'You beast,' she hissed, incensed. Acting on pure instinct, she spun round and her hand came up to deal him a slap, but he caught her wrist before she landed the blow. His hold was inescapable, his eyes as hard as granite.

'Don't even think about it. My hand still smarts from the bite you inflicted on it last night. That was the first time you drew my blood and 'twill be the last,' he said, his voice harsh. 'No woman has ever bested me and none ever will.'

Twisting the fingers of his other hand in her hair, he snapped her head back. Half-stifled, her head reeling, she found her lips sealed by a hard demanding mouth that bore down relentlessly on hers. His lips were meant to punish, and Lorne was too stunned by what he was doing to react. When he raised his head the only sound was the burbling water and their rapid breathing as they gazed at each other. The air crackled with emotion.

'What a pity you are a McBryde and I have to miss the chance of making love to you,' he drawled. 'You are made for it. Were you any other wench, I might well be tempted.'

Outrage exploded in Lorne's brain. Her cheeks scarlet with embarrassment and shame, she glared at him, her eyes spitting venom. 'You rate yourself too highly. You are arrogant in your assumption that you are some magnificent gift to womankind. I would sooner bed down with a ravening beast than bed down with you.'

Iain's jaw tightened. 'Are you always such a shrew?' He

gave her a long-suffering look, as if she were being unreasonably difficult. Reluctantly he released her, feeling a desire to kiss those lips again—but this time to feel those lips respond and return the kiss.

'A shrew!' Lorne gasped, appalled that he had kissed her so brutally. 'How do you expect me to behave? You have your men kidnap me—threaten my life—you insult and degrade me every time I am in your presence—and now you have the gall to kiss me. My reputation might mean nothing at all to you, but it certainly does to me. When this is over and word gets out that I have been with you, there is bound to be a scandal over it,' she berated him with bitter scorn. 'I will be despised for something that isn't my fault.'

Iain stared down at her irate face in shock and amusement. 'Reputation? Since when did Highlanders concern themselves with young ladies' reputations?'

Lorne seethed. There was nothing more definable than this man's clear and absolute self-possession. He had no understanding of what it was to be tormented, afraid, alone, to hope for salvation in the form of someone he knew, someone close. These things belonged to another breed, and in that he held nothing but contempt.

'For the past seven years I've been away from the Highlands, living in England with my grandmother.'

Iain's eyes danced with mirth and his teeth flashed white from between his parted lips. 'Why? What did you do? Are you so unmanageable and undisciplined that even your own father cannot control you?'

Her eyes clouded. 'I didn't do anything. He—he thought it best to send me away after—after that day. My grandmother lives near York. From an early age she instilled into me a moral code—and you, Iain Monroe, have violated that code by abducting me and kissing me. In my grandmother's world the reputation of an unmarried young woman matters.'

Iain looked at her hard, his expression becoming thoughtful. He knew she had visited her relatives in England several years ago, but he had no idea she had lived there for so long. However, he found it ironical that she should be so concerned about her reputation, for he recalled the scandal that had erupted when she had been caught philandering in the most intimate manner with a strutting young rake by the name of Rupert Ogleby. Normally London society wouldn't have batted an eyelid at such an incident, but because the young lady in question was just fifteen years old and Lady Barton, her grandmother, a well-respected member of society and highly thought of by King William himself, the incident had been sensationalised.

Hearing the little catch in Lorne's voice and suspecting that she must have been deeply affected by the scandal, and having no wish to remind her of the incident, he kept the fact that he knew about it to himself. He realised how his actions and those of his men had humiliated and hurt her. She suddenly seemed so very young and vulnerable that he felt a twinge of conscience. Deep within him the wall of ice he'd kept around his heart for seven years suffered its first crack.

'I'm sorry,' he capitulated on a gentler note. 'I didn't know. What I don't understand is that if your father sent you away—ignoring you for seven years—why do you want to protect him?'

'Because whatever he is guilty of in your eyes, to me, first and foremost, he is my father to whom I owe allegiance and am duty bound—and I hate you. I hate you all for kidnapping me and giving him no alternative but to rescue me. It's a coward's way of capturing his enemy and unworthy of you.'

Iain stared at her, caught somewhere between anger and amazement at her defiant courage. 'You might see it that way, but it doesn't change anything. I agree that I've broken all the rules of etiquette where you are concerned, but the fact remains that you are my hostage and I intend keeping you with me—if only for your own protection. Considering the mood my fellow companions are in, there is every possibility that you will suffer if I let you go—so I advise you not to try anything foolish or bold. You might just as well relax and accept the situation.'

'Relax?' she flared. 'Is that what you expect me to do? How can I relax in this Godforsaken place with no clothes and no friends—and with just a bunch of heartless vengeance seekers who look ready to draw my blood at any minute?'

Iain's eyes narrowed dangerously. 'One word from me and they will do just that,' he warned in a silky, ominous voice.

Lorne recoiled from the hard glitter in his eyes. She did not doubt that one glance from this arrogant, noble lord, and every member of the hunting party would be more than happy to do his bidding. 'Tell me, Lord Monroe—is there a dungeon beneath this ruin you intend to incarcerate me in until you finish your hunt?'

He considered her for a moment. 'Don't be ridiculous. I am not entirely heartless. My friend Sir Hugh will continue with the hunt without me and those in my party. I have decided to return to Norwood today. I can promise you ease and comfort there.'

'If you intend that to be a kindness, it isn't. It's a curse,' she flung at him with stinging scorn, her mind already ranging far afield in its search for some avenue of escape. Tossing her head imperiously, she turned to negotiate the rocks she had clambered over to get here. Automatically Iain reached out to help her, but she jumped out of his reach, avoiding his touch as she would the plague. 'Don't you dare touch me,' she warned him. 'You may have made me your prisoner, but understand this. You keep your hands to yourself.'

When she had clambered over the rocks and her feet were back on the green sward running alongside the burn, she strode off without a backward glance. She realised she was famished and those oatcakes were suddenly very appealing. When she'd eaten she would think of a way to escape.

Rolling up his shirtsleeves and tucking the hem into the waistband of his breeches, Iain watched her go, admiring the flowing, long-legged grace of her stride and gentle sway of her slim hips, and the way her hair tossed in the breeze. He shook his head, trying to concentrate on the change he had made to his plans to return to Norwood early, but after his brief encounter with his hostage and the taste of her lips, and remembering how his starved senses had wanted to feast on them again, he was more inclined to dwell on the amazing quirk of fate that had caused Lorne McBryde to reappear in his life. No longer a child, but a woman full grown—and still a McBryde, a woman bearing a name that had insinuated itself into his soul from an early age, a name that stirred his hatred and mistrust.

Lorne sat quietly on a grassy knoll on the edge of the courtyard close to the trees, watching the proceedings as some of the men prepared to escort her and the trophies of the hunt back to Norwood. Preceded by a dozen or so hunt-servants, whose duty it was to find the deer and drive them towards the hunt, under the leadership of Sir Hugh, it was a rather reduced number of sportsmen who were preparing to start out for a final day's pursuit of the red deer and wild boar.

Lorne's eyes were alert, watching Archie, who was supposed to be guarding her, but had left her side for a moment to saddle his horse close by and away from the rest.

She observed Iain, clad in a dark brown leather doublet, black breeches and knee-high boots, moving among the men. He never looked her way once, and anyone would think he had forgotten her existence, but of course he hadn't.

He was the most handsome, fearsome man Lorne had ever beheld, bent on coldly and unemotionally capturing her father and destroying her family, and she ought to hate him. But she could not. He had just cause to despise every one of the McBrydes, herself included, and for that she felt profound regret.

Her gaze shifted to Archie, who was tightening the girth on his horse's saddle. This done, he looped the reins over a wooden post and went to assist in securing the carcass of a splendid young deer over the back of a sturdy garron. It proved awkward. Attracting the attention of the others, Iain included, they went to help, their attention momentarily diverted from their captive. Lorne glanced at Archie's horse. The opportunity was not to be missed.

She found herself getting up and walking slowly towards the mount, trying to keep her nerves under control. If Iain should look towards where she had been sitting and find her gone, she was too afraid to imagine what he would do. On reaching the horse, she glanced towards her captors. No one had noticed she had moved. The sun vanished as she led the horse into the dense woods. Out of sight, she brought the mount around and climbed into the saddle, digging her heels into its flanks and setting off through the trees. Her route lay east and she headed towards it.

Satisfied that the carcass of the young deer was well secured over the back of the garron, Iain stood back and smiled when Hugh rode up to bid him farewell.

'I go to London in a few weeks, Iain—before the hard weather and dark days of the Scottish winter begin. Come with me. The company would be appreciated—and I know for a fact...' he chuckled, with a conspiratorial lowering of his lids '...that the fair Mistress Fraser is to be in town. Couldn't keep your eyes off her the last time you were together. Come, what do you say? It might be just what you need.'

'I'll let you know, Hugh. I confess the idea is appealing and the thought of meeting Maria Fraser again extremely tempting, but this latest development might take longer to settle than I care for.'

Iain's gaze unconsciously sought out Lorne where she had been sitting on her grassy knoll, her hands clasped around her knees and a long lock of golden hair hanging heavily over one shoulder.

Finding the place empty, he froze. He was momentarily unable to believe she wasn't there, his gaze ricocheting from the place where she had been sitting, around the courtyard and back again. He thought he could never be as angry as he had been last night when he had come face to face with her, but the explosion of rage and foreboding surmounted even that. Immediately he turned his blistering gaze on Archie.

'Where is she?' he thundered. 'Your primary job was to guard her. God damn the woman! Where the devil has she gone?'

Archie looked around in consternation, afraid that his master was losing his hold on that precarious temper of his. His gaze was drawn to where he had left his horse. 'My horse—it's gone! She—she—'

Rage continued to explode in Iain's brain. 'Must have taken it,' he bit out in a soft, murderous voice.

Striding swiftly towards his horse, he felt his emotions veer crazily from apprehension to fury. Apprehension because she had obviously gone careering off into the forest where she might get lost or meet with an accident, and fury because where most men would quake in his presence, this chit of a girl had openly defied him. As a demonstration of headstrong defiance, disobedience and rebelliousness, it was supreme. He had foolishly believed she would be too afraid to try escaping in this inhospitable countryside—but she was a McBryde, he reminded himself bitterly, who would dare anything.

Cursing her to perdition, within seconds he had swung himself on to his horse and was in hot pursuit, correctly assuming she would go in an easterly direction. His men followed, some dispersing in other directions.

Lorne had deliberately avoided looking over her shoulder as she picked her way amongst the hollies, the birch and the alder, but, coming to the end of the wood, she glanced back. She was unable to see the rider who pursued her, but heard the thunder of following hoofbeats becoming ever louder and nearer.

Emerging out of the trees into the full glare of sunlight, she rode like the wind. There was nothing ahead of her but a wide expanse of forest and sunwashed heather-emblazoned hills, and no sign of life. Her face set, her eyes blazing, she urged the horse to greater speed.

Behind her Iain saw a girl whose golden, unbound hair streamed out like a silken flag. She was a good horsewoman, riding in a way that would have done credit to her father and brothers, and in that unlikely moment he was overwhelmed with admiration.

Suddenly, from somewhere not far away, came the long, ululating blast of the hunting horn and the baying of hounds. Panicked, Lorne's already excited, panting and sweating horse instantly reared and bolted. Struggling to bring it under control and at the same time outrun her pursuer, Lorne clung on in desperation. Ahead of her there loomed a narrow plateau with a steep incline on either side, the ground littered with outcrops of loose stones. Unable to turn and take a safer route, she found herself riding along it, trying not to look down the steep slopes to her right and left. All she could hear was the horse's laboured breathing and the hollow thud of hooves.

Suddenly another blast of the hunting horn caused the horse to balk, pitching her over its head. The fall knocked the breath out of her body and she lay still, dazed and disoriented and fighting for air, while her horse galloped away. Through a haze she saw a rider appear along the plateau. Her heart almost stopped when she recognised Iain on his huge white hunter, riding low over its neck and looking like an ominous spectre of doom. Terror and rage and an acute sense of fear overriding everything, recovering her senses and getting her breath back, she scrambled to her feet, and, as quick as a harried fox, took flight.

Iain flung himself off his horse and gave chase. Lorne turned and looked back, trying to remain upright on the loose stones. Iain almost stopped in his tracks when he beheld her face and saw her eyes sparking with green fire. She was like a tempestuous goddess, wild and beautiful in all her fury, and alive with hatred as she courageously tried to outrun her enemy, refusing to be broken. She was truly amazing, and in that moment Iain thought she was the most magnificent creature he'd ever laid eyes on.

When he was close he snatched at her, jerking her back, his fingers digging cruelly into her arm. She whirled round, stubborn and unyielding as she tried to get free of his iron hold.

'Damn you,' he bit out savagely, trying to prevent her nails from raking his face. 'Stop fighting me, you little hellcat. It's plain to see you share the blood of the McBrydes.'

Lorne continued to struggle against him as if her life

depended on it. She saw his face, terrifying in its rage, his jaw clenched tight and his silver eyes as hard as granite. A cry broke from her lips when suddenly she lost her footing and began to fall, taking him with her. They hit the ground, tumbling and rolling over and over down the steep incline, a shower of dislodged stones accompanying them to the bottom.

Lorne found herself pinned beneath Iain's powerful frame, unable to move, her chest straining in her need for air. His head was buried in the hollow of her neck and he was breathing hard. In breathless tension she waited for him to move, wondering if he was hurt.

With blood welling through his beard from a cut on his cheek, slowly he raised his head and looked down at her, his face just an inch from her own, his breath hot on her face. Their eyes became locked in a mesmerising web, and the fire that swept through Iain at having her womanly body pinned beneath his almost deafened him to any resistance. Immediately he recollected himself. Angry frustration ran rampant through every fibre of his being, as his argument was about to burst forth in a torrent.

Taking note of the taut set of his jaw and the undiluted fury blazing in his eyes, tendrils of fear coiled in the pit of Lorne's stomach and her pulse accelerated wildly. Never had she encountered such cold, purposeful rage in her life—not even from her father and brothers.

Levering his body off hers, Iain got to his feet. 'Get up,' he snapped. Without waiting for her to obey he reached down and grasped her arm, jerking her roughly to her feet. Lorne winced when a pain shot up her forearm into her elbow, realising she must have hurt it in the fall, but Iain was so furious he was blind to her discomfort. Again he grabbed her injured arm in a powerful grip. She gasped in protest at feeling another shooting pain, but he was dragging her in his wake towards his horse, which had made a more dignified descent than its master. Placing his free hand on the saddle, Iain loomed over his captive, his gaze a cold blast, his expression intense.

'How far did you think you'd get alone and defenceless, you little idiot? Is it that you are hell bent on self-destruction, or merely out to thwart me?'

Without waiting for her to reply, he placed his hands on her waist and lifted her effortlessly on to his horse, before hoisting himself up behind her and wrapping his iron-thewed arms tightly round her waist in a grip that was meant to hurt and retaliate.

'I will give you a warning, Lorne McBryde—just one,' he said in a low, savage voice close to her ear. 'If you ever try anything like that again or do one more thing to exasperate or anger me, I will personally see to it that you await your father's arrival at Norwood in my deepest, darkest dungeon. Do you understand?'

Lorne swallowed convulsively and nodded. 'Yes,' she whispered, glad when his arms relaxed their iron hold.

'I have your word?'

'Yes.'

'Say it.'

'You have my word.'

Chapter Three

Silence lay heavily between them on the ride back to the castle, but each was conscious of the closeness of the other. With her back moulded to the hardened contours of Iain's body, Lorne was more shaken by what had happened than she had let him see. Her throat ached and her eyes burned, but she would not cry.

They rode into the courtyard where a knot of men stood around waiting for them to return. Iain swung himself on to the ground and roughly pulled Lorne down after him. When she took a step back, his hand clamped down painfully on her forearm. Her face contorted with a new wave of pain, but Iain had his head turned away and didn't see.

Archie rushed forward, relieved that Lorne appeared to be unhurt, but the same could not be said of his master. 'My lord, your face is bleeding. It must be tended.'

Iain wiped his beard with the back of his hand, scowling when he saw the blood. He directed a single look at the woman by his side, his rapier-sharp gaze holding hers. 'It will be tended, Archie, but not by you. Take someone with you to look for your horse. It bolted on hearing the sound of the horn.'

Still gripping Lorne's wrist and forcibly pulling her behind him, Iain strode with long purposeful strides across the courtyard, through the trees and down to the burn. Once there he let go of her wrist and looked at her coldly. Lorne set her jaw and tried to fight the sudden fear that threatened to engulf her. She knew the folly of her escape effort, and retribution in the form of Iain Monroe had come swiftly for her foolishness.

'Stay there,' he snapped, knowing he would have to guard her carefully in the days ahead. She was impulsive and headstrong, and so unpredictable that he never knew what she would do next. Kneeling on one knee, he bent over the water and washed the blood from his beard. Standing and then resting his hips on a large boulder, which brought his face on a level with hers, he produced a small dirk from his belt, testing its sharpness with his thumb. His eyes were merciless when they settled on Lorne.

'Come here.'

Mutely she obeyed and moved to stand in front of him, her eyes riveted on the knife. When he handed it to her, she took it with trembling hands. 'What do you want me to do?'

'Shave me.'

Her eyes widened until they were two great green orbs, and her soft lips parted in disbelief. 'Shave you? But—I—I can't,' she whispered shakily. 'Oh, no. Certainly not. I won't do it.'

'You can and you will.'

'But—I've never—'

'Now is the time to learn,' he bit back, refusing to let her off the hook lightly. He noticed her shaking hands and his eyes narrowed. 'And if you draw a single drop of my blood you must be prepared to suffer the consequences.'

Lorne's eyes snapped to his, stormy once more. His tone threatened terrible consequences should she commit such a crime a second time. She did not know him well enough to discern what thoughts and intentions his face was reflecting, and she was unable to imagine what form his reprisals would take. However, hurt that he might believe she truly intended to harm him had the effect of subduing her nerves and reverting her to her former state of proud rebellion.

'Are you not afraid that I might use this knife to slit your throat?'

Despite the stubborn tilt to her chin and her rebellious tone, there was a tiny quiver of fear in her voice, and when Iain heard it his heart softened. She had shown so much daring and amazing courage, so much indefatigable spirit in running away and fighting him so relentlessly, that he'd actually thought she was fearless. Now, however, as he looked at her, he saw the strain of the last twenty-four hours on her face, the mauve smudges beneath her eyes and her pallor.

'No. I trust you,' he said gently, deciding that helping her to relax while she held the knife was in both their best interests. 'Just stay calm and you'll do just fine.'

The soft words coming on the heels of his sudden change in persona from captor to carer took Lorne by surprise. It sounded nice, but she continued to glare at him in furious silence.

'Now—come closer.'

Amazed by his unflappable calm, Lorne moved to stand to one side of him, intending to perform the dreaded task with as little contact as possible between them, but Iain had other ideas. Gently but firmly he took hold of her hand, drawing her closer so that she stood directly in front of him between his thighs. Placing his hands on her hips to prevent her moving away, his eyes laid siege to hers. In the circle of his arms he could feel the alert tension of all her muscles. Her stillness was like that of an animal poised for flight.

'I want you where I can see you. Now—stop glaring at me and start shaving.'

Conscious of his hands holding her firm, with a militant look in her eyes she tipped his head back with her finger and began to ply the blade carefully to the lean contours of his jaw. Shaving the uninjured side of his face first, she passed the blade over his cheek, wiping it after each stroke on a kerchief which Iain provided.

'If you cooperate, life will be much easier for you when we reach Norwood,' he told her, his eyes tracing the classically beautiful lines of her face, thinking that she really was extraordinarily lovely, her skin fine and soft.

Lorne sighed, feeling inclined to do just that. For one thing she was in no fit state to continue sparring with him—not that she wanted to. She was also physically exhausted and her arm was hurting.

'Have you never shaved your brothers?' Iain asked conversationally, liking the feel of having her close. His gaze was able to dwell on her hairline, on the fine bloom of pale blonde hair, which was like a newborn babe's.

Preoccupied with her task and gnawing on her bottom lip in deep concentration as she carefully applied the blade to that vulnerable area beneath his nose, she shook her head slowly. 'I told you, I was sent to England to live with my grandmother. I haven't seen either of my brothers for seven years.'

She paused in her task and frowned irately when she felt his hands slide further around her hips and tighten slightly on her bottom with the practised ease of a born seducer. The movement shocked her to the depths of her virginal innocence and made her heart pound in her chest.

'I think you're beginning to enjoy this. Do you have to hold me in quite that way? Please remove your hands,' she said, meeting the enigmatic gaze of the man who was nine years older than her in years but centuries older than her in experience, who had done and seen everything there was to do and see, and who knew exactly the effect his intimate hold was having on her.

Her prim reprimand brought a reluctant smile to Iain's lips and urged him to draw her a bit closer, settling her thighs intimately against his loins, the action flicking a fiery brand across his senses. 'Not a chance. Not until you've performed your task to my satisfaction. I don't want you taking off before you've finished removing my beard,' he murmured teasingly, his warm breath touching her face.

Lorne began again, oddly relaxed by the low timbre of his voice and the steadiness of his gaze. 'Do you always wear a beard?' she asked softly.

'No. Only when my military duties keep me away from home for any length of time—or when I'm hunting, as now. I find it tedious always having to shave.'

'You have a manservant. Couldn't he do that?'

He chuckled at that. 'I wouldn't trust Archie anywhere near my face with a sharp blade. I prefer to do it myself—unless there happens to be a pretty maid with a steady hand willing to perform the task for me.'

The softening of his voice caused Lorne's heart to skip a beat. 'I seem to recall you gave me little choice,' she replied, avoiding his eyes by wiping the blade once more. 'You—you are a soldier?' she asked, not really surprised, for there was an aura about him of a man who had often confronted danger—and derived pleasure from it.

'Was. When peace was restored between England and France, I returned to Norwood and vowed to live an untroubled life running my estate and pursuing life's simple pleasures—which I was doing nicely until you came crashing into my life with all the force of a tribe of Highlanders. Unfortunately, peace at Norwood will not be restored until this business with your father is settled.'

'I didn't ask to be kidnapped,' she retorted sharply. After a moment's silence in which she was uneasily conscious of his eyes perusing every detail of her face, she said, 'During the war with France, did you serve in Flanders?'

'I did.'

'Robert, my brother, was there, too.'

Iain scowled with derision. 'I know—fighting for King Louis.'

Lorne was quick to defend her brother. 'To be fair to Robert, he fights for what he believes to be right—just as you do—and his prime concern is for the Highlands and the High-landers' way of life. But I remember what you said when you came to Kinlochalen that day. You spoke the truth when you said the Highlanders were enmeshed in the ways of the past, settling scores by the old methods. You also said that the world is changing, that Scotland is changing, but Robert's ob-stinate and independent spirit will never accept change.'

Iain regarded her in amazement. 'Considering the short time you spent with your brother before you were sent to live with your grandmother, you appear to know him well. You also remember a great deal about that day I rode into Kinlo-chalen, Lorne McBryde.'

'I remember everything about that day,' she said quietly, meaningfully, a faraway look entering her eyes as she paused in her task. Her eyes settled on his. 'I may have lived in England for the past seven years, but I was born a Highlander and my memory is long. Both Robert and James wrote to me on a regular basis at Astley Priory.'

Iain caught her gaze, and regarded her intently. 'But when your father was sentenced to hang, to prevent the forfeiture of Drumgow and his estate, your brother signed an oath of allegiance before the start of '92, submitting himself and his dependents to King William and his indemnity.'

'Robert swore that oath in shame and bitterness in the presence of the Sheriffs at Inveraray, where my father will hang if he is caught. It is no secret that Robert is prepared to work towards a second Stewart restoration. For the most part he keeps his thoughts to himself, but his hatred of being ruled by an alien Protestant southern government is shared by many West Highland clans who, as you will be aware, form a hard core of implacable, obstinate dissent and remain loyal to the Stewart cause.'

Having removed most of his beard, Lorne paused to gaze at the face that was beginning to emerge. She saw arrogance in the jut of her captor's jaw, and an indomitable pride and strength etched in every finely moulded feature. She was also beginning to sense a powerful charisma that had nothing to do with his handsome looks and powerful physique, or that mocking smile of his and brilliant flashing eyes.

Unbidden, another face floated before her eyes, a face so like this one, but without the arrogance and hard-bitten edge of experience and age. It was the face of his brother David, with features so fair and so perfect. She realised that David would have looked like the boy Iain had once been. Tears misted her eyes and a hard lump appeared in her throat.

'What is it?' Iain asked warily, seeing her distress and suspecting the reason for it.

She swallowed down the lump in her throat and whispered, 'You—you look like—'

Iain's features tightened and he stiffened, embracing her in a glance that was ice cold. 'Don't say it,' he warned quietly.

Heeding the warning note in his voice, Lorne lowered her gaze and, resigning herself with a little sigh, continued with her task in thoughtful silence. Unwilling to let her stop talking and in an attempt to relieve the awkward moment, with his eyes fixed compellingly on her sweet, downcast face, Iain asked, 'Did you enjoy living with your grandmother?'

She nodded, glad that he was no longer angry with her for reminding him of his brother. The mood of conviviality between them was a relief and she welcomed it. 'I love her dearly. It may surprise you to know that my grandmother is Scottish by birth. Her family lived in Leith—but they're all dead now. When my grandfather came to Edinburgh during the Civil War, he met and married her and took her to live at Astley Priory—his home near York.'

'And your mother? How did she come to meet Edgar McBryde?'

'When she came to Scotland with my grandmother on a rare visit to her family. She met my father in Edinburgh.'

Iain shifted his position to make himself more comfortable on the rock, his arms still folded around her in what had almost become an intimate embrace. 'When this is over, will you ever forgive me for kidnapping you, Lorne McBryde?'

His question was so unexpected that Lorne searched for something to say. After a moment she shook her head, her hair rippling down her back like water from a pump, and she slanted him a smile so wide it was like the sun rising over the Scottish mountains. 'Well,' she said, trying to sound severe despite the mirth shimmering in her eyes. 'I might forgive you for kidnapping me, because I understand why you are doing it, you see—but it's a hanging offence to make me shave you.'

Iain laughed out loud at that, and the unexpected charm of his white smile that followed did treacherous things to Lorne's heart. She was glad to discover he had a sense of humour.

'Then I may repeat the offence by asking you to shave me again tomorrow—and each day after that while you remain at Norwood. Now—continue telling me how your parents met.' Iain was amazed by his own curiosity to know everything about her, and sublimely content to let her beauty feed his gaze, creating within his being a sweet, hungering ache.

'They were attracted to each other from the start, but my grandparents were against them forming any attachment. They did everything they could to keep them apart, but my mother was determined to have her way.' Lorne smiled wistfully. 'For all his blusterings, my father loved her deeply, and he was quietly proud of the way she would stand up to him and speak her mind. I recall him telling me how stubborn she could be—that she was as hot-headed as any man, and that she had a temper that could make a mountain tremble.'

'She must have been a rare jewel, your mother.'

Lorne met his gaze, seeing his eyes were warm and smiling. 'Yes, she was, although I don't remember her very well.'

'And she had traits that have been inherited by her daughter.'

'It looks that way, I suppose. Anyway, she was set on marrying my father and in the end my grandparents gave in—but it broke their hearts. They never saw her again—or Robert and James. When my mother died I was three years old. Determined to abide by my mother's wishes, my father made sure my education was taken care of and that I was taught English, although for most of the time I was virtually ignored and left to do very much as I pleased. If I had been a boy, it would have been different,' she said in a matter-of-fact way, having accepted the truth of this at an early age.

About to attack the tuft of hair growing around the cut on his cheek, which she had left until last, she said, 'After—after what happened—when my father was outlawed, as I have already told you I was sent to live with my grandmother.'

'And now? Is there a reason for your return?'

She nodded, growing cold on being reminded of what awaited her at Drumgow.

Iain's brows drew together into a slight frown as he looked at her, seeing her eyes were tinged with sadness. 'Is it so very terrible?' he asked gently.

'It is to me,' she replied quietly. 'It is Robert's wish for me to marry one of his neighbours.'

'I see.' His expression sombre, Iain considered her for a space, then asked, 'And is this prospective bridegroom known to you?'

'Yes—and to you, too, I believe. It is Duncan Galbraith.'

There was a moment's silence as Iain digested this news and then he looked deep into her eyes. 'So that's the way of things. And do I detect a reluctance on your part?'

She nodded, seeing something in his eyes akin to compassion. 'Because I was so far away I was unable to participate in the betrothal negotiations. With my father's permission Robert proceeded without me. Duncan is Laird of Kinlochalen now. His older brothers were killed in a skirmish with a rival clan. Both Robert and Duncan welcome a union between our families and are eager for the wedding to take place as soon as I arrive at Drumgow.'

'What I see in your eyes tells me that the bride is not so eager to sacrifice herself on the altar of matrimony merely to unite two ancient bloodlines. Why don't you want to marry Duncan Galbraith?'

Lorne's eyes fell from his. 'I have my reasons. I am not obliged to share them with you,' she answered quietly, wondering what his reaction would be if she told him that it was Duncan who had betrayed the whereabouts of Iain's brother that day to Ewan Galbraith, and that because of it she had sworn an oath never to speak to Duncan again for as long as she lived. She could never forgive him, but nor could she convey the knowledge of what he had done to Iain Monroe either.

'I don't want to marry him—and I will beg my brothers' understanding, but I fear my protests will be to no avail against Robert's determination—and my father's, if, as you say, he has returned to Scotland. In fact, I strongly suspect that it is my father who is behind it.'

Iain gave the proud young woman within the circle of his arms a long, assessing look. By kidnapping her he had inadvertently, but effectively, ruined all her chances of acquiring a decent husband in her grandmother's genteel world—unless the scandal her liaison with Rupert Ogleby had caused had already put paid to that—but his instinct told him that these things would not concern Duncan Galbraith.

She was the precious property of Edgar McBryde, and—if young Ogleby was to be believed, at least in part, which he was inclined to do, for he strongly believed there was never smoke without fire—had already been enjoyed by one man. A lazy grin suddenly swept over his rugged face, for he would derive immense satisfaction and a good deal of pleasure in tasting for himself the delights of Galbraith's lovely young bride before she reached the marital bed. It was the most exciting thought he had entertained in many months.

'If you were hoping for a turn of fate, then perhaps I have inadvertently brought it about,' he said, his iron-thewed arms tightening slightly about her slender waist and a slumberous expression appearing in his heavy-lidded eyes.

'Oh? In what way?' Lorne asked, becoming much too conscious of being held too close, and the magnetism of his powerful frame, that made her heart leap into her throat.

'The way I see it, I may have done you a favour by kidnapping you. I may be saving you from a fate worse than death. Perhaps Galbraith will not be so eager to wed you when he knows I—his sworn enemy—am keeping you, since I am the one responsible for bringing his father to the gallows. He may even find someone else to marry.'

Lorne sighed, shaking her head slowly. 'No, he won't. Duncan and I were friends once. He was fiercely protective of me and always there. I was grateful to him—in fact, if it hadn't been for Duncan and Rory, his younger brother, I don't know how I would have survived when my mother died. But I remember him as an arrogant, possessive youth, and when he made up his mind about something, he would not let go easily.'

Iain looked down at her, his gaze attentive. 'You have an interesting past, Lorne McBryde.'

'I'm glad you think so, my lord. I would call it extraordinary.' She focused her attention on the few remaining hairs around the cut on Iain's cheek, eager to complete her task so she could break free of his hold, for she was aware of a gnawing disquiet settling on her at being held too close for too long. Somewhere deep within her a spark flickered and flared, setting her skin ablaze and filling her body with liquid fire. Despite her rioting nerves, outwardly she remained calm.

'Now, hold still,' she breathed. 'Apart from the hairs around the wound I'm almost finished.'

A slow smile curved his lips. 'Are you sure you have the stomach for it?'

A rueful smile brought up the corners of her lips. 'I have a cast-iron stomach, my lord—although I must warn you that if you do not hold yourself still, it will hurt more before I'm through with you. I might even be tempted to mar your features permanently and make you look like Lucifer, as recompense for kidnapping me—which would certainly put paid to your handsome looks and *amours* with the ladies.'

'Or enhance them,' Iain countered softly, his eyes capturing hers with an intimacy that made Lorne's blood run warm.

'To be so disfigured might intrigue them—and make them wonder what it would be like to bed with the devil.'

As Lorne gazed at his proud aristocratic face, unable to conceal her naïveté, visions of such a thing happening brought two bright flags of scarlet to her cheeks and an uneasiness coursing through her. He was speaking to her as if he had ceased to think of her as his enemy, but as a lover, almost, and she was at a loss to know how to react. Deciding it was best to make light of the situation, which she always did when she was presented with an awkward moment, she gave him a beguiling smile.

'And it will be their hell to pay if they do. Still—I'm sure you know what's what.'

He gazed at her, eyes amused, a smile curving on his lower lip. 'I've never had any complaints.'

'I'm sure you've had a lot of practice. Maybe you and the devil aren't so very different after all—and I must consider myself fortunate that our relationship is already established.'

'And what is our relationship?'

She cocked her head to one side and looked at him squarely. 'We are enemies, of course. What else?'

His eyes glowed wickedly. 'What else indeed. I do not claim to hold your family in any esteem—but you—you are a different matter, Lorne McBryde. You intrigue me and I have a yearning to get to know you better. For the time we are together, can we not, in common agreement, strive to be as gracious and mannerly as it is possible for enemies to be towards each other?'

'That depends on whether or not you hold still and allow me to finish the task you gave me. And do not forget that I still hold the knife,' she reminded him quietly, with a glint of mischief sparking in her bright green eyes, and a puckish smile on her lips.

'Then I am yours to command and surrender myself to your ministerings completely.' Iain chuckled, unmoved by her gentle chiding.

Lorne's hands trembled slightly as she bent her attention to her task, having to use all her concentration to steady them as she passed the blade close to the wound. She gazed at it through a blur of hot tears. With her own deep sensitivity, she hated to think she had caused his injury.

'What's the matter?' he asked. 'Is it horrendous?'

She shook her head. 'No. The wound is quite deep, but it doesn't need stitching. Although—it might leave a faint scar.'

''Twill not be my only scar—although the others are mementoes of the wars.'

'And do they attest to other men's deaths?'

'I will just say that I have survived better than my adversaries.'

'I'm sorry,' she whispered, suddenly overcome with remorse when she focused her eyes on the wound. 'I'm so—so sorry.'

Iain heard the sincerity in her tearful voice and he was touched that she could express so much compassion and gentleness for her enemy. He suddenly felt vaguely ashamed of what he was doing to her. 'Don't cry,' he murmured achingly, his voice hoarse. ''Tis only a scratch.'

Hearing the strange, compellingly gentle quality in his deep voice, Lorne lifted her eyes and met his steady gaze. 'It isn't. It's much more than that. I didn't mean to make you so angry or for you to hurt yourself—or for Archie's horse to go galloping off like that.'

The tender apology of her reply almost demolished Iain's reserve and his throat constricted around an unfamiliar knot of emotion. Paralysed by what he was thinking and feeling, he stared at her soft mouth with a hunger that he was finding difficult to control. Her eyes were awash with tears and when they began to spill over her lashes and run slowly down her cheeks, it almost unmanned him.

'Please don't cry,' he murmured, pulling her into his embrace and wrapping his arms around her, his one desire being to calm her, to hold her, but in that moment another kind of desire, potent and primitive, swelled inside him, one he wanted to savour and enjoy. Lowering his mouth to hers, he succumbed to the impulse that had been tormenting him and kissed her long and deep and undemanding, feeling the softness of her lips and tasting the salt of her tears. His arms tightened across her back, pressing the contours of her body to his, and he almost lost his head entirely when he felt her lips open under his and she kissed him back.

To Lorne, being kissed like that was like being cocooned in a warm world of sensuality. His lips were teasing, tormenting and provoking—not at all like that other kiss, which had been brutal and meant to punish. Her world began to tilt and the searing lips sent tremors rippling through her body, touching every nerve until they were aflame with desire. She was aware of nothing. All that mattered was the closeness of this man and the protection of his arms.

After what seemed like an eternity, Iain raised his head and tenderly gazed down into her melting green eyes. The woman in his arms affected him like a heady wine. Her warm, open face was unable to conceal her innocence. 'I wonder,' he murmured.

'What?' she breathed, struggling to release herself from the trance-like state induced by his kiss. 'What do you wonder?'

'If you are as guileless and innocent as you appear to be.'

She laughed lightly, the sound as merry and relaxed as a child at play, and as pure as the water running over the pebbles close by. 'I don't think so. You must have noticed that I have a tendency towards disobedience and defiance.'

His dark eyes narrowed, studying her with quiet intensity. 'You're a most perverse wench, that's for sure.'

'I am merely protecting my honour,' she countered. 'I have also often been accused of being far too wilful and head-strong for my own good.'

His look was one of wry amusement. 'Aye. You have not been with us twenty-four hours and already my experience with you leads me to agree. You are Edgar McBryde's daughter for sure.'

When he released his hold she backed away from him. Bringing himself up to his full height, he reached out to draw her back, but when his hand touched her arm she winced and gasped. Immediately he was concerned.

'What is it? What's wrong?'

'It's nothing. I—hurt my arm when I fell—that's all.'

'Let me see,' he ordered quietly, awash with guilt when he remembered how roughly he had handled her. He had been so wrapped up in his own anger that not once had he thought to ask if she was hurt. Taking her arm, he saw her sleeve was torn and dark with dried blood. Gently he rolled it up to her elbow, seeing the flesh was grazed, sore and bruised.

Lorne tried to draw her arm away but he held on to it. 'Please—don't concern yourself. As you can see, it's nothing, I assure you.'

'Yes, it is. I should have realised you might be hurt. My mother was always telling me that my temper and my thoughtlessness are my worst enemies.'

'You are not to blame. The horse balked and threw me on the sound of the horn—I assumed that he would be familiar with it on the hunt.'

'Archie doesn't ride to hunt on that particular horse. He purchased it just before we set out, and had no idea it would shy at the sound of the hunting horn.' He grinned. 'Which is fortunate for me that it does, otherwise I might still be chasing after you.'

'What? On that magnificent beast of yours? You would have caught up with me in no time at all.' She sighed resignedly, pouting her lips prettily. 'Trust me to pick the one horse that has no stomach for the hunt.'

'Nevertheless, I shouldn't have gone hurtling after you like I did.' Deftly his fingers felt the bones. 'There's nothing broken, but it's bruised and you have a nasty graze there. Still, it's nothing that a cold compress won't help,' he said, having dressed many a wound in his years as a soldier. Placing his hands on her waist, he lifted her effortlessly on to the rock he had just vacated. 'Sit there. It's your turn to be ministered to.'

With her permission he tore a strip of material from the hem of her petticoat. After dipping one half in the burn, he cleansed the graze carefully, washing away the dried blood with long, cooling strokes, before binding it with the other half. His hands were gentle and he didn't speak as he bent his head over her arm, which gave Lorne a moment to dwell on what had just happened between them.

Without his beard and with his hair falling forward in roguish curls over his brow, Iain Monroe looked youthful and more vulnerable. As she watched him she felt drawn to him, wanting to taste his kisses again—and more, knowing she would be unable to resist the desires that begged for fulfilment.

But then, hadn't her body betrayed her? Had she really forgot he was holding her by force and would not release her until her father was caught?

Was she really so weak?

Yes, she realised with startling clarity. Where Iain Monroe was concerned she was. But he was not her enemy. He never had been. In fact, he made her want to get to know him better, to step beyond the hatred he carried in his heart for the McBrydes, to tell him she had not betrayed his brother's hiding place to the Galbraiths or her father. But how was she ever to burst the festering abscess of misunderstanding when he ordered her to be silent?

She was confused. Last night she had sworn to make this man's life hell while ever he held her hostage—but that was before the kiss.

And therein lay Iain Monroe's appeal.

That kiss had changed everything, and she had to admit to her change of heart. Was that all it had taken, for him to kiss her? It had changed things for him, too, she sensed that. Last night, when he had realised who she was, his hatred had been intense—but now, not twenty-four hours had passed and he had kissed her with such tender passion.

When he'd finished bandaging her arm, she held it up to inspect his handiwork and smiled. 'I'm impressed. You should have been a doctor.'

'I was a soldier, don't forget, and used to dealing with the broken bones and wounds of my men.'

His expression changed as he perceived John striding towards them. Lifting Lorne down, he waited for him to join them.

'Andrew's back,' John said abruptly, scowling darkly from one to the other. His disapproval of the intimacy that was fast developing between Iain and the girl was plain in the firm set of his jaw and the blistering glare he threw Lorne.

John's mood conveyed itself to Iain and his manner became brusque. 'Good. Now we can leave for Norwood. I want to be there before nightfall. Andrew returned to the inn to give your maidservant a letter to take to your brother in Edinburgh,' he told Lorne. 'He's also brought your baggage, which should make life more comfortable for you at Norwood.'

'Thank you,' she replied, warily searching his implacable features, already mourning the loss of her lover of a moment before.

For a moment Iain's gaze held hers with a penetrating intensity. 'There's no need to thank me,' he said curtly. 'Time for that when your father is caught and you are allowed to go home.'

Chapter Four

When Iain turned and strode on ahead of them, John looked at Lorne. Her glowing cheeks and eyes large and warm with the emotions Iain had aroused in her caused him some unease. 'I warn ye ta have a care, Lorne McBryde. When a pretty wench comes within Iain's reach, he canna keep his hands off her.'

Lorne's green eyes snapped with anger as she bore the impertinence of his expression. 'You are mistaken. I have no illusions about my situation or Iain Monroe's intentions where I am concerned. I am his prisoner, and I am hardly likely to forget it. Do you honestly think I would let him bed me while he schemes to capture my father and see him hanged? I will be no man's mistress—least of all Iain Monroe's.'

'Aye, well—be careful in yer dealings with him. I ken Iain better than any man alive. He's not an easy man ta cross. It takes a very brave man, or a fool, to try. But he's persuasive,' John told her honestly, lightening his mood and smiling lazily. 'He wears many faces. Not all of them are kind. He can warm a female heart with just a look—but he can also burn,' he warned.

'You appear to know him well.'

'Aye, I do—and his father before him. Iain's mother was my cousin, and when my kin was odiously butchered by the Galbraiths and yer grandfather and his sons and their retainers, Iain's father brought me ta Norwood—where I've remained ever since.'

'The McBrydes killed your family?'

'Aye—all of them. Not one man, woman or child was free from molestation. Come dawn, when I returned after spending the night at the home of a neighbour, when frost clung to my hair and my clothes, and to breathe deeply was like having a knife thrust between my ribs, I discovered the slaughter.'

'For what it's worth, I'm sorry,' Lorne murmured, feeling a lump of constricting sorrow in her chest. Small wonder John Ferguson held a grudge against her and her kin. The pain she'd seen vanished, and his features were already perfectly composed when he looked at her.

''Twas a long time ago, but I canna forget the barbarous butchery and slaughter committed by the McBrydes and the Galbraiths.' He fixed Lorne with a hard, cynical gaze. 'Yer own father was still a youth—but experienced in the brutal ways of the Highlanders for all that. He played his part well—and will answer for his actions—as we all do in the end,' he said with the calm conviction of what he believed. 'No man escapes.'

Reaching the others, who were mounted and ready to leave, Lorne was pleased to see that Archie had retrieved his horse, and relieved when he helped her to mount another that she wasn't to ride the beast that had thrown her.

Iain watched her mount, suddenly furious with himself for having succumbed so easily and foolishly to his captive's charms. He had let himself be mindlessly borne away on a rush of passion. Was the wench some kind of sorceress who had cast a spell on him? He, Iain Monroe, had succumbed to the compelling force of Lorne McBryde's warm femininity like some over-eager young lad.

But never had he met a woman who possessed so much freedom of spirit and courage, who was so open and direct. He knew she would never be anything other than honest, and the brightness in that steady, often disconcerting gaze, was an intelligent brightness that proclaimed the agility of an independent mind. She had the wild, untamed quality of her Highland heritage running in dangerous undercurrents just below the surface that found its counterpart in his own hot-blooded, impetuous nature.

Unfortunately, the realisation of who she was banished his pleasure, for he must never forget that the McBryde blood flowed thick and strong through her veins. Nor must he forget how her betrayal of his brother had brought about his death. She was his hostage and he had no right to think about her in any personal way. But he could not escape the fact that from the moment she had sunk her teeth into his flesh and kicked his shin, she had fascinated and intrigued him.

As Lorne was about to join the column of men, a voice rang out.

'Wait. A word, if you please, before we leave.'

She glanced at Iain, who was striding towards her, her heart contracting painfully when she heard the hard edge to his voice. Looking down at him, she waited for him to continue, feeling by the coldness of his voice, by the very intonation with which he addressed her, that it was a stranger who looked at her.

'What happened between us just now was a mistake,' he said coldly, out of Archie's hearing. 'It was nothing but a pleasurable moment of shared ardour—and I do not pretend that it was anything but that. I behaved in a manner that I now regret.'

Lorne bristled, but pride prevented her from showing any

emotion. Her head went up and her eyes were like dagger thrusts. 'Why? Because I am Lorne McBryde?'

'Precisely.'

Lorne was ashamed, deeply ashamed that she had yielded to him so willingly. How could she have forgotten why she was here? But for one endless, wonderful moment, she had been able to forget that she was his hostage. She had belonged to him, but then he had snatched away that brief glimpse of heaven with his cruel words.

'Damn you, Iain Monroe. I didn't deserve that. But you are right. It shouldn't have happened and I will thank you to keep your hands to yourself for the time I am your prisoner.'

'I shall endeavour to do just that.'

His eyes focused on her with a clarity that seemed to gain power from his anger. Lorne could see something fearsome that rang a hollow bell deep inside her, frightening her. Then he turned away and she knew he was closing a mental door on her. Angrily she dug her heels into her horse's flanks and moved on, hoping she wouldn't have to speak to him again for the duration of the journey.

Set against a magnificent backdrop of scattered woodlands and gently sloping hills, the massive edifice of Castle Norwood, with a blue flag emblazoned with the Monroe coat of arms flying aloft, came into view. The splendidly varied skyline of steep roofs, projecting corner turrets and gables showed the influence of France, of that country's chateaux. Five storeys of solid, time-stained impenetrable granite, with relatively tiny windows burrowed through the thick walls, seemed to grow out of the circling, high defensive wall. The huge structure was a place of destiny and foreboding.

With the arrival of the Earl of Norwood the castle had awakened from its temporary slumber. Lorne rode through the massive gates, which yawned open like a huge mouth waiting to swallow her up. The clatter of iron shoes against the cobbled courtyard jarred her out of her weariness. As the long line of travellers approached the iron-studded doors of the castle, a woman stepped out and ran across the cobbles, her bright green skirts flying out behind her. With a grin stretching his face from ear to ear, John reined in his horse and dismounted. It was plain that the woman was pleased to see him, for she had eyes for no other.

In fascination Lorne watched John gather her to him in a bearlike hug, finding it hard to believe this was the same brute of a man who had roughly bundled her on to his horse and galloped off with her into the night. Tenderly stroking the woman's cheek, John exchanged a few brief words with her and then watched her go back inside.

Bone weary and longing for a bed where she could lie down and sleep for ever, Lorne vaguely saw Iain swing down from his horse and speak to the men. They began to dismount and move away to unsaddle and wipe down their sweating steeds. Iain came to help her down. She was too weary to protest.

'Archie,' he called to the young man. 'Take Mistress McBryde inside and see that she is made comfortable,' he commanded, before spinning on his heel and striding away from them.

Lifting her skirts to climb the short flight of steps, Lorne followed Archie, knowing she was about to enter a prison, but she was too tired to care. Despite being who she was and looking for all the world like a vagabond, she was so beautiful that it brought an unmistakable look of admiration to the eyes of the servants who saw her. Her arrival was met with interested murmurs of speculation, for each of those assembled knew of the importance of her presence at Castle Norwood.

With a morbid sense of doom Lorne entered the lofty, stone-vaulted hall, passing between halberds with red plumes that flanked the doorway. The interior seemed extremely bright in comparison to the deepening dusk outside, for pine torches had been lit and burned straight up in sconces. They cast a brilliant light, enriching the plaids and banners and bouncing off the steel blades of a lavish armaments display— a copious arrangement of equipment for killing people that adorned the walls and dominated the hall.

The woman Lorne had seen in the courtyard crossed towards them. Perhaps close on thirty in age, she looked to be a person of strong character and bore herself with a dignified confidence. Her hair was the colour of the bracken that clothed the autumn hills, and her attractive features were marked with a strong squarish jaw. She greeted Archie with a brief smile before assessing Lorne, her blue-grey eyes bright and alert and surprisingly friendly as she hastened to minister to this unhappy young woman her husband had captured.

'I am Flora—John's wife. He has told me why you are here and that I must make sure you are made comfortable. I expect you are exhausted after being in the saddle all day. Please come with me and I will show you to your chamber.'

Lorne gave her a curious glance. 'You speak as if you were expecting me,' she said with stilted coolness.

'I was. Iain sent a man on ahead to proclaim your coming.'

Despair filled Lorne as she followed the older woman across the hall and up the stairs. Climbing to the third storey of this massive tower house, she was shown into a comfortably furnished chamber, which was heated by a blazing fire.

Flora's gaze was soft when she looked at Lorne. 'I'm sure you'll be comfortable in here. I'll have some food sent up for you—unless you'd care to eat with the rest of the household in the dining hall?'

'No—I think not.'

'I understand. Perhaps you would welcome a warm bath,' she suggested after making a brief assessment of Lorne's appearance. 'One of the maidservants will unpack for you and see to your needs.'

Lorne's chin went up belligerently. 'Thank you, but I am perfectly capable of seeing to my own needs.'

Flora felt her resistance. 'Iain has stressed that while you remain under his roof you are to be treated as his guest—and guests at Norwood are not left to fend for themselves.'

'I am his prisoner, not his guest,' Lorne stated, her voice laced with sarcasm.

Flora offered a tentative smile and her eyes betrayed her sympathy as she looked at the younger woman with sudden liking. Lorne McBryde was resentful and frightened, of course, even though she was trying to disclaim it to bolster her courage. And what girl wouldn't be upon finding herself snatched by kidnappers in the dark and forced to travel miles to an unknown destination with hostile strangers against her will?

'Guest or captive, we will do our best to make your stay at Norwood as comfortable as possible. I know why you have been brought here, and I realise how extremely difficult this must be for you—and, for what it's worth, I am sorry. I don't agree with grown men kidnapping young women to aid them in settling old grievances—and I am none too pleased to discover that my husband is capable of such villainy. I am well used to John's impulsive acts, but he can often be so infuriating—as are all men.' She sighed deeply. 'At times all that male posturing wearies me. They are like small boys playing out some game.'

'I can assure you that this is no game to me, ma'am,' Lorne retorted coldly.

'Please call me Flora. Whatever you imagine, I wish you no harm.'

If Flora thought Lorne would succumb to her kindness, she was mistaken. The young woman's face remained expressionless, nor did she lower her gaze, but her rejection couldn't have been plainer if she had put it into words.

'Thank you,' was all Lorne said.

Flora directed her a level gaze. Her voice was stilted when she spoke. 'I do understand how you must be feeling, and I speak with your best interest in mind. Excuse me. I'll arrange to have some food sent up.'

Lorne watched Flora cross towards the door, feeling a touch of remorse. Her smile had been so genuine, so guileless, that she felt ashamed. She wasn't naturally rude to people, especially when they were being kind. Besides, she would rather have this woman as a future ally than foe. 'Wait—please.'

Flora paused at the door and turned.

Lorne took a tentative step forward. 'Ever since I was captured I have been surrounded by so much hostility that I've been at my wits' end not knowing what to do.' Suddenly her lips broke into a smile. 'Actually, that isn't entirely true. Archie has gone out of his way to be nice to me. He was the only person civil to me after I was captured. I will not forget his many kindnesses.'

Flora moved back into the centre of the room, touched by Lorne's change of attitude. 'Archie's like that—quite the young gallant, in fact.'

At that moment a pretty, bright-eyed young maid in starched white linen entered the room. Despite Lorne being kin of the despised McBrydes, the maid's manner was subservient to the point of bobbing a curtsy.

'Arrange to have hot water sent up, will you, Janet,' Flora ordered. 'Mistress McBryde would like a bath.'

* * *

Lorne submitted without protest to the young maid's ministerings. The journey to Norwood had been long and tiring and she felt weary and dirty. The bath was invigorating, and when she had been towelled dry she felt much better. While Janet unpacked her belongings she ate a little of the food that was brought to her, but the fatigue of the past twenty-four hours was beginning to tell on her. Her bed was an invitation to rest, but her head was still reeling from the events of the day and she was too restless to sleep. Instructing Janet to snuff out the candles and leave her, she covered her nightdress with her robe and went to the window, looking out at the dark, listening to the sounds of the night beyond.

As she felt the huge castle wrapping itself round her, the dire reality of her predicament hit her like a heavy weight. What dangerous folly it had been to leave Mrs. Shelly at the inn and wander off into the night as she had. How long would she have to remain in this place? How long before her father and brothers came to rescue her? She knew that as soon as Mrs. Shelly handed James the note in Edinburgh telling him of her capture, he would lose no time in returning to Drumgow. Her family would certainly make haste to set her free from her gaolers—and become gaolers of a different sort.

Aware that she hadn't heard Janet close the door behind her when she went out, but feeling eyes boring through her back, she spun round, sensing that she was not alone. In the gloom she was startled upon seeing Iain's tall figure propped in the doorway with his arms folded casually across his chest, the perfect image of relaxed arrogance and elegance. He was attired in breeches and knee-high boots, and a sleeveless, brown leather jerkin hung loose over a white shirt, which was open at the neck, showing the corded muscles of his throat.

He had a hard look about him, with a firmly muscled chest, lean waist and narrow hips, and, recalling the agility and easy strength he had shown when he had come hurtling after her when she'd escaped into the woods earlier that day, she could only guess at the discipline he practised in keeping himself in such fine, fighting form. Beneath raised brows he was regarding her in cold silence, and his grim expression boded ill.

'So, the Earl of Norwood felt duty bound to welcome me to his house, did he? What an honour and an extraordinary mark of esteem from a man of such tender pride! However, you are either unaware of the impropriety of such a visit to a lady's bedchamber at this hour, or you are out to strip me of what little dignity I have left. What you have to say must be of the utmost importance to justify such behaviour—or am I to assume you have ventured into my room with sinful intent?'

Iain loomed in the doorway like a dark, ominous shadow, his expression remaining hard. 'Banish the thought. I've merely come to see if you are comfortable.'

'You have servants to see to that. I do not welcome your intrusion into my privacy.'

Lorne's heart began to beat in deep, fierce thuds when her unexpected and highly unwelcome visitor relinquished his stance in the doorway and strolled casually into the room. His size made the room appear smaller, and he cast huge shadows on the wall. She faced him bravely, her hands clasped demurely at her waist to prevent them from trembling, conscious that she wore nothing but her nightdress beneath her robe, and of the intense physical awareness she felt at his nearness. The warmth he had shown her earlier was still absent. It was as if the closeness, the tenderness they had shared, had never been.

Iain's eyes were drawn to her graceful figure. The light

from the fire fell on her small, proud head, and even in the shadowed room softer lights glowed within the shining depths of her hair loosely falling about her shoulders. Her face was like an icon, exaggeratedly so in the dim light, and the silken robe covering her nightdress moulded itself to her curvaceous form, presenting such delights to Iain's closely attentive gaze that he felt his senses leap. He cursed himself for his weakness. He might covet her, but he would not allow himself to be affected by her.

'Why is there no light in the room?' he asked sharply, taking his annoyance out on her.

'Because I prefer it this way. The fire offers light enough. Please understand that you cannot come marching in here whenever you feel like it,' Lorne chided, unable to believe the absolute nerve of the man and refusing to let the matter drop until he understood this.

He arched a sleek black brow. 'Can't I? Try me,' he said, his voice as cutting as steel. 'This is my house—and you are hardly in any position to summon the servants to throw me out.'

'Much as I would like to,' she replied with contemptuous scorn.

On hearing her uncompromising antagonism, Iain very slowly, very carefully, moved closer, a cruel smile on his face and his eyes glittering silver shards. 'I don't doubt that for one moment, Lorne McBryde, and should you decide to tie the sheets together, climb out of your window and scale the three storeys to the courtyard below, I feel I must warn you that my rooms are next door—and that I am a light sleeper. I advise you to think very carefully before you make the mistake of doing anything to antagonise me,' he said in an unnaturally quiet voice. 'I promise you, you'll regret it.'

Despite the icy tingle of alarm his silken voice caused in her, Lorne lifted her chin courageously. 'And if you think I am some complaisant female who will do your smallest bidding, who will be content to reside in this grim heap of stones where the servants are as mad as their master, you can forget it. I shall give you neither rest nor respite while I am here. That I promise you. If my brothers hear one whisper of mistreatment of me, they will tear this castle apart with their bare hands if necessary to free me.'

'It will be a cold day in hell before they hear such rumours,' Iain stated coldly. 'You have only yourself to blame for the situation you find yourself in.'

'I would have thought it to be physically impossible to abduct oneself,' Lorne scoffed with a harsh sarcastic laugh.

'If you behave yourself, I promise that you will be given every courtesy as befits my guest.'

'My definition of a guest is one that can come and go as one pleases. If you do not choose to make mourners of your friends, my lord, I suggest you release me immediately.'

A mildly tolerant smile touched Iain's handsome visage, but the glint in the dark eyes was hard, his voice as smooth as polished steel. 'I did not go to the trouble of bringing you here simply to let you go.'

'I realise that would be too much to expect of you,' she mocked. 'I gather from your cold manner, my lord, that you didn't mean what you said to me this morning.'

'Remind me,' he drawled arching one sleek black enquiring brow. 'I said a great many things I shouldn't have.'

'Yes, you did. But you did say that for the time we are together, we should strive to be as gracious and mannerly as it is possible for enemies to be towards each other. However, it is clear to me that we are adversaries once more. Is that right?'

'Correct. However, providing you give me no trouble, there is no reason why we can't be civil to one another.'

Staring down at her soft mouth, Iain felt a hunger stirring inside him he knew he would find difficult to control if he stayed much longer. He had felt the warmth of holding her in his arms and the exquisite pleasure she had made him feel. He had tasted the sweetness of her mouth, and when he recalled the way she had responded, it made him want to feast on the entire banquet and made making love to his adversary seem almost plausible.

Recognising the brief softening in her captor's eyes, Lorne smiled inwardly. 'I confess to being confused,' she remarked with a haughty lift to her chin, her eyes full of a cruel, sweet joy to find she might have the power to make herself irresistible to this powerful, commanding man if she had a mind. 'I am your enemy. You have made the hatred you feel for me and my family plain—and yet earlier you seemed incapable of any kind of restraint and discrimination. That is not normal behaviour from a man of your inflexible will, who I have come to understand is normally able to master his passionate nature,' she taunted, throwing back her head insolently, wanting to laugh triumphantly and mockingly in his face.

It gave her a feeling of bitter satisfaction—a satisfaction tempered with unease, because when she gazed at the compelling, achingly handsome man who had teased her earlier, when those mobile lips had kissed her with such tender passion, she knew that if Iain Monroe were to repeat his earlier behaviour, she would be like putty in his hands.

'Everything ceased to be normal when John took you hostage. In the meantime, everything will be done to capture your father. In that, as in everything else, I am firmly committed to accomplishing my goal. These are things that are beyond your power to change.'

'I don't believe that.'

'Yes, you do. McBryde is already brushed by the wings of

the Angel of Death. He will think his daughter of such value that I can hardly imagine he would allow you to languish in my hands. Until he arrives, extra guards have been placed around the castle and the surrounding area. Some have been mustered from my retainers who are experienced in the field.'

'How fortunate that you have so many loyal men to do your bidding,' Lorne scoffed in angry derision.

'In clan tradition we are no different from the Highlanders. The land hereabouts is Monroe land. Tacksmen are bound to the Monroes by age-old tradition, by kinship and by the terms of their leases. They pay me rent and bring their sons and people as officers and swordsmen in times of strife, and in return they are given protection and loyalty. While we await our common enemy, a strong guard will be mounted at the castle and you will be kept under strict surveillance. Should you decide to make a run for it, those men will cut you down. Is that clear?'

Swallowing the lump of humiliation in her throat, when Lorne looked into that harsh, sinister face, she firmly believed his men would do just that. 'No doubt I am not your only victim and your dungeons are full of innocent corpses. Tell me, Lord Monroe, do people cross themselves when they go past your accursed castle?'

Iain glared at her. 'You, Mistress McBryde, have wild imaginings. For your own safety I trust you will not try to escape. You gave me your word.'

Lorne stared at him hard. Her father's life depended on her escape, but she had given Iain Monroe her word that she wouldn't attempt it. He had told her he trusted her, and for some reason she could not explain, in all honesty she couldn't bring herself to jeopardise that trust. In which case she must rely on her father's and brothers' ability to rescue her and make good their escape. Having no wish to be humiliated, she would do whatever she had to do—and she would do it with dignity.

'I am a woman of my word. But that does not mean I will passively endure the situation for long.'

'If you do just one thing to inconvenience me or anyone else at Norwood, I won't be responsible for the consequences. I swear to God. Do you understand me?' She glowered at him, but remained stonily silent, and her arrogant refusal to submit to his will enraged him even more. 'Answer me,' he ordered mercilessly.

Realising that her defiance was pushing him beyond reason, Lorne nodded. 'Yes.'

Observing the firm, rebellious thrust to her chin and seeing the flash of fire in her green eyes, Iain knew she wouldn't quietly resign herself to captivity. He must be wary of her at all times. The wench was like a powder keg. She seemed so innocent, so eager, so loyal to her kin, so convinced of the rightness to help her father escape the noose—and these things made her doubly dangerous.

'Perhaps it would be wise after all to incarcerate you in my deepest dungeon. At least there you would be unable to give me trouble.' He turned and strode towards the door. Pausing, he looked back at her. 'We will meet at breakfast in the morning. In the meantime I will leave you with this instruction. You will remain within the castle at all times. Is that clear?'

Lorne tossed her head, pure mutiny blazing in her eyes. 'You are a tyrant, Iain Monroe.'

'I disagree.'

'Yes, you are, and I hate you. Tyranny is tyranny and I, for one, do not propose to bow to it. I prefer to take my meals in my room. You can't possibly expect me to eat my breakfast with my gaolers. It would be like stepping into a nest of vipers—with everyone looking at me, hating me. No—I can't possibly.'

Iain's jaw set with implacable determination as he said in a flat, authoritative voice that belied the leaping fury in his eyes at the thought that she would openly defy him, 'I don't think you heard me. I *expect* to see you in the dining hall at breakfast. I have brought together as many local lairds, tacksmen and their vassals as can be assembled at short notice. There are approximately one hundred men in and around the castle, most of whom believe it is my duty to offer you my hospitality regardless of who you are. If you do not appear, you will leave me with no alternative but to come to your room and drag you out in front of everyone. I told you not to leave the castle, but I will not have you skulking in your quarters twenty-four hours a day.'

Lorne's heart shrieked her resentment of his commands, but she kept her silence, glad when he opened the door and strode out, confident in his arrogance that she would do as she was told. She was unaccustomed to being ordered about by anyone, yet she knew Iain Monroe would insist and that, eventually, she would be forced to obey.

The following morning found Lorne selecting what she would wear, knowing that if she didn't appear at breakfast her captor would do exactly as he'd threatened and come and find her. Determined to avoid a public humiliation, she selected a blue velvet dress that had been made for her to wear at a special occasion on her visit to London with her grandmother. She dressed with care and instructed Janet to brush her heavy hair until it gleamed, before arranging it in thick coils about her head. Despite her look of innocence and the seductive allure of the gown, the hairstyle accentuated her classical features, her high cheekbones and slanting green eyes.

In a whisper of velvet and enveloped in a subtle cloud of perfume, taking a deep breath and holding her head high,

Lorne swept down the stairs to the dining hall. She was a McBryde and bore herself like a queen, for on no account would she appear before these Lowlanders baying for her father's blood humble and meek.

It was a long time since Castle Norwood had entertained so much activity within its walls. Not for forty-five years, in fact, when the Civil War had torn the people of England and Scotland apart. But the Earl and his stewards coped well, summoning loyal retainers to assist in what had to be done to capture Edgar McBryde when he eventually showed his hand. And here they were, like steadfast soldiers pressed into service as of old.

With a constant stream of servants emerging from the kitchens laden with trays and jugs and chambermaids carrying water and logs up to the bedrooms, Iain sat in pensive pose impatiently looking towards the stairs, struggling with his mounting annoyance that his captive might demonstrate her rebellion and remain in her room to defy and provoke him. She was late, deliberately so, and just when he was on the point of going to fetch her, his gaze froze on the tantalising apparition that suddenly appeared on the stairs. He stared at her, caught somewhere between amazement and admiration for her defiant courage.

The wench looked stunning, and Iain knew that this was what she had set out to achieve. Despite the crushing chain of circumstances that had bedevilled Lorne McBryde since she had returned to Scotland, it was plain to every man present that she was undaunted and of no weak spirit. With her head held high and her shoulders back, she showed no fear as she prepared to enter the 'pit of vipers'. What Iain saw was courage and poise and all the things he admired about her. His heart began to hammer in deep, aching beats as his eyes glided over her from head to toe in a lingering appreciation of everything they touched.

Lorne reached the hall, her nose pleasantly titillated by the most appetising smells. Her slender feet propelled her across the floor in a dazzling blur beneath her velvet skirts. With her heart pounding, she moved with a quiet ambience and a new-found tolerance for the assembled company seated at the hastily erected trestle tables, groaning beneath the weight of milk and butter and pots of honey, barley cakes and bannocks and oatmeal brose. Fine pewter plates, silver and glass goblets gleamed as they caught the light slanting through the high windows.

She saw the gazes of the gentlemen privileged to eat within the castle flicker simultaneously to her movement across the hall and become riveted there. A tingle of delight swept through her as, shocked into silence, their surprised expressions gave way to reverent admiration before a soft buzz of speculative conversation began among them. They shuffled awkwardly to their feet as she walked imperiously towards them, and she was quietly pleased that her efforts were having the desired effect. So many faces shifted before her eyes that she was incapable of recognising anyone that she knew, and she didn't see Iain's lips twitch into a thin smile from where he lounged, as if cynically amused that her appearance should have given rise to so great a stir.

With immense relief Lorne saw Flora coming towards her, her face wreathed in a smile, clearly approving of the way she looked.

'You look perfect,' she murmured for Lorne's ears alone. 'Come and sit by Archie and me. Grace has already been said so you can start eating.'

Seated on the bench between the only two people who had shown her any real semblance of courtesy and friendliness, Lorne collected her thoughts sufficiently to respond with a gracious smile to Flora's warm welcome. She saw Iain at the far end of the table eating salt herring off the end of his dirk, and next to him the falcon eye of John Ferguson was watching her with arrogant attention. Iain was regarding her from beneath hooded lids with cynical amusement. Their eyes met and Lorne's reaction was to stiffen her back and look away. Moved by a feminine impulse of coquetry, by the need concealed in every woman to deal blow for blow and return hurt for hurt, she turned to Archie and bestowed on him a melting smile.

Seated beside her, Flora took one look at Lorne's carefully composed features and gentle smile, and was not fooled, but she admired the way the young woman courageously hid her true feelings from prying eyes, defiantly pretending all was well and eating her steaming oatmeal brose drenched with a deep amber honey off her horn spoon as though she were dining in one of London's most fashionable establishments.

'To have so many men inside the castle is not usual,' Flora explained to Lorne, breaking the silence that had fallen as they ate. 'The housekeeper and her maids are working around the clock to prepare such monstrous quantities of food to feed their gargantuan appetites. But while things are so unsettled—'

'You don't have to explain, Flora,' Lorne said with more force than she intended. 'I do know the reason why. Do you and John live in the castle?' she asked, eager to divert the conversation away from her personal catastrophe and discuss something else.

'No. Since our marriage six months ago, John and I have lived with my father and mother at the Manor House in Norwood village. My father is the procurator fiscal for the parish of Norwood.'

Lorne was impressed by this, for the procurator fiscal—a legal officer who performed the functions of public prosecutor—was a man of great power.

'We are living at the castle until this business is settled, when I shall be relieved to return home.'

'But why must you be here?'

'To ease Mrs. Lockwood's burden of looking after the needs of so many inhabitants at the castle. Mrs. Lockwood is a dear, and has been the Monroes' housekeeper for many years,' Flora explained. 'Also, Iain and John are of the opinion that you will benefit from some female company, and I agree with them.'

Accepting a platter of steaming bannocks on behalf of Lorne from a gentleman seated opposite, Flora glanced with quiet amusement at the other gentlemen in their immediate vicinity who were devouring Lorne with eager curiosity and no longer looking at her with unhidden scorn. Her eyes twinkled with satisfaction.

'You certainly appear to have worked wonders on some of the gentlemen present, Lorne. They have scarcely removed their eyes from your face throughout the repast. It's amazing what effect a beautiful and talented woman can have on men—even men such as these. Despite being who you are, before too long you'll have every one of them eating out of your hand and you might break several hearts.'

Glancing down the table, Lorne caught Iain's eye. Even now he was bombarding her with signals of his powerful, vibrant sexuality that set her senses on edge. She could feel them all about her, engulfing her. He wasn't smiling and his eyes looked at her seriously for a moment, then lightened and slid over her face with a kind of lazy insolence, one eyebrow lifted almost imperceptibly.

'There is one heart in particular I would truly like to render into little pieces,' she said quietly, a hint of savagery in her tone. 'For if I cannot slay that mocking, silver-eyed devil watching my every move from his end of the table with a weapon, I would enjoy doing as much damage to his pride and self-esteem that would prove irreparable. I would delight in dragging him down to his knees, to make him crawl and grovel at my feet, and when he offered me his heart I would trample on it and spurn him, and there would be nothing left but the empty shell of the proud and arrogant man I first saw riding into the village of Kinlochalen.'

Glancing sharply at Lorne, Flora could see where her attention was fixed, and the identity of the gentleman who roused her to such bitterness. 'Poor Iain. I'm beginning to feel sorry for him already,' she murmured, laughing softly, thinking it a shame in many respects that this young woman was a McBryde, for this was the type of woman who would make Iain a perfect wife. 'I fear you are going to need to keep your wits sharp and all your courage in future dealings with the Earl of Norwood. But take heed. With those looks of his and enough charm to crumble Stirling Castle and the rock upon which it sits, you may find yourself out of your depth— and you will not be the first woman to do so.'

Lorne's eyebrow flicked upwards as she agreed with her new friend. 'I have already made an accurate assessment of my captor's character, Flora,' she said, speaking with confidence, for it did not occur to her that she was already falling under the spell of a practised seducer, such men being beyond her realms of her experience. 'I have learned to be wary and will endeavour to keep out of his way while I am forced to remain under his roof.'

Chapter Five

From where he sat Iain was taken aback by the depth of Lorne's composure and the delicate, almost ethereal beauty in the young face. In repose she was the quintessence of the beautiful female animal, her face and body as perfectly formed as they could be. Her sensuality was so malignant that even her enemies' eyes seemed to burn with evil pleasure as they lingered on her.

He gritted his teeth in what might have been jealousy as he watched these men, who had been so ready to condemn their captive yesterday, pander to her every need, covet her. He watched the appreciation in their eyes as they regarded the creaminess of her skin and the simple elegance of her gown, the scooped neckline offering a tantalising view of smooth, voluptuous flesh. The next thing he could expect, he thought bitterly, was that they would exonerate her from the part she had played in his brother's death and forget the name she bore.

His eyes narrowed as he continued to watch her. What was the minx up to? If it was a ploy to charm them all into sub-mission, she was succeeding superbly. The stupid charade was beginning to chafe against his patience, but he was no different from the others and found his gaze drawn to her like metal filings to a magnet, and he knew he was in danger of becoming as enamoured as the next man—if he wasn't already. She had evidently had a good night's sleep because she looked sharp and bright and flushed with the compliments being showered on her by that young pup Archie Grogan.

Breakfast over, the men began to rise from the long tables and disperse. They would take up their allotted duties around the castle should the enemy come calling.

Iain observed Lorne slipping from the hall like a graceful, drifting waif. Uncoiling his tall, lean body from his seat, he swiftly moved in her direction.

'Wait. You needn't hurry away.'

Lorne turned to find Iain immediately behind her. She was unable to prevent her heart from doing a somersault on finding herself in such close proximity to him once more— so close that she could see that the wound on his cheek looked to be healing nicely.

'I was glad to see you at breakfast, and that you've decided to be reasonable.'

'Considering the circumstances, you could hardly reproach me if I choose to be unreasonable.'

'I must congratulate you. You have succeeded in charming every one of the gentlemen who attended breakfast, but I warn you to have a care. To compel their admiration is a foolish course of action to embark upon when you are their prisoner. It is not a game I find amusing.'

The look Lorne gave him was one of mock, wide-eyed innocence. 'Game, my lord? I play no game.'

'No? Yesterday these men would gladly have seen you horsewhipped—and today, after using your feminine wiles on them, they worship at your feet. I compliment you, madam,' he drawled. 'You are an artist.' His expression was grim. 'It cannot have escaped your notice that they've been smitten by Cupid—the lot of them.'

His wry tone almost made Lorne burst out laughing. She looked at him obliquely, her smile provocative. 'Really? And does that include the mighty Earl of Norwood? I have heard that you are given to breaking hearts yourself, my lord,' she remarked glibly.

'Hearts mend,' Iain replied sharply.

'And do you speak from experience?' she asked with a smile. 'Has your heart ever been broken?'

'I have never allowed a woman to get that close.'

'Heaven forbid if one does and you become her absolute slave,' Lorne quipped, turning away to proceed up the stairs, annoyed when he fell into step beside her. She paused and snapped her head up, intending to launch into a tirade. 'Don't you have work to do, my lord?'

Her impudent remark brought a chuckle to his throat. 'Plenty—but all in good time.' Reluctant to leave her now she was away from the others, he crossed his arms over his chest and leaned casually against the newel post, one brow arched in speculative enquiry. 'Since you are likely to be living at Norwood for some considerable time, please feel inclined to call me Iain. Is my name so difficult for you to say?'

'I think "my lord" will suffice for now.'

'For now? Does that mean you intend to get to know me better?' he asked, distracted by the golden lights in her hair and the deep curl of her eyelashes silhouetted for an instance against the light.

'What makes you think I want to?' In utter disbelief Lorne watched a slow, satisfied grin sweep across his handsome face. She tried in vain to see beyond the darkness of his magnetic, shameless gaze. He looked so very different to the man of last night who had been so harsh and unfeeling towards her that she experienced great difficulty in suppressing a smile.

'A small matter of a kiss.'

'Which you lost no time in telling me was a mistake,' she reminded him. The path down which he was leading her filled her with a trembling disquiet.

'It was. But that doesn't alter the fact that I enjoyed kissing you and would enjoy teaching you how to do it better.'

Lorne tilted her head to one side and glanced up at him obliquely. 'So, you think I'm in need of instruction?'

'I'd be surprised if you weren't. It's considered improper for a maid to be well versed in the art of kissing.'

'Perhaps if you hadn't taken me by surprise you might not have found me so bereft of knowledge,' she countered sharply, tossing her head haughtily. 'The times I've been kissed are too numerous to count,' she lied, 'and I certainly don't need to be taught how to do it from the likes of you.'

Iain's eyes narrowed as they settled on her lips. He nodded slowly as he contemplated her statement. 'Kissed and often! Have you, now?' he crooned. 'Then it would be interesting to discover how much you've learned from your experiences.'

'I have learned quite enough—so don't you dare touch me—you—you vile, unprincipled lecher,' she flared hotly.

'Pray continue,' he chuckled. 'I haven't had such a dressing down since I was a lad.'

'There are other things I could call you, but I shall refrain for the sake of decency,' she bit back furiously.

Iain gazed at her, a slight, infuriating smile curving his firm lips. His eyes plumbed the depths of hers, reliving the experience of kissing her as he had done so often in his fantasies. He saw a spark of sensuality below the surface of her charm. It caressed him like an old acquaintance, and the way it made his heart quicken and his blood run warm was worth more than coupling with any other woman.

'When I kissed you, I recall you kissing me back,' he breathed, reluctant to let the incident that had given him so much pleasure drop, 'which tells me you enjoyed the experience.'

Gathering her shattered senses, Lorne glowered at him as much to rebuke him for his impudent reminder of his own behaviour by the stream as to declare her own response to it. 'You allow your imagination too much liberty, my lord. Perhaps it is time you gave it a rest.'

Iain's lips twitched with humour and the twinkle in his eyes slowly evolved into a rakish gleam. 'I assure you, my dear, I have no intention of reining in my imagination, not when I find the subject so appealing. And do not ask me to explain my imaginings to you, for they are of a most sensual nature and not for the ears of an innocent—if, indeed, that is what you are,' he said, recalling her association with young Ogleby.

Lorne struggled to remain calm, but she was unable to do anything to prevent the burning flush that rushed to her cheeks. She had no idea what had prompted his remark, and knew better than to ask. Battling with her composure she brushed a stray lock of hair from her brow with her slender fingers. Had she given vent to her true feelings, she would have used those attractive members to wipe the smirk from his lips.

'Pray excuse me,' she said, picking up her skirts. 'This conversation is not to my liking and I think it wise to put an end to it right now.'

The smile disappeared from Iain's lips, and a heavy, deeply troubled frown creased his brow as he watched her go. He was painfully aware of what he was doing and realised that it was madness to encourage what he was feeling. As a soldier he understood the strategy of moving with caution. He had tra-

versed the road of conquest, be it on the field of battle with
the enemy, or in the bed of a woman. He knew the rules of
the game, and when no resistance was offered by one or the
other they were susceptible to surrender.

But whether Lorne McBryde was susceptible to surrender
or not, when he looked to where John still sat and he caught
his disdainful expression, it reminded him that she was still
his prisoner and he was behaving like a besotted fool to the
daughter of his enemy.

Iain thought he had solved the problem of his captive by
avoiding her as much as possible, but his plight became unbearable when he found her round every corner and in every
room of his great house. He came to recognise her footfall on
the passageways, the swish of her skirts, and her delicate
perfume that lingered like a fragrant cloud in her wake. He
observed her from afar without meaning to—sitting in a
window recess looking out, reading or industriously stitching
at a sampler, which Flora had provided her with to occupy her
hands.

Iain observed that the spell she cast was not reserved for
him alone. With every passing day it found new victims, each
one hopelessly vulnerable to it. Somehow she had inveigled
her way into his household, dazzling his servants, who tripped
over each other to be of service to her—fetching her refreshment from the kitchen, or a stool on which to rest her small
feet while she read or stitched. Becoming abnormally sensitive to every nuance of her presence, he dealt with the
enforced situation by working relentlessly, as if to burn his
desire for her and his anger from his system.

At night he lay awake in his great bed, restless and tormented as he thought of the beautiful young temptress on the
other side of the wall. It was as if his whole being was trapped

on the edge of something. He was pulled deeper into a mael-
strom of desire that had a hold on his senses, tightening with
each passing day she remained beneath his roof. Furious with
himself and fate for having thrust him into this untenable
situation, it was with an effort of will, which amounted almost
to hypnosis, that he would blot her image from his mind and
fall to sleep.

Lorne's life at Castle Norwood assumed a routine. She rose
at dawn and breakfasted in the dining hall with the other inhabitants. During the morning and afternoons she mended
linen or helped Flora with some of her chores, mainly in the
stillroom, which smelled delicious with the spicy scent of
herbs. After supper she would usually escape to her chamber
to read before going to bed, but there were evenings when she
would return to the hall with Flora, where others not on
lookout were gathered.

She would sit quietly, sipping wine as she listened with
interest to the stories that were told. They were spellbinding
tales and legends that refreshed their hearts and enriched their
spirits, that thrilled and entertained everyone present. They
were of magical folklore, beautiful and dramatic, telling of a
world of beguiling witches, elves and fairies and evil
monsters, stories that had been told in Scotland for centuries
and handed down by word of mouth from generation to generation.

And then they would listen to the music of the harp and
pipes. When prompted, Archie would sing a lament, some-
times to the accompaniment of a fiddle or the soft strumming
guitar. Melody sprang naturally to his lips, and his songs
made the heart stir.

As everyone became used to her presence, often she would
fall into conversation and be included in others. She began to

relax, but she was forever conscious that she was still the subject of her captors' vigilance.

Finding herself more and more in John Ferguson's presence, torn between an intense dislike and a growing respect, she gradually revised her opinion of him. Away from the wildness of the forest and soberly clad, his hair neatly brushed and tied back, he was no longer the intimidating ruffian who had captured her and carried her off into the night. He sat across from her slumped in a chair. Idly he toyed with a drinking cup full of whisky.

The huge log that had been hauled on to the fire in the great hall had burned down to a red glow, but its light and the light from pine torches did not dispel the black shadows that accumulated high up in the medieval hall. Wine, ale and whisky flowed and the atmosphere was thick with the aroma of food and sweat and smoke from the fire. Those gathered had settled down to listen to an old man recount tales of his youth. John turned his head to find Lorne surveying him from the seat opposite.

Lorne met his gaze squarely. 'You watch me a good deal, John Ferguson. Are you afraid I might vanish beneath your nose if you look away?'

The whisky he had imbibed had mellowed John's mood and he gave her the closest thing she had ever seen to a smile on his dour countenance. 'So closely are ye guarded, Mistress McBryde, that ye would have to possess the powers of a witch to do that.'

'Be assured that if I had such powers I would have used my witchcraft to my advantage and spirited myself away long before now. I would have cast a spell on you and everyone else in this accursed pile and sent the lot of you to the devil. Or maybe I have been blessed with the second sight and have foreseen what is in store for us all and am content to bide my time.'

'Have a care what ye say, lassie, lest yer words be miscon-

strued by those not familiar with Highland superstitions.'
John's rugged face was expressionless as usual when he
looked at her, but this time his eyes crinkled at the corners.
''Tis not uncommon for witches to be scourged and burned
at the stake, ye ken.'

Lorne smiled. 'I see you have not forgotten your Highland
upbringing entirely, so tell me, John Ferguson, as a Highlander, do you believe in the second sight?'

His lips twisted scornfully. 'Only babes and animals and
ancients see the second sight.'

Lorne permitted herself the luxury of a smile. 'Ah, but you
know the superstition of the Highlanders. It is said that there
are those who can read the future and believe in black cats
scheming to do mischief on All Hallows Eve, and malevolent
goblins roaming the hills. They believe in men and women
with the evil eye who can wither crops, shrivel a body at a
glance and dry the milk of a cow.'

Surprised by her knowledge of Highland superstitions after
so long an absence and the light humour with which she
spoke, John smiled his dry smile. 'Aye, and dry the lochs and
see through time and converse with people from the past
and beyond the grave.' Falling silent, he looked at her long
and hard, his expression serious. 'I was weaned on Highland
superstitions, lassie, and there's na a thing ye can tell me that
I dinna already know—but whether or not I believe them is
another matter. They're sinister tales passed down to us
through time and founder in ridicule on non-believers' ears.'

'Are you a Catholic, John—or have you recanted your faith?'

'Sanctimonious hocus-pocus doesna interest me.'

'And if my father is captured, can he expect no mercy?'

'Edgar McBryde is unworthy of compassion, and the
only mercy the chief of a sept of murderers and thieves can
expect is a kindly executioner who will na prolong his

passing. Whatever he does will aid him not at all. The end of his life has already been ordained. He knew that when he returned to Scotland. An awareness of the violence of his death as punishment for his sins is a destructive force in any man's life, so I can only assume his need to be back in the Highlands is greater than his fear of what he will suffer.'

'Contrary to the opinions of you and the Earl, my father will assess the situation carefully before launching an attack against you. At the cost of his pride, he will not run away.'

'He's either left the field and returned from whence he came, or the redcoats are hunting him. In which case he'll have gone to earth.' The smile on John's lips deepened into mockery and then into an icy contempt. 'But be assured they'll dig him out.' He shrugged nonchalantly. 'Whatever— our aim is to defeat him by any means, to bring him low and not to let him escape the noose a second time. And that'll be the end of it. I witnessed what ye did that day in the glen of Kinlochalen,' he said suddenly. 'With me own eyes I saw ye betray David Monroe's whereabouts to Ewan Galbraith.'

'Then your own eyes deceived you, John Ferguson,' Lorne said, with all the satisfaction of one telling the simple truth.

John stiffened, an imperceptible frown furrowing his heavy brow. His bright blue gaze was penetrating when he looked at Lorne. 'If they did then explain ta me what I did see.'

Lorne rose and looked across at him, her expression hard. 'You have prejudged me. I refuse to give you my confidence now. On pain of death the Earl has forbidden me to speak his brother's name, so I will abide by that. Besides,' she said, her voice laced with sarcasm, 'you don't want to be swayed from what you believe, do you, John Ferguson?'

With a quiet dignity she turned and left the hall, leaving John with a perplexed, uncertain frown staring after her.

* * *

Iain would have been surprised to know that Lorne was no more immune to him than he was to her, for as time went on and she waited to be set free she could not prevent her eyes from searching him out or her thoughts from straying in disquieting directions. Nothing in her limited experience had prepared her for such a man as Iain Monroe. If she had found him impressive before, to see him now in his own castle, surrounded by the men and women of Norwood who depended on him in every sense, made him grow, in her estimation, to an almost invincibility.

The effect he produced was not merely the result of his incomparable handsome looks—it was more than that. The monumental energy he seemed to possess was volcanic, and the discipline and courtesy of his manner, and his occasional sardonic humour, made him distinct from any other man she had ever known.

Often she would glimpse him through the window in her chamber, either talking with the gentlemen who were guarding the castle or riding out beyond the walls, and even when he was not in the castle she felt his dominating presence everywhere. She told herself that nothing he could do could tempt her, but she always looked for him, as if the sight of him was reassuring, quelling her fear and anxiety. As the days slipped by she realised with shock that, despite uncertainties in her life, and the unpleasantness of her abduction, which had made her Iain's prisoner, she was content at Castle Norwood. After a while, however, being confined indoors and with little to occupy her time, she became tense and irritable.

She had been a prisoner for two weeks and Iain hadn't spoken a single word to her in two days. Oh, if only she could go outside, she wished, as she paced the floor of the hall in angry frustration, looking around as if searching for some way to escape her confines. It was quiet and there wasn't a soul about, but even when she was alone she was not naïve enough to assume she wasn't being watched. Whether by tact or order, someone would be hovering close by.

'Based on the way you are hellbent on wearing out my floor,' said a deep, hearty and commanding voice from the shadows, 'I gather you're angry about something.'

Lorne turned with a start, surprised to see Iain and so relieved to have him speak to her at last that her heart began to beat in deep, fierce thuds of pure joy. However, she was startled and impressed to see him attired in a blood-red tartan shaded with yellow and green. A leather sporran was fastened in front, and wool stockings encased his muscular legs. A snug-fitting dark green jacket added to the ensemble, and the woollen plaid slung across his chest was secured at one shoulder by a large, circular bodkin enriched with precious stones. Any man in full Scottish regalia was a splendid sight, and a man of Iain Monroe's physique was breathtaking. Taking a step back, she placed her hands on her hips and cast an exaggerated, mocking eye over the well-groomed Earl of Norwood from head to toe, her expression that of a mischievous, wily minx.

'Why! 'Pon my word! Very fine. Very fine indeed.'

Iain's clear eyes gleamed beneath his captive's gloating pleasure, and he made no effort to limit his own perusal.

Lorne felt herself flushing, for at that moment nothing was more obvious to her than that imperious gaze taking in every detail of her own appearance, a most outrageous, devilish smile tempting his lips when his eyes lingered overlong on her breasts.

'You look rather fetching yourself,' he crooned, murmuring his appreciation as he made a leg and swept her a bow of impeccable elegance.

'I am glad I meet with your standards, my lord,' Lorne retorted scathingly, deliberately presenting her back to him and folding her arms.

The smile faded from Iain's lips and was replaced by an ominous frown. 'You're angry.'

'Of course I'm angry,' she cried as he turned her round to face him. 'I'm angry about everything and with everybody—as you would be, too, in my position.'

Iain regarded her from beneath an arched brow with mild amusement. 'Including me?'

'You most of all,' she replied in a long-suffering voice. 'I'm not used to being confined to one place for so long.'

'But Castle Norwood is enormous—big enough for an army to disappear into.' Iain felt slightly guilty for ignoring her these last two days and like a hundred kinds of monsters for what he was doing to her.

'You know what I mean,' Lorne said in exasperation, turning away from him and going to the window. She looked out longingly. 'It looks such a lovely afternoon and I'm almost half-crazy for some fresh air.'

'But it's freezing outside,' Iain told her, moving to her side.

She glared up at him as she tried to make him see her point. 'Then I'm quite prepared to die of exposure,' she quipped crossly. Immediately she tempered her tone and expression as she became prepared to wheedle and pander to accomplish her goal. 'I just need some fresh air. Please be reasonable and let me go outside for just a few minutes. I'm hardly likely to try to escape with so many big, brawny men guarding me, all armed to the teeth.'

Iain hesitated, staring down in fascination at her eyes sparkling with anticipation. Momentarily he became preoccupied with how adorable she looked, dressed in that particular shade of rose pink that warmed her complexion. In all honesty he couldn't blame her for being tired of her confinement to the house.

'I might consider it.'

'Consider it?' she cried, disappointment written all over her face. Planting her fists irately on either side of her minuscule waist, she thrust her face forward 'Thank you—you— you ogre—you insufferable, unspeakable gaoler. What pleasure can you possibly derive from denying me some fresh air? I'm not asking you to let me go beyond the courtyard.' Suddenly Iain threw back his head and laughed, which only heightened Lorne's fury. 'Oh—you beast,' she flared in exasperation. 'How dare you laugh at my mortification?'

She stepped past him, fully intending to leave him standing there, but his hand shot out and captured her own.

'Come with me,' he said, his amazing laughter still ringing out as he led her towards the stairs. 'If it's fresh air you want, my lady, then fresh air you shall have in abundance.'

'Where are you taking me?' she demanded, having to run to keep up with his long strides.

'I have something to show you,' he replied without slackening his pace.

As they climbed up from one floor to the next, Lorne became more and more intrigued. Telling her to follow him when they reached a narrow landing, Iain mounted a spiral stair that took them up to one of the turret rooms. Stepping inside, she gazed around the small circular room in wonder. Light filtered in through three narrow slits. Bracing her hands on the wall on either side of the one closest to her, she looked out over the roof of the castle.

'Come,' said Iain. 'There's a better view outside.'

'Outside?'

He opened a little door in the corner. Taking her hand and

ducking his head to pass through, he led her out on to a small balcony. The cold air hit her face with an icy blast, and the wind, stronger at this great height than down below, snatched the breath from her lips. With a gasp of dizzy delight and quite undaunted, Lorne leaned against a low parapet and looked down the sheer granite walls of the castle to the courtyard below and out to the countryside beyond.

'Oh!' she gasped, completely awestruck, startled when a group of ravens lifted as one to find a more peaceful place to roost. 'If whoever built Castle Norwood meant to impress, he certainly knew what he was doing. The view is quite magnificent.'

Standing behind her, alarmed that she might lean over too far, Iain placed his arm firmly about her waist. 'Careful—not too close.' He laughed. 'I've no stomach for picking your pieces off the flags below. That would take some explaining to your brothers.'

Too exhilarated to show any objection at being so familiarly handled, Lorne allowed him to keep his arm about her waist as she absorbed the view. From the parapet she could look down into the courtyard. Men and horses looked so tiny they resembled ants going about their work. Beyond the surround walls she saw the township, with its many rooftops and smoking chimneys, and large enough to boast a considerable number of shops, two taverns and a chapel. How beautiful it was in the afternoon sunlight. She shifted her glance round to the north, beyond the crofts to the hills and forests. Somewhere out there was the ancient town of Stirling, and even further to the north and west, the Highlands, where the purple heather and russet and gold bracken poured down the mountainsides like an elixir.

'We're so high up,' she gasped, experiencing a heady sense of freedom and laughing like a young girl as she felt the wind take hold of her hair and whip it about her head. 'It's unreal—just like being on top of the world.'

'You could be right,' Iain agreed, trying to ignore the way she felt in his arms as he lowered his head so that his mouth was close to her ear. 'I often came up here as a boy. No matter what the season—whether it is raining, windy or the sun is shining—nothing ever changes. The air is always clean and fresh and there is a feeling of complete freedom.'

'Weren't you ever afraid of being so high up—that you might fall or be blown away?' Lorne enquired, feeling a little light-headed from the unaccustomed height.

'Never. In fact, all my life I not only went looking for danger, but I thrived on it.'

Lorne looked down into the courtyard once more, seeing men milling around the wellhead close to the kitchens, behind which she could see the kitchen garden. Just beyond that, surrounded by a square-sheltering wall covered with ivy, was a graveyard. She knew that it was in one of those graves that David Monroe's body mouldered in the earth. Bitter memories flooded her mind, stirring a sadness inside her, but having no wish to goad the man behind her to a black fury by referring to his brother's death, she shifted her gaze back to the village.

'I'm surprised at how large the village of Norwood is. I always thought large villages a rarity in Scotland, where rural settlements usually take the form of scattered cottages or small hamlets.'

'That's usually due to the emphasis being on pastoral farming, which does not require extensive co-operation between neighbours,' Iain informed her. 'You can see from here that the land around Norwood is fertile and therefore able to support a large, concentrated community.'

'Show me where Flora and John live—when they're not

at the castle guarding me,' she remarked pointedly. 'Can you point out the house to me from here?' Her eyes scanned the maze of tiny streets and narrow lanes that made up the village.

Ignoring her jibe, which was intended to remind him of her position at Norwood, Iain obliged, pointing out a half-timber-framed three-storey house with a slate roof next to the chapel in a large square. Even from this distance Lorne could see it was a handsome residence.

'I've just come from there,' Iain told her. 'No doubt Flora has told you that her father is the procurator fiscal for the parish of Norwood. Today was the occasion when as the Earl, and being law and judge of my domain, I had to hear complaints and settle disputes among tenants and tacksmen and dispense justice. Normally it is done at the castle, but the situation being what it is, and because there were some pressing matters to be dealt with, the fiscal's house was the appropriate place to hold the proceedings.'

'I am happy to see that you are inclined to leniency when you dispense justice, my lord.'

'And how do you know that?'

'Because even from this distance I can see that the whipping post and the pillory in the square are mercifully empty at this present time.'

Iain grinned, admiring her perception. 'That is because there were only two cases of relative minor disputes. The youths involved saw the error of their ways and were duly pardoned.'

'I wish you could see your way clear to interceding with the Privy Council, and arranging a pardon for my father,' Lorne whispered daringly, steeling herself for the blast of fury this might provoke, but when Iain spoke his voice was surprisingly grave.

'I can't, Lorne. You know I can't.'

She looked straight ahead, swallowing the lump that had appeared in the back of her throat. 'I should have known better than to ask.'

'It would have been better if he'd never returned to the Highlands.'

'Perhaps, but I can understand why he has,' she said softly. 'Neither time nor distance could efface his attachment to the country of his birth. He is old and battle weary, and to die and have his bones consigned to the grave among strangers—far away from family and his native land—he could not endure.'

Eager to dispel the unease her request had placed between them, on a more cheerful note she asked him to tell her about Castle Norwood. He told her how it had been built in the sixteenth century by an ancestor of his who had played a distinguished part in Scottish history. Of Anglo-Saxon origin, his family could be traced to the days of King David in the twelfth century. Two centuries later his ancestors had given loyal service to Robert the Bruce and been awarded with extensive estates. As he recounted colourful and exciting stories of the people who long ago had lived in the castle, Lorne drank it all in, warming with the excitement of the adventures, and she could almost believe the spirits of these men of old still existed in the heart of the castle.

'In the past, in times of war, from up here boiling oil and missiles would be thrown down on invading forces,' he told her.

Lorne turned her head and met his eyes on a level with her own, eyes that were warm and danced as though he found their closeness and isolation up here on the roof vastly entertaining. Her antipathy towards him seemed to melt in the most curious way, for she found herself quite intrigued by this confounding man. Even when he was being hostile towards her, when he angered her intentionally, she never forgot the tragedy he felt over his brother's death, and she felt a bond with him far deeper than her occasional resentment.

'Would these invading forces be the McBrydes or the Galbraiths—or both, by any chance?' she asked teasingly, her mouth trembling in the start of a grin to match his own.

'Both, I should think, considering that everything they do they seem to do together.'

Conscious that Iain's hard frame was pressed against her back and his arm firmly fixed about her waist, Lorne turned round and, pulling back, looked up at him. A heavy lock of black hair tumbled over his brow and blew about in the wind. The colour on her cheeks was gloriously high, which owed a great deal to the cold north-easterly wind. Her eyes were sparkling like twin emerald orbs. They were the most brilliant eyes Iain had ever seen, of a green so bright they seemed lit from within.

Iain was not a man of such iron control that he could resist looking down at her feminine form, which she held before him day after day like a talisman. Noticing things like how her gown clung to her round curves so provocatively, concealing the bountiful treasures beneath, gave him a clear sense of pleasurable torture. Now she was so close he could feel her warmth, smell the sweet scent of her body, all in such close proximity, and the memory of her responsiveness to his kiss by the stream sent heat searing into his loins. Why did this explosion of passion happen every time he was near her? Why could this one girl make him lose his mind? It dawned on him as he looked down into her face upturned to his that he wanted her more now than he had ever wanted her before, if that were possible.

'I—I suppose we ought to go back down,' Lorne said when a moment had passed, and his silence became unsettling.

In answer Iain frowned and gazed at her hard, looking like

a man in the throes of some internal battle. 'Is it possible that you are even more beautiful now than when I first saw you?' he said in the lazy, sensual drawl that always made Lorne's heart melt.

She laughed uneasily. 'Fancy waiting until I'm perched on top of the roof with nowhere to run, to tell me that—with my hair all messy and my face red from the wind. It puts a woman at a disadvantage.'

'I like you with your hair all messy and your red face,' he breathed.

Lorne realised just how perceptive this man was. She was disturbingly aware of those warm spheres delving into hers as if he were intent on searching out her innermost thoughts. He held her at arm's length, his eyes, full of intensity, refusing to relinquish their hold on hers. The hands on her shoulders were so powerful that Lorne felt like a child in his grasp. For an instant she thought he was angry, but then she saw a troubled, almost tortured look enter his dark eyes.

'I've known many women, Lorne, and ventured far and wide, but no maid has provoked my imagination to such a degree as you do. You are a temptress, dangerous and destructive in your innocence. 'Tis hard for me seeing you day after day, knowing you are almost within my arm's reach night after night, and not touching you as I want to do.'

His voice had softened to the timbre of rough velvet and made Lorne's senses jolt almost as much as the strange way he was looking at her. Suddenly her sense of security began to disintegrate. 'Did you really bring me all the way up here to take in the air and to look at the view?' she asked quietly, feeling a treacherous warmth slowly beginning to seep beneath her flesh.

'I wanted to be alone with you.'

'And why should you think I want to be alone with you?' she whispered shakily.

His relentless dark gaze locked with hers. 'Neither of us has anything to gain by pretending the other doesn't exist—that the kiss we shared by the stream never happened. I remember it, and I know damn well you remember it, too.'

Lorne wanted to deny it, but she couldn't lie to him. He was right. The burning memory of that kiss lay between them, which had become a source of hideous anguish to her now, and increased her pain and wretchedness. 'I haven't forgotten it. How could I?' she added defensively.

'So far I have managed to convince myself that my memory of how sweet it was is exaggerated. Now I'm curious to know if it really was that good and ardently wish it might be repeated—and to finish what we began.'

'Are you telling me you want to make love to me?'

The sweetness of her question was almost Iain's undoing. 'It is my most fervent desire. It is not just a question of wanting you, but of wanting you too much. The mere fact of being alone with you now is torture for me.'

He spoke in that cajoling tone that charmed Lorne. She shivered when she recalled the touch of his lips, which she was consciously yearning for. Breathing deep, she savoured it once more, feeling the hour of her defeat approaching. He entices women and they come eventually, John had told her, and she was no different. She smiled faintly. 'Then you must be cautious, my lord, lest you forget who I am and why I am here.' She became thoughtful, observing him with earnest attention. 'I don't want to fall in love with you.'

'I have no intention of making you.'

'Good.'

'Why?'

'Because that would never do. Besides, I don't think I could bear it.'

Suddenly, like a waif, she slipped out of his arms and into

the turret room, but before she began her descent down the spiral stair she turned and looked back at him. It was a special look just for him. It seemed to beckon with strange energies. It seduced him absolutely and left him bewildered in the most sensual way. He was intrigued by the enigma of this young woman, whose naïve personality concealed a mysterious core of which Lorne herself was perhaps not aware.

Iain followed her, heeding her words and forcing himself with an effort to shift his thoughts to who she was and why she was here, but somewhere in the caverns of his mind, he knew he was going to possess her before she left Castle Norwood.

Slipping inside her chamber before Iain could catch up with her, Lorne crossed to her dressing table and sat before the mirror, contemplating her features as she had done so often in the past. She was deeply disturbed by what Iain had said as she tried to see what he saw in her. He had said she was a temptress. Was she? Somehow the wide, lustrous eyes staring back at her looked alien to her, but determinedly she plunged her gaze into their depths.

And suddenly, like a will-o'-the-wisp, it seemed that someone else gazed out at her, someone almost childlike in her innocence, but at the same time seductive—a temptress, who seemed to grow from a tiny seed in a recess of her personality, a seed that had lain dormant in fertile soil until this moment. But she vanished as quickly as she appeared, too shy, too coy, to be caught, but far too real to deny.

Lorne sighed wistfully, continuing to study her face. Iain Monroe had cast some magical enchantment over her. His dominance was accomplished by tenderness rather than by force, and she instinctively sensed that once she succumbed to the mesmeric force of his personality, she would then be at his mercy.

Chapter Six

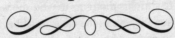

A strange kind of existence reigned at Castle Norwood. As time went on everyone tensed themselves for the moment when the McBrydes would launch an attack, so when Duncan Galbraith rode up to the heavily guarded iron gates on a cold and misty afternoon, with just one gillie as escort, having passed through the sprawling village of Norwood and the surrounding district unmolested, everyone was taken by surprise. He had ridden south with a great tail of gillies for protection, having left them camped in the woods some five miles west of Norwood.

Duncan had learnt through the McBrydes what had befallen Lorne, and fury such as he had never known pressed down on him with merciless gravity. The mere thought of the woman he hoped to wed being held captive by Iain Monroe chafed in unbridled restlessness on him. Two weeks into her captivity, impatience gnawed at him as he waited for Edgar McBryde to decide what to do.

Edgar's whereabouts in the Highlands was known to many but revealed by none.

According to Robert, Edgar's initial reaction on learning

of his daughter's capture had been to gather a large band of loyal men and ride south to take Castle Norwood by storm, but, on being warned that a party of government soldiers was waiting for him to show himself, and reluctant to feel the hangman's noose about his neck—and not even to free Lorne from her captivity—he'd decided that no casually planned attack would be carried out for the present.

Since Duncan was Lorne's prospective bridegroom, through Robert, Edgar had urged him to go to Castle Norwood, which was a day and a half's ride from Kinlochalen, and present himself to Iain Monroe. Edgar's instructions were that Duncan was to demand to see Lorne and inspect her prison for himself, to see if it was possible for them to launch an attack and bring about her rescue.

No matter how much Duncan wanted to see Lorne, he would have preferred one of her brothers to undertake the journey and confront Iain Monroe, but, having no wish to anger Edgar McBryde, whose disapproval he feared above all else, he'd agreed to travel to Norwood himself.

The Earl was not at home when Duncan reached the castle. Men at arms, whose duty it was to guard the gates, looked him over with a curious wariness, while his cold pale eyes took stock of his surroundings. Three giant hounds bounded menacingly ahead of John Ferguson's bulky figure as he crossed the courtyard to inspect the visitor. The hounds jumped up, unsettling Duncan's horse, but he held it on a tight rein as John warded them off.

With one hand resting on the hilt of his sword, the other on the dirk at his belt, John looked up and surveyed the man on horseback and his gillie suspiciously, feeling the blood curdling in his veins on recognising the Laird of Kinlochalen—young, tall and robust and dangerously vigorous. ''Tis a brave man who rides up to the gates of Castle

Norwood—or a foolish one, at a time like this—especially if his name happens to be Galbraith.'

'I am Laird of Kinlochalen—'

'I ken who ye are. Are we to assume ye are here on an errand from that murdering villain Edgar McBryde?' The contempt in John's voice was too conspicuous to go undetected.

'I come on behalf of Robert and James McBryde. They demand their sister's immediate release.'

'Until Edgar McBryde surrenders himself or the redcoats drag him from his lair, this is where she will stay.'

Mistrustful and resentful, after insisting that Galbraith leave his horse and gillie at the gate and making sure he was unarmed, he granted the Highlander permission to enter the castle to see Lorne for himself.

She came unsuspectingly, having no idea who awaited her, but on seeing the man standing beside John watching her descend the stairs, her heart missed a beat, the cause being an unpleasant sensation more akin to revulsion. There was no mistaking Duncan Galbraith. He had grown from the tall youth she remembered to a large man whose body was all brawn. There was an authoritative air about him and a conscious swagger of arrogance. Lorne sensed correctly that he enjoyed the influence and superiority his new status as Laird of Kinlochalen had brought him.

Confident and self-assured, his face was not unhandsome, but it was spoiled by the permanent menacing expression he wore. Instinctively she took a step back to avoid coming too close, and studied him as dispassionately as if he had been a stranger.

'Duncan! You take me by surprise. I am astounded that John let you in—considering who you are.'

'Are you not pleased to see me after so long, Lorne?'

'I confess that I would have been better pleased to see Rory,' she answered truthfully.

'Aye, ye always were too soft where that lad was concerned,' Duncan growled, meeting her forthright stare, disappointed that the years had done little to relieve her antagonism towards him. The unconcealed hostility in her eyes and the lack of warmth in her voice aroused his displeasure. She didn't look like a captive should.

However, he was surprised by her appearance. The last time he'd seen her when she had left Kinlochalen, distraught following the brutal death of David Monroe, she had been a girl, pale and wan. Before him now stood another Lorne, vibrant in health, and more beautiful than he'd imagined she could be. She met his gaze proudly as he absorbed the sight of her. He was not disappointed. His home at Kinlochalen would be a brighter, warmer place with Lorne McBryde as its chatelaine.

'How is Rory?' Lorne asked calmly.

Duncan shrugged. 'Rory's a scholar at the university in Edinburgh. He's one of those who believe in compromise and tolerance.'

'Which will always be mocked and scornfully rejected by you,' Lorne spat.

Duncan ignored her remark and glanced impatiently at John. 'I'll speak to her in private.'

'I'm sure ye'd prefer the delights of a nice little tête-à-tête,' John said sardonically, 'but ye'll say what ye have to say before me. Believe me, Galbraith, my own preference is to throw ye out on yer backside, but if seeing McBryde's daughter helps ta bring about his surrender, then it will be worth it.'

'I am here to make sure Monroe is not ill treating his captive.'

John's smile was wicked, his words full of meaning. 'On the contrary,' he mocked, 'the Earl of Norwood is renowned for his hospitality and treats Mistress McBryde like an honoured guest. See how well she looks for yerself.' He extended his arm with a courtly flourish to where Lorne stood. 'I think that when the time comes for her to leave, the wee lassie will object most strongly.'

Duncan looked at the silent young woman under drooping lids, angered because she didn't appear to be suffering any discomfort as Monroe's prisoner. Quite the opposite, in fact. 'Come, Lorne—are you not pleased to see me? Your greeting is as cold as a Highland winter. Surely this is a most affecting moment for close friends reunited after so long an absence? Shall you find warmth for me in the future as my wife?'

Lorne looked into his face with cold eyes. 'Wife? My God,' she whispered. 'You truly expect that of me?'

'Aye, why not? We are not strangers.'

'I've little faith that a union between us would be blissful or that it would last. I have been summoned by my brothers to return to Drumgow to marry a man who, if he resembles his warring brothers, considers women as little more than chattels. You have selected to marry me because of my bloodline and for no other reason—so do not insult my intelligence by expressing false affection. After all, what could be more satisfying after years of friendship, than for the McBrydes and the Galbraiths to be united by marriage? I will not live a lie, Duncan. I will not bind myself for life to a man I have no liking for.'

Duncan's eyes flashed with burning ire. 'After two weeks in the hands of your profligate captor, to spare you the humiliation and speculation you will experience on returning to Drumgow, you may be glad to marry me following this unfortunate affair. You will be hard pressed to find another who will take you after a Monroe has sullied you.'

Undiluted anger leapt and blazed in Lorne's eyes. 'How dare you insult me? He hasn't touched me.'

'There are those who will not believe you, no matter how hard you protest otherwise.' Duncan looked at John. 'Monroe would be advised to note that I want a virgin bride and will not settle for less.' His pale eyes flashed a warning that the older man would be ill served to ignore.

John felt a surge of smug satisfaction and his smile was contemptuous—it was plain that Galbraith knew nothing about the lassie's affair with Rupert Ogleby. He was tempted to rectify this by telling this arrogant young pup that he would be sorely disappointed on his wedding night when he discovered his bride was not the virtuous young maid he imagined her to be, but when he looked into Lorne's big green eyes gleaming her hatred at her betrothed, he had no doubt that she would have her own way of telling him.

'If you have forgotten the circumstances of our parting, I have not—and never will. I shall never forgive you for what you did that day,' Lorne said quietly. 'And nor am I some helpless victim to be coldly sacrificed on the altar of matrimony into the hands of a heartless and unscrupulous man.'

Duncan's jaw clenched and his cold eyes glared at the young woman standing proud and defiant before him. 'Silence. 'Tis your father you speak of with disrespect and does you no credit.'

'Aye, my lord—my father,' she uttered with scornful contempt, looking Duncan squarely in the eye. 'And how is my father and where is he?'

'He has seen better health—but he asks you not to worry yourself unduly on his account.'

'I don't,' she replied coldly. 'Does my father worry himself on *my* account?'

'That is why I am here.'

Lorne laughed softly to hide the hurt in her voice. 'Really! His concern is touching and most surprising. So—tell me,

Duncan, how long will I have to remain at Castle Norwood—
a prisoner?' she demanded. 'How much longer before my
father surrenders himself and puts an end to this madness?'

'Is that what you want, Lorne?' Duncan hissed, thrusting
his face forward and glaring at her with outrage. 'Are you
blithely telling me that you would betray your own kin and
see your father hang?'

His cruel, fierce accusation pierced Lorne's heart to the
core and she paled beneath the force and implication of his
words. It was as if a net had been thrown over her. No sound
issued forth from between her lips. In shock she opened her
eyes wide and searched Duncan's face as if fervently seeking
a denial of what he accused her of, before lowering them
beneath his unrelenting, piercing gaze. She was overwhelmed
with shame and struggling with pangs of uncertainty and dis-
loyalty, for she no longer knew what she wanted.

Of course she did not wish her father's death—no daughter
would wish that—and where her captor was concerned her
thoughts were all awry with confusion. Iain had vouchsafed
her entry into his world, and she was neither able to leave it
nor desirous of doing so, for when she did she would never
see him again.

'I have not seen your father since he returned to Scotland,'
Duncan went on harshly. 'What his plans are are his affair. I
have not been made privy to them. I have merely come to
Norwood on his request—passed on to me by Robert—to
assess your situation, and to make quite certain you are well
and not being mistreated.'

Suddenly a voice rang out like the crack of a whip in the
vaulted hall. 'What are you doing here, Galbraith?'

Duncan's face paled considerably, and it was obvious that he
was wary, if not a little afraid, of the man advancing with long,
purposeful strides towards him, the heels of his high boots re-

verberating off the stone flags of the hall. The Earl of Norwood's face was set as hard as the granite of the Scottish hills.

When Iain stopped, the two men were only three feet apart. Arriving back at the castle after checking the defences to the north, Iain had been told immediately of the arrival of their visitor. On stepping into the hall, he had stopped short, every colourful oath he could think of running through his mind on seeing Lorne speaking to Duncan Galbraith, looking like the ravishing beauty she was, her unforgettable green eyes raised to his. He saw the way Galbraith was looking at her, and the sight sent a sudden surge of cold fury through him. The intoxicating beauty before the Highlander would arouse lust in any man. Did the wench have to look so damned lovely?

Standing close to the Highlander, Iain saw there was expression in those cold pale eyes assessing him—disbelief, then hatred. He dropped a haughty glance at Galbraith and he did not trouble to disguise the poor esteem in which he held him. The hall was full of tension, which everyone present could feel. Duncan trembled and perspiration broke out on his brow on meeting Iain Monroe for the first time. The man's size put him at a disadvantage. He felt intimidated and vulnerable, but he was determined to have his say.

'You ask me what I want, Monroe?' He pointed with a shaking finger at the young woman standing like a beautiful carved statue. 'Lorne McBryde, no less. She is betrothed to me. She will be my wife and you cannot treat anything of mine in such a manner without answering to me.'

Iain's eyes were like hard, cold steel as they met his enemy's, and the muscles in his cheeks tensed with ire as his gloved hand gripped the riding crop he carried. 'I answer to no man, Galbraith—and least of all to you.' He turned his wrathful eyes on John. 'You should have consulted me before you let him past the gates. No doubt he's made a detailed inspection of the castle and our defences and will report back to McBryde. As a result he will be better equipped when he launches his attack.'

John's eyes narrowed in annoyance beneath the younger man's blistering attack, but he remained silent. Besides, he now considered it unlikely that McBryde would be in any position to storm Castle Norwood if it were true that the redcoats were on his back.

Iain's rapier gaze stabbed into Duncan's pale eyes once more. 'McBryde's daughter will remain safely in my care for the present. She is basing all her hopes on her father giving himself up so that she can be released.'

Seeing Lorne take a small step towards Iain, as if seeking his protection, Duncan eyed her with a strange mixture of angry insolence and hungry fervour. 'You seem at ease with your captivity, Lorne, and completely oblivious to the dangers pressing on your father.'

Lorne raised a lovely brow in chiding admonition. 'You are wrong if you think that. I would not see him hang, but what does he care for me?' she cried brokenly. 'A man who would leave his daughter all alone among his most despised enemies. As Lowlanders the Monroes are your enemies too, Duncan, so I advise you to be careful lest the Earl of Norwood and John Fergusson here remember all the terrible wrongs inflicted on them in the past by the McBrydes and the Galbraiths and it costs you your life.'

Her firm reminder of his family's past crimes and the threatened repercussions deepened Duncan's anger and chilled his pale eyes to a piercing darkness. 'And do not forget that you too bear one of those names before you become too comfortably ensconced at Norwood,' he flung at her. 'Your capture has had vast and unfortunate repercussions on your kinfolk. I think, perhaps, that the Earl of Norwood's hospitality has overreached itself, for your loyalties appear to have become somewhat misplaced of late,' Duncan accused scathingly. 'You stand beside him like an accomplice instead of his arch-enemy. You will be telling me next that he is not responsible for your capture and incarceration and that you exonerate him from all blame. Your father will be deeply disappointed in you, Lorne. Deeply. The sooner you are returned to Drumgow and you are under your brothers' guidance and protection, the better.'

Duncan had the satisfaction of seeing Lorne's defiant expression crumble. His words went straight to her heart and she stared at him with all the nauseating reality of someone who has just been hit by a truth they would prefer not to hear. The cocoon of sensuality she had existed in since she had left Iain in the tiny turret room yesterday began to disintegrate. Nothing was the same now Duncan had arrived at Castle Norwood. She wasn't sure of anything anymore, least of all her feelings about herself.

Any decent, self-respecting woman would despise her captor, an enemy of her kin, and do everything within her power to escape him. Bitter self-revulsion rose up like bile in her throat and almost choked her, for that wasn't what she had done. Instead she had allowed him to kiss her, to fondle her and speak soft endearments of desire and want—and worse, she had enjoyed it, encouraged it, even, because she was hopelessly attracted to him and had responded with shameless fervour. Her behaviour had been unforgivable and inexcusable.

'Castle Norwood will offer Mistress McBryde refuge until her father sees sense and surrenders himself, at which time due provision will be made for her safe transport to Drumgow,' Iain bit out before Lorne could reply.

Iain looked at her, sensing her distress and self-castigation. Her face was guilt-stricken, her eyes alert and oddly tortured by shame. Too late, he realised that Galbraith's words of reproach had penetrated her heart and mind and that she had withdrawn from him. Iain seethed with indignation, over-whelmed with an animal instinct of possessiveness. The antagonism he felt towards Galbraith filled him and he couldn't wait to be rid of him. Clenching his jaw so tightly that a muscle jerked in the side of his cheek, he addressed Lorne.

'Return to your chamber.'

Lorne's eyes flamed with revolt. 'I have every right to stay to hear what is said.'

Iain's jaw tightened at this final piece of defiance. 'I told you to go to your room.'

'But I—'

'Do as I say.' He jerked his head in the direction of the stairs.

Frustrated by his commanding tone, Lorne clenched her fists. At that moment Iain Monroe was every inch her gaoler, and as icy and indifferent as justice itself. Any fears she might have of what would result from Duncan's unexpected arrival were because she knew what power this ruthless Earl of Norwood possessed to make her and her kin suffer. She glared at him as their eyes parried for supremacy in a silent battle of unspoken challenge. Iain slapped his riding crop impatiently against his leg. It was Lorne who looked away first, and without further argument she swivelled on her heels and left.

Duncan was struggling to control his manic fury as he watched her go. 'I command you to let her go,' he snarled, his hands bunched into fists by his sides.

Iain's look was one of cold contempt. 'Let her go? I have no intention of doing any such thing.'

'You dared,' Duncan uttered through clenched teeth, 'you dared abduct her, and by doing so think by this means to bring Edgar McBryde to heel.'

'Precisely.'

'Then you do not know him.'

'No—and I thank God for it,' Iain drawled. 'He knows the score. If he gives himself up, then I promise to restore his daughter to her brothers at Drumgow unharmed.'

'Do you expect me to believe the word of a—'

'Lowlander,' Iain finished for him. 'It seems to me that you have no choice. McBryde is taking his time over this and I grow impatient—but not too impatient. His daughter is proving to be the most charming diversion,' he added smoothly. 'I'd be willing to wait a while longer for McBryde to give himself up if it allows us to become better acquainted.' His mockery was both subtle and direct, its meaning bringing a furious purple flush to Duncan's cheeks—and a sudden alertness to John's eyes.

'I imagine you would,' Duncan seethed. 'Damn you, Monroe. I'd sooner see her burned in hell than see you get your hands on her.' The words were spat from his lips.

Iain smiled. 'I believe you, Galbraith. It seems to me that her father is too fond of his own hide to submit to the authorities and suffer the ultimate penalty for his past crimes, but if he cares one whit about his daughter, he will do just that.' Impatient to put an end to the audience, Iain turned away. 'There is nothing more to be said. The way out is behind you.' He turned on his heel and strode towards the stairs.

Incensed at being dismissed like a lackey, Duncan glared after him. 'You'll get what you deserve one day, Monroe.'

Iain turned and regarded the younger man with disdain. 'I live in hope,' he drawled.

'I demand that you remember Lorne is not a prize to be won or conquered. If you think she is, then you will answer to me with your sword.'

Iain grinned, fingering the hilt of his sword. 'You tempt me to put you to the test, just for the sheer hell of it.' Noting the alarm that sprang to Galbraith's eyes, and how he suddenly stepped back before the threat, his lips curled with contempt. He was beginning to suspect that the man was all noise, a coward at heart, and to face down an enemy, let alone wield a sword, was beyond him.

'If you harm one hair of her head,' Duncan shouted in a fresh burst of bravado, his voice ricocheting off the walls in the vaulted hall as he slowly backed towards the door, 'there is no hiding place in all Scotland safe enough to keep you from my vengeance.'

Fury ignited afresh in Iain's eyes. 'You spout brave words, Galbraith. But have a care what you say. You will do well to remember that I have a vengeance of my own to exact if I have a mind.' So saying, he climbed the stairs and disappeared from view. Who could blame him if he let his lust for revenge drive him to consort with his enemy in the tenderest way? Would he not be justified in using Lorne McBryde for that purpose?

Gnashing his teeth in a savage snarl, Duncan turned and strode out of the hall, knowing it had been a mistake to come to Castle Norwood. Nothing had been gained—or had it? He had not reckoned on John Fergusson following him out to the gate.

John had become increasingly alarmed of late by the interest Iain was taking in their captive, an interest John suspected would soon become an obsession if she remained at Castle Norwood for much longer. John knew that if Iain became completely enamoured of the girl he would be hard to deflect from his purpose, and he wouldn't let Galbraith or her brothers stand in his way. This was unthinkable to John, who hoped for Iain to wed a healthy young woman with a Lowland pedigree worthy of his own.

And yet John had come to like the lass, the vital and bonny

daughter of their enemy, who had captured Iain's heart. But a liaison between them would never do. Never. John was determined to steer them away from each other, though it would sour his soul to do it.

When Duncan was mounted, he glared down at John. 'Is there anything else you have to say to me?'

'Word has reached us that McBryde is too busy trying ta outmanoeuvre the redcoats to give much attention to his daughter.'

'True—but don't let that lull you into relaxing your guard. The Laird of Drumgow can handle a dozen redcoats single handed,' Duncan sneered. 'What of it?'

'You didna ride south alone, Galbraith. Where are the gillies who rode with ye?'

'Encamped five miles north-west on the drove road,' he told him, not bothering to conceal the fact.

'Then perhaps ye should remain close to Norwood for a couple of days or so—in the event that McBryde is captured and our prisoner is released. She will require an escort to Drumgow.'

With her senses reeling dizzily and with tears in her eyes, Lorne returned to her chamber, holding them back until she had closed the door behind her. She sat on the bed and covered her face with her hands and cried wretchedly, the hurt and shame that engulfed her past bearing.

Never having seen anyone so distraught, in alarm Janet sent for Flora, who came immediately, but she could find no words to reconcile the heartbroken young woman.

Cradled in Flora's arms, Lorne wept, her emotions tearing her heart in two. Flora's voice, as she muttered soothing words in her ear and smoothed her hair with one hand, was so full of sympathetic concern that she cried all the more.

Biting despair, bitter self-recriminations, fear and confusion,
guilt, hate and helplessness—she felt herself consumed by all
these emotions and others she could not define. She wept
bitterly, surrendering to her heartbreak and confusion until she
was drained and empty, trapped in some kind of void between
her past and her future and unable to live in the present.

Astley Priory, her grandmother and the wonderful life she
had known were denied her, and her brothers and Drumgow
were strangers. And here at Castle Norwood, her sanctuary
from her future was also her prison—she was an outsider, an
enemy, not wanted. As she wept she felt a loneliness such as
she had never known.

When she could cry no more she removed her head from
Flora's chest and mopped her eyes with a handkerchief.

'Better now?' The older woman brushed the hair from
Lorne's wet cheeks. 'I know it can't be easy for you here
among strangers, but you'll soon be going to Drumgow.'

Lorne's expression became grim. 'To be among more strangers,' she retorted bitterly. 'I feel so confused. Duncan accused
me of betraying my father—and he's right. I have, and I feel
swamped with guilt and deeply ashamed. He may be every kind
of devil, but no matter what terrible things he has done in the
past, he is still my father and I have no wish to see him hang,
but I would do almost anything to avoid going to Drumgow.'
Suddenly an alert expectancy gripped her and there was a new
kind of urgency in her voice when she spoke. 'Flora—what
would you say if I asked you to help me escape from here?'

Flora's face was blank as she replied. 'I can't, Lorne. I may
not agree with what Iain and John are doing, but if I were to
do as you ask it would cause enormous contention between
my husband and I.'

Disappointed, Lorne nodded slowly, having expected her
to refuse. 'Of course—forgive me. I should not have asked.'

'John knows my feelings on the matter—I have made them plain a thousand times, but I cannot interfere. Besides, it could not be contrived with the castle so closely guarded. It would also be an incredibly stupid thing to do. Iain would soon discover your absence and ride after you.'

'I know, but it is because of him that I must go,' Lorne said quietly.

Flora looked at her with a sad, knowing smile. 'I know. I understand far more than you may have guessed.' She folded Lorne's hands in her own. 'No matter where you are—be it at your grandmother's house, here, or at Drumgow—it is only a matter of time before your father is taken. It is extremely doubtful now that he will attack the castle in the hope of rescuing you.'

Lorne paled and her eyes flew to Flora's in alarm. 'How do you know that? Flora, tell me—tell me the truth. You know something, don't you? Has something happened? Is he captured already? Is he dead?'

'To the best of my knowledge he still lives. But word has reached us that a large party of government soldiers is scouring far and wide in the Highlands for him. It is also rumoured that he is not a well man—that he suffers greatly from wounds inflicted on him in battle when he fought in Flanders.'

Lorne could not remain unaffected by this news. 'I see,' she whispered, overwhelmed with a crushing sense of guilt that she had not asked Duncan more about her father's health. Feeling dreadfully ashamed, she hung her head, swallowing a hard lump of painful emotion.

'Poor Father. He has been the cause of so much suffering— so much spilling of blood—and now it is his turn. It is right that he should be punished, but he is my father, and the idea of him hiding and being hunted like a wild animal and hanged like a felon is repugnant to me. I should hate him with all my heart for his treatment of others—of me—for rejecting me and sending me away—but I don't. I want to see him—I want to see him before—' She sighed, too emotionally spent to utter those final words. 'Can you understand that, Flora?'

'Yes, I can. It is an attitude I approve of. I'm so terribly sorry, my dear.'

Lorne shrugged and gave a sad sigh of resignation.

Towards evening Flora had a tray brought up to Lorne's room; though her appetite was lacking, Flora insisted she ate a little before helping her into her bedclothes. She then brought her charge a hot toddy and urged her to drink it.

'It will help you to sleep and dispel any bad dreams.'

Gulping it down and handing the glass back to Flora, Lorne's heart gave a leap when she heard the gentle rap on her door. Instinctively she knew it was Iain, and she was proved right when Flora admitted him. He wore the same grim expression she had seen earlier when she had left him with Duncan.

Iain looked to where Janet was turning the bed down. 'You may go to bed,' he said stonily before fixing his gaze on Flora. 'I would like to speak to Lorne, if you don't mind, Flora.'

'She's very tired, Iain, and I hardly think—'

'It's all right, Flora,' Lorne said quickly. 'Really.'

Flora glanced dubiously from one to the other before settling her eyes on Iain's implacable gaze. She was familiar with that look and knew it would be futile arguing. She gave Lorne's hand a gentle squeeze. 'Goodnight, my dear. Sleep well.'

When the door had closed on Flora and Janet, Iain moved towards his captive. He was a towering, masculine presence in her bedchamber. Taking judicious note of the taut set of his jaw and the small lines of ruthlessness around his mouth, Lorne felt the first tendril of fear curl round her heart. There was something controlled and purposeful about him, which, she suspected, had a great deal to do with Duncan's visit. His long muscular frame looked resplendent in a heavily embroidered midnight blue, the rich material of his coat moulding his powerful shoulders. His hair was smoothly brushed and tied back with a leather thong.

It was the first time Lorne had seen him since he had coldly dismissed her earlier, and it was like coming face to face with a stranger. She was uneasy, especially when those thoroughly dark eyes locked on hers. She had forgotten how brilliant and piercing they were, so piercing that they seemed capable of stripping her resolve not to succumb to him. He appeared to be relaxed, his stance casual; in fact, he was treating his visit to her room with a cool nonchalance that seemed inappropriate. The closer he came towards her, the more of an effort it took to face his unspoken challenge and not summon Flora back to protect her. She glanced at him with nervous apprehension, his mere presence bringing her senses alive.

'Whatever you have to say to me, please tell me and go,' she pleaded, pressing trembling fingers to her temples and turning away from him. 'I am tired and wish to go to bed.'

'I have a matter to discuss with you and it must be said tonight.'

'Why now? Why not tomorrow?' she argued tonelessly.

'Tomorrow I ride to Stirling to inquire after your father's whereabouts.' He turned from her and moved towards the hearth, kicking a log further into the flames with the toe of his boot, causing them to leap and the log to snap and spark vigorously. 'Are you aware that government soldiers are scouring the Highlands for him? When he heard they were on

his tail, he took to the hills like a fox,' he said, with his back
to her.

Displaying a calm she did not feel, Lorne nodded. 'Flora
told me. If you should find out that he's been taken, will you
release me?'

Iain gazed at her for an instant. With her hair floating like
a cloud about her shoulders and down her back, she was
standing straight before him with the candlelight gently caressing her form, the folds of her robe falling and forming a
circle round her feet. Her face was still flushed from the tears
so recently shed, and her eyes were watching him apprehensively. She looked breathtakingly lovely and demure in her
lace-trimmed robe and stunningly arousing. He had only to
reach out and take her in his arms and wipe away the anxiety
from her face. He could feel himself responding, a fact that
only increased his anger, for since Galbraith's visit he was in
one of his tyrannical moods when no power on earth could
have made him succumb to that desire.

'I gave my word that I would,' he said at length, in answer
to her question. 'You will be taken to Drumgow—unless you
would prefer to remain at Norwood for the present.'

Confused by what he said, Lorne stared at him in surprise.
'I can't do that. Ties of kinship bind me. I cannot betray my
father and brothers by allying myself with their enemy.'

'Then you must beg your kin's forgiveness for being attracted to their enemy,' Iain said, turning his head to look at
her and cocking one elegantly shaped brow. His eyes captured
hers against her will, holding them imprisoned and challenging her to deny it.

Treacherous warmth was beginning to creep into Lorne's
body. The meaning in his eyes was as clear as if it were
written in the stars. With trembling fingers she shoved a
wayward lock of hair from her face, an innocent gesture that

made Iain's blood run warm. 'I confess that what my heart yearns for goes against everything I deem honourable,' she whispered, her voice trembling.

Crossing his arms, Iain leant his hip on the arm of a chair and calmly looked at her in impassive silence, before saying in a voice that was as soft as velvet, 'And what does your heart yearn for, Lorne McBryde? Tell me.'

Drowning in the seduction of his gaze she shook her head slowly. 'I can't.'

Her reply brought a curve to his lips. 'My dear Lorne— you are transparent. I read you well. I know what it is you want.' He looked at her thoughtfully for a moment, touched by her innocence—in fact, her innocence was so convincing that he wondered for a split second if he could be wrong about her. She possessed a tender femininity that touched a deep chord in him. He was so desperate to have her, to bury himself in her, that he could feel his control slipping like gossamer threads under too much strain.

Standing upright, he shifted his gaze to the fire once more, watching with indifference as the flames took hold of the log he'd just fed into it. 'Were you surprised to see Galbraith?' His question was a casual one, belying the anger and torment he felt at the mere thought of Galbraith wanting her for his wife, of touching her in any intimate way.

'Yes—of course I was.'

'And pleased?'

'No,' she replied quietly and without hesitation, wishing he would tell her his real reason for seeking her out in her room at this hour. Her delicate eyebrows lifted in mute question as she waited for him to end his preoccupation with the fire.

'So,' he said at length, turning his head towards her, 'you have no desire to be his wife, even though he is determined to have you.'

'My feelings where Duncan is concerned have not changed.'

'Tell me, would he still want you if he knew you were not the virtuous maid he believes you to be?'

Lorne frowned, bewildered by his question. 'I—I don't know,' she answered hesitantly. 'Perhaps not.' A few steps brought her just within arm's reach of him. She looked up at him intently. 'My lord, what is it that you want to speak to me about? What is it you want?'

Iain paused, hesitating to say the word, which, in the presence of her questioning gaze, seemed monstrous. But he wanted her too much to stop now.

'You.'

Chapter Seven

The word hung in the air between them, piercing Lorne like an arrow from a bow. She stared at Iain, thinking he had lost his mind, but he seemed so cool, so self-assured.

'Tell me. Are you truly as innocent as you seem?' he asked, watching her closely and noting her agitation as she considered the question.

Frowning, she looked at him curiously. 'You seem to have a preoccupation with my innocence. May I ask why?'

He nodded. 'When I was in Flanders there was a young soldier under my command by the name of Rupert Ogleby. His father had bought him a commission in the army to get rid of him. He'd been involved in a rather unsavoury scandal with a young woman, you see—a young woman of beauty, good connections and a certain notoriety.' He looked at her pointedly. 'You, I believe.'

For a moment, surprise left Lorne speechless. She felt as if a blow had been delivered to her stomach and she recoiled instantly, her two hands flying to her neck. Her throat dried and her eyes burned with shame when she remembered the gossip and the scandal that had ensued as a result of her visit to Rupert's house. This was the last thing she had been expecting. White to the lips, she stared at Iain, unable to believe what he was saying.

Iain responded with a questioning lift to his brows. 'Do you deny having known him?'

'No. I have no reason to, but I have since had reason to regret ever meeting him. I was fifteen years old at the time, and extremely foolish.'

'It would appear you were—although I agree that, with his easy charm and handsome looks, any maid would be hard pressed to resist him,' Iain continued coldly. 'You may have observed that he was of a boastful nature. He claimed to have been your lover—that he made love to you on several occasions and that you were an eager recipient, and in an attempt to whiten his own character, he alleged that you had done the pursuing. Soon the entire regiment was talking of the affair between the two of you.'

'Then it's a pity they hadn't a war to fight instead of indulging in mindless, malicious gossip about a fifteen-year-old girl,' Lorne retorted drily, feeling as if something were shattering inside her as she tried to steady her voice. 'And no doubt every one of your men—you, too, it would seem—believed Rupert's lurid version of events.'

Iain lifted his broad shoulders in an indifferent shrug. 'I had no time for Ogleby. He was morally corrupt, a knave and a conceited braggart. There were times when I would have booted his backside out of the regiment if his father hadn't been a gentleman and a friend of mine.' He fixed Lorne with his piercing gaze. 'Have you nothing to say for yourself?'

'And just what would you have me say?' she demanded, her magnificent eyes shining with humiliation and wrath, her wealth of hair tumbling down her back like molten gold.

'I would think that nothing but the truth will do in a situation like this.' His tone was merciless and cutting.

Lorne glared at him furiously, tears of outrage springing to her eyes. 'Anything that happened between Rupert and I is not worth repeating and has got absolutely nothing to do with you. But what I will say is that you shouldn't always believe everything that you hear. Apart from being ordered to Drumgow, I have never in all my life done anything I didn't want to. I have also never regretted anything I've ever done.'

'Regardless of whether it's right or wrong?'

'Of course not, but it depends on one's standards. You've clearly summed up the situation and decided that what Rupert told you was the truth.'

'And was it? Come now, just one honest admission. Was Ogleby lying?' The corner of Iain's mouth twisted wryly in a gesture that was not quite a smile, and his biting tone carried anger and frustration.

Lorne was deeply hurt that Iain had known all about the scandal she had thought was over and done with all this time and had never said a word to her, and the hurt deepened when she realised that he really did believe Rupert's sordid version of events. Dear Lord, she thought, her mind reeling as she tried to concentrate on the lies Rupert must have concocted for some kind of malicious reason of his own to degrade her in the eyes of the whole world. Stiffening her spine, she looked at her tormentor squarely, two bright flags of burning colour having replaced the pallor on her cheeks. As hurt as she was, her anger was greater, and her sense of pride made her unwilling to tell him anything.

'The circumstances of my relationship with Rupert Ogleby are none of your business. What I may or may not have done has no bearing on the case—and after what you have done to me, you are the last man on earth I should have to explain myself to. How dare you sit in judgement on me,' she flared, her voice trembling with fury. 'Despite making me your prisoner, I thought you were a gentleman, with an established standard of decency. But I can see nothing decent about you now, Lord Monroe. You have tried, convicted and sentenced me on Rupert's version alone, which, in my eyes, makes you no better than him.'

Iain eyed her relentlessly, his jaw tight and his mouth a resolute line. Searching the green depths of this proud and scornful beauty for the truth, he was tempted to strangle her for keeping it from him and for defiling her body with other men—if indeed she had. He was astounded how the image of her coupling with any other man but him tore his mind to shreds, and he was driven by a violent compulsion to have her with an urgency and hunger that stunned him. In frustration he turned away, his face taut.

'And following this,' he said after a lengthy silence, 'Galbraith still wants to wed you?'

'In fear of me being ordered back to Scotland, my grandmother didn't inform my brothers, so I doubt the scandal reached Kinlochalen—not that they would have paid much attention to it if it had, low as I am in their esteem. But even Duncan would find no joy in marrying a woman of questionable virtue—a woman sullied by other men. He is a man, after all,' Lorne bit back, stung by the contempt in her captor's voice.

'Maybe you're right. Galbraith might be strongly averse to his betrothed cavorting about in beds with the likes of Rupert Ogleby,' Iain jeered cruelly, glaring down at her, the hard line of his mouth tightening as he exulted wickedly in his power to hurt her—although why he should wish to do so was beyond him.

Her eyes sparked with emerald fire. Hating him for believing she had the morals of a whore and looking like a tempestuous goddess in all her fury, Lorne stepped forward and dealt a crashing blow to the side of his face with the flat of her hand. It was so hard that it snapped his head around and she thought her wrist might snap.

Iain was thoroughly stunned. He didn't say a word. A pulse began to drum at his temple as he stood there looking into blazing green eyes and a face alive with rage. A pink stain burned on his cheek in an otherwise ashen face.

Automatically Lorne took one step back from his silent rage and stood her ground, her chest heaving with fury and her palm stinging following its contact with his cheek. 'You had that coming—you loathsome, heartless beast.'

'So, you are not Edgar McBryde's daughter for nothing,' Iain bit back scornfully. 'Brutality must be inbred in you. I trust you feel better now?'

Lorne tossed her head challengingly and set her soft mouth in a stubborn line. 'No. I will never be able to forgive my stupidity for stepping out of the inn that night, which placed me in your hands. I wish I'd never set eyes on you.'

A lock of black hair had come loose and fell across Iain's brow in rakish disarray. His penetrating eyes held hers, full of accusation and distaste. Lorne held his gaze, refusing to look away or to utter one word in her defence. Like everyone else, Iain Monroe had listened to the gossip and decided it was true. He had made up his mind about her—she was soiled, used—and anything she might say would be futile.

There was no trace of softness or affection in the marble severity of Iain's face, but she could still see the distaste in his eyes, knowing he despised her, but she realised there was something else lurking in those mysterious dark depths, something that had been there from the first—he wanted her, despite his opinion of her. Hadn't he just told her this? she recalled, as his sensuous voice still sang through her treacherous mind like a recurring refrain. His desire was purely a physical thing, but there was no mistake. His next words confirmed this.

'I think it is time we reached a clear understanding about what is happening between us—'

'Nothing is happening between us,' Lorne jumped in quickly, her heart contracting with alarm.

'If you will allow me to finish,' Iain went on, annoyed at the interruption. 'I was about to say—and what we want to happen between us. We are two people from opposing camps. We are enemies—or supposed to be—and the physical desire I feel for you is a totally unreasonable thing under the circumstances.' He fell silent, plumbing the depths of those magnificent eyes upturned to his, knowing that when he took her their mating would be wild and primitive, and no matter how many lovers had feasted on her ripe form, he was determined to use all his sexual experience to shatter the defences of this proud young woman who had no idea how to withstand it.

'Despite the things Rupert said about you, half the time I feel you are too naïve and innocent to be nineteen years old, that you are a little girl pretending to be a woman, and the other half you make me feel like *I* am a youth. But neither of us are children. This isn't a society ball in London, where protocol dictates I must approach your grandmother for her permission to ask you to dance, knowing it could be weeks before I could steal a kiss. We are both adults, with adults' needs. I want you, and I can see in your eyes that you want me. Before I leave this room tonight I intend to remove your clothes and take you to bed and make love to you. You told me you have been kissed and often,' he informed her bluntly, 'and just now you implied that you are no innocent. I'd like to discover just how much you do know.'

'You will force yourself on me?' Lorne cried in panic and

disbelief, beginning to realise that when Iain Monroe set his mind on having something, he was not easily dissuaded from that end.

'No,' Iain stated firmly. 'I will not do that. But I will forewarn you. When I take you in my arms I will not force you to do anything you don't want to do. Whatever happens must be your decision. Tomorrow there will be no accusations. You must know that what you did was of your own free will.' His dark eyes regarded her seriously for a moment, then a faint, almost teasing smile, so very persuasive, lightened his face. 'When I recall the manner in which you kissed me by the burn, I do not believe you are too reluctant to continue where we left off.'

His words defused Lorne's ire and confused her at the same time. She could feel her resistance ebbing. Tears of humiliation burned the backs of her eyes. She stepped back to widen the space between them, trying to keep a grip on her fragile self-control, and fighting desperately to hold on to her shattered pride. This man was her enemy, yet the physical desire she felt for him continued to ache inside her.

A small insidious voice whispered a caution, reminding her that any liaison with this man would bring her nothing but heartbreak, but another voice was whispering something else, telling her not to let the moment pass, to catch it and hold on to it. The intensity of feeling between them was evident, but not easily understood, but what she did know was that it offered a new excitement, as though the future held a secret and a promise. But still she hesitated.

'This is too much,' she whispered, weak from the turbulence of her emotions. 'We can't—I can't. It wouldn't be right.'

Watching her closely, Iain saw something move and glow a little in her eyes, and a tiny flame of triumph licked about his heart. Beginning to relax now he had his prey within his sights, he smiled then, that unnerving, lovely white smile that could charm and melt the stoniest heart.

'Since when did a prisoner have rights?' he mocked tenderly, moving closer.

'Please—do not jest about it.' Lorne knew he could read the fear in her eyes, for instantly all trace of mockery vanished.

'I'm sorry.' He watched her struggle for control of her emotions not without some sympathy, but he didn't show it. 'You were wasted on Ogleby. What was he—eighteen? And you no more than fifteen? Both inexperienced in the art of making love, and Ogleby never one to look beyond his own gratification. You want someone who can give you pleasures in return.'

'And you think that someone is you?'

'I've never had any complaints.'

Her stomach churning, Lorne wrapped her arms around her waist and turned away from his piercing gaze. 'Allow me a moment to understand what it is you want. What you really mean is that for you, a night spent in my bed will mean no more than a moment's pleasure. I wonder at your scruples,' she retorted with a trace of sarcasm, sick at heart, 'that you can disrupt the life of a woman you do not know by kidnapping her, and then dishonour her in the basest fashion.'

'In the light of your affair with Ogleby, he has already seen to that. The damage to your reputation was done long before you came to Norwood. Are you afraid that as the daughter of the Laird of Drumgow you will be condemned for associating with his vilest enemy?' Iain asked gently, noticing how the dancing flames on the logs brought the golden tresses of her hair alive.

Lorne felt a red flush of indignation sweep over her face. She spun round to face him once more, speaking passionately.

'I came to your house because I had no choice. My father and brothers know that and will hold me blameless. I have done nothing to betray my people.'

'No—it is your own people who have betrayed you,' Iain stated firmly. 'Your father cast you out as a child, rejecting you and abandoning you without mercy.'

'He did not abandon me,' Lorne cried. Already riven with so much guilt in the wake of Duncan's visit, she was quick to defend her father, but Iain was right. Her father and brothers had cast her out, only to recall her to Scotland when marriage to Duncan Galbraith would be beneficial to both families; it was a business arrangement about land and the uniting of two families and clan succession. If she produced a son, in due course he would succeed as chief of the Galbraiths, the process linking the two families even more closely. It had nothing to do with wanting each other. So why should she refuse so passionate a plea from Iain Monroe, feeling as she did about him?

'Well?' Iain prompted. 'Is what I suggest offensive to you? Or is it that you find me repulsive?'

'Neither,' she replied honestly.

'For one night I am asking you to forget everything else. Do you not find that appealing?' he murmured, his black eyes raking her from head to toe. There was an enormous amount of subliminal sensuality in her every gesture, and seeing her bite her lower lip as she struggled apprehensively with the decision that faced her, plucked a deeper chord within Iain than watching another woman remove her clothes. With the lightest touch he ran a fingertip along the soft line of her jaw, down her neck and along the shoulder covered by her robe.

Lorne shivered inwardly, her lips parting on a breathless gasp, and she tried in vain to see past the darkness of his magnetic, shameless eyes. Protests tried to form themselves on her lips, and died instantly. She wanted to find words to stop him from touching her anywhere else before it was too late, but as his eyes beckoned her to him, becoming narrow and assessing, she felt resigned and defeated.

Shocked by his revelations about Rupert, and confused and apprehensive at his consequent proposals, she'd had a little time to consider what she should do. In the grip of some powerful emotion she suddenly recalled what Duncan had said—he wanted a virgin bride and nothing less would do. A virgin bride! And that's what he would get—unless… Unless she gave herself to Iain Monroe.

Immediately Lorne's conscience reared up to do battle, for what she was contemplating went beyond anything she had ever contemplated before. She was more frightened than she had ever been in her life, and she was both appalled and ashamed that she could even consider doing such a monstrous thing. But, Duncan aside, wasn't this what she wanted, what she had thought about ever since Iain had kissed her? All she wanted was for him to hold her like that again, to speak in that same tender tone that had made her heart melt, and to kiss her into insensibility. She had found such pleasure in his arms, such bliss—and something else, too, something dangerous and pagan to her. It was a feeling she hadn't realised could exist, a feeling she wanted to experience again—and only with this man.

As if her need communicated itself to Iain, with his eyes fastened to her lips he said, 'I am wondering if your mouth will taste as sweet on mine as it did before. And I also wonder if your skin feels as soft as it looks.'

Lorne's heart skipped a beat. She felt herself melting, ready to experience whatever lay ahead. She was sinking into a deep, sensual spell as he reached for her, his hands tightening imperceptibly on her arms.

'Perhaps this will help you to decide,' he breathed when she didn't answer.

His arms came round her with stunning force, and his mouth came down on to hers with a deliberate ruthless expertise, searing her lips with such a burning kiss, just as devastating as the one before, that it kindled a fire in her blood with exquisite slowness and silenced her conscience. She recaptured the storm of sensations unbeknown to her. There was a promise of fulfilment that nothing could hinder. At the height of her beauty, Lorne was made for love—not until later would she be able to judge how Iain had restrained the violence of his desire in order to assure his conquest. Tasting brandy on his lips, she closed her eyes and listened to the awakening of her own body, feeling things that made her long for more than kisses.

With his mouth against hers, he whispered, 'You want me. Say it.'

'Yes,' she breathed, trembling and breathless, sliding her arms round his neck to draw him closer, all her senses becoming limited. 'I want you. Though I may be damned tomorrow, I do not want you to leave me tonight.'

'And you are sure of that?' he asked, giving her one last chance to call a halt to what was about to happen.

Lorne nodded, unable to form that tiny, one-syllable word.

Iain's eyes burned dark with passion as his lips brushed her cheek. 'Dear Lord, you're exquisite. My desire craves appeasement.'

'Your desire has the taste of strong liquor, my lord,' Lorne whispered, unable to still her racing heart. 'I can taste it on your lips.'

'My predicament would not abate with one dram—it took several,' he chuckled, sweeping her hair over her shoulder and nuzzling her neck.

'Which only succeeded in whetting your cravings.'

'Aye. Do you not realise what a temptation you are to me, my sweet, having you near me day after day, night after night?'

Again his mouth laid siege to her own, taking her lips in a fierce, devouring kiss that sent jolt after jolt of exquisite sensations rocketing through her, filling her with a fever of longing. Releasing her just long enough to remove her robe and nightdress with the dexterous ease of long practice, murmuring to her between kisses, which he dropped on her creamy flesh, and somehow managing to remove his own attire in the process, at last he pulled her down on to the bed beside him. Her cheeks grew hot beneath his devouring gaze and she tried to cover herself with the quilt, but he pulled it away, the mobile line of his mouth quirking in a half-smile.

'There's no need for modesty, my love. Tonight I will see all of you.'

Janet had already drawn the heavy curtains round two sides of the bed before she left, so the lovers were cocooned in a warm and wonderful world of their own. One of the two candles spluttered out, leaving them in shadow—neither of them noticed. Lorne felt resigned about what she knew was to happen to her; she also felt defeated, afraid and apprehensive, and yet beneath it all was a wild elation that went surging through her and singing in her blood.

Her flesh burned as she felt Iain's eyes caress her, tease her, and she shivered and drew in her breath in a half-startled gasp when his strong fingers gently explored every inch of her, cupping, touching, tracing the line of her waist and over the curve of her hips with sure mastery of his subject. Shyly she allowed her own gaze to stray over the contours of her lover's godlike body stretched out beside her, from his shoulders and deep chest, matted with crisp black hair, to the muscles of his arms and down to his tender fingers.

Proud, savage and determined, his splendid form gleamed in the soft light. She saw herself reflected in his eyes, eyes filled with complex hints of his mood. His kisses acted on her like a balm, blotting out the hostile world, annihilating her fears and loneliness, as his fragrance and his lips filled her mind and soul. Gradually she discarded her prudery and surrendered and gave back in turn, each time more yielding.

Suffused by the scent of the temptress lying beside him and finding her too bewitching to resist, Iain pulled her closer, desire, primitive and potent, pounding through his veins. Her sighs caressed him as he touched her, and little gasps escaped her throat at the ecstasy he aroused when his fingers penetrated her most secret place. He knew instinctively that, unlike all the other women he had bedded, though no longer innocent she was sexually untutored. He gloried in her, and the soft yielding of her body was redolent of his passion. She slipped her tongue into his mouth so daringly that he moaned with the pleasure of it, no longer the seducer but the seduced. It was like being kissed by an angel.

By now all rational thought had flown from Lorne's head. With an abandon that shocked her, she melted against him, the perfumed mass of her hair resting on him like a golden coverlet as her senses clamoured for him to possess her. Responding to the need he was so skilful at building in her, yielding to the exquisite pleasure of his touch, she soon realised that Iain Monroe was a man of extraordinary skill and power as he rolled her on to her back. Suddenly his weight was on her, and the desire burning in those silver eyes looking down at her was like a savage force devouring him from within. Kissing her with a raw, urgent hunger, he wedged his knee between her legs, and suddenly Lorne felt a fierce stab of pain as he entered her, filling her.

Feeling her body jerk and hearing the cry of pain she tried

to muffle in his shoulder, Iain froze as the shock of what he had done was hammered home. In confusion he looked down at her, seeing her eyes were damp with tears.

'Sweet God in heaven! You're a virgin.'

She gave him a watery smile. 'Did you really think I wasn't? I told you that you shouldn't always believe what you hear.'

With immense relief Iain saw neither accusation nor victory in her eyes. 'For what reason do you surrender your virginity to me when I have nothing to offer you?' Drowning in self-loathing for taking her innocence, he was about to pull away, but she sensed it and coiled her arms round his neck like twin serpents.

'It's all right—truly,' she whispered against his cheek. 'Don't stop now. It's too late anyway.'

Overwhelmed with mindless pleasure and unable to break the contact and relinquish the exquisite feeling of holding her in his arms, Iain complied. There was no holding back and he took possession of her with an ungovernable surge of dominant desire.

When he began to move inside her that was the moment Lorne ceased to think. Something began to uncoil in the pit of her stomach, which gathered momentum with each deep thrust. His hands were beneath her, moulding her hips to take her deeper, and her flesh clutched in spasms at his invading force, sending her to the point of total surrender. The shooting darts of bliss penetrating the depths of her belly loosened her joints so that her arms encircling his shoulders went limp. She arched her back, the soft globes of her breasts pressed flat against his chest.

Wave after wave of exquisite torture washed over her, and only Iain's steadying rhythm kept her from journeying beyond herself. Exulting silently, she felt herself being ruled by him, possessed by him, feeling his need burning through her with infinite power, igniting her female flesh with new life. They were wrapped in the pure rapture of their union, with no quarter given as senses were besieged, man and woman as close as it was possible to be, yielding and merging with each other.

'I love you,' she murmured breathlessly into the warm cords of his neck where a pulse was throbbing frantically. She was unable to do anything other than cling to him and listen to the fading echo of those three words that had passed unguarded from between her lips, as the explosion of pleasure engulfed everything, banishing the past, and she lost herself in the man who had brought her to such heights of incredible bliss.

This man to whom she had given herself had become her lover in every sense of the word. He had made her into a woman, had given her true knowledge of herself, and she was glad it had been him. She struggled upwards out of the warm, pulsating, wonderful world she was reluctant to leave.

The golden glow of the candle washed over them as they lay clasped together, their moist skin cooling in the night air. They were breathing heavily as they waited for the slow and powerful beating of their hearts that follows climax to return to normal, and to preserve the moment of their union a moment longer, as though afraid to disturb their fragile link by moving.

It seemed a long time before Iain stirred and shifted to his side, taking her with him, pulling the quilt over them both against the chill. Gazing at the incredibly lovely young woman nesting in the crook of his arm, her satiated body aglow from the force of her passion, he felt strangely humble and possessive. The enchanting temptress who had yielded to him without reservation, who had writhed beneath him as he had made love to her, was gentleness and goodness personified. He revelled in the sweetness of her as he stroked her spine, trying not to think and to hold on to the fading euphoria.

'Did I hurt you?' he asked quietly after a while, having an odd feeling that for reasons of her own Lorne had cleverly manipulated what had just happened between them.

Her cheeks turned a rosy hue. 'Yes,' she whispered. 'At first.'

'Forgive me,' he said with a trace of sarcasm. 'I don't have any experience deflowering virgins. Why did you do it, Lorne? Why did you deliberately mislead me into believing you were no longer virtuous? I would like to understand why you did. I insist on your honesty. Lie to me,' he warned silkily, 'and I will make your father seem like a saint.'

His threat made Lorne almost sick with fright. Ruefully she slanted her eyes up at him, feeling a prickling of fear that escalated to panic the moment she met his gaze. In contrast to the quiet of his voice, his face was hard. Her mouth went dry and she made as if to shrink away from his protective embrace, but his arm tightened.

'Stay where you are. I have no intention of letting you go just yet.'

Wordlessly she turned her head away.

When she said nothing, Iain correctly interpreted her silence as reluctance. He caught her chin and turned it back. 'Look at me.'

Slowly she raised her eyes to his. 'Why did I do what?'

'Intentionally let me believe that all those disgusting things Ogleby said about you were true? Do you realise the enormity of what you've done?'

'Yes. I have allowed my father's arch-enemy to make love to me,' she whispered, glad that, even though he was angry with her for deceiving him, he continued to hold her.

'It was rash—suicidal, in fact. You knew what you were doing, didn't you?'

She nodded miserably.

'Couldn't you wait for Galbraith to initiate you?'

She stiffened at the callousness of his words. 'I have already told you that I will not marry him.'

Iain gave her a long, assessing look. 'Don't make assumptions, Lorne. It won't be the first time a woman has insinuated herself into my bed with marriage in mind. But I won't marry you,' he warned quietly, and she felt his hand tighten on her arm like a steel band.

'Is this all you want from me?' she asked softly. 'To have me in your bed?'

'It's all I can take. Do not tempt fate beyond this night, for it would grieve me sorely to see the intimacy we have shared turn into bitterness.'

Lorne actually flinched at the bite in his voice. She hadn't expected him to make any undying declarations of love to her and offer to marry her—not when David's ghost would always be between them. He simply wanted her in his bed, but not his life. She knew this, so why did it wrench her heart to hear him say it?

'Don't worry. I don't want to marry you either,' she retaliated crossly, glaring up at him through a haze of wrathful tears, and suddenly wishing he would loosen his hold so that she could escape to the other side of the bed. 'The last thing I want is a barbarian for a husband. Whether his name happens to be Galbraith or Monroe, they are the same to me.'

Briefly Iain's eyes blazed into hers. 'Barbarian? Listen,' he warned through gritted teeth, his voice a deep rumble in his chest, 'when I begin to act the barbarian you'll know it. I assure you, my pet, you don't want to be my wife.'

'No, I don't. I knew that when I let you…well…you know,' she mumbled, an embarrassed flush sweeping her face when she recalled the intimacy they had shared. 'With all that is between us, I know you couldn't possibly marry me—and neither will Duncan now.'

The silence was inaudible. Iain's entire face instantly became hard and shuttered. So, that was what the insufferable, conniving little wench was up to! He should have known. Rolling her on to her back, he pinned her shoulders to the bed and loomed over her, his eyes snapping on hers. 'Now I know what game it is you're playing, I will tell you that I don't like it. Are you telling me that you sacrificed yourself to me to avoid marriage to Galbraith?'

Terrified of what he would do when she confessed the truth, Lorne kept her eyes on a small pulse beating rapidly in his throat and her voice was a strangled whisper when she shakily confessed, 'Initially.'

A grim smile touched his mouth. 'Somehow I knew you'd say that.'

'But when I gave myself to you it wasn't Duncan I was thinking of,' she said quickly, gazing at him meaningfully.

'And I am to feel grateful for that, am I?' he rasped bitterly.

'I thought you might like to know.'

Unable to stay angry with her when her flesh was pressed so intimately against his, a slow, roguish grin dawned across his handsome features. 'Your generosity warms my heart,' he chuckled softly. 'When I decided to make love to you, I wanted you to be everything I believed you to be—everything Ogleby accused you of being.'

'What? A clever whore?' she replied bitterly.

'Not exactly.' He looked at her with quiet gravity and his voice softened unmistakably. 'I'm glad I was wrong.'

'So am I,' she whispered with a throbbing ache in her voice, and when Iain saw the expression in those smouldering eyes gazing up at him, he saw a feeling so intense that he was humbled by it.

'Rupert was a popular man of great personal charisma and an exaggerated ego that fed itself on women,' Lorne went on quietly. 'He was a charming man until he was angered—and angered he was when he was about to force himself on me but was interrupted when his mother, accompanied by three of her friends, came calling. They found me in complete disarray and assumed the worst. Even now the memory of it makes me feel physically sick. I later found out that I was the only female to reject Rupert's advances, so I can only assume that in anger he set to work maligning my character to anyone who would listen.'

'I'm happy to see you survived the ordeal.'

'I was humiliated, but not destroyed, by it—although at the time I had no idea how thoroughly he tried to besmirch my reputation until you told me. Before the scandal broke my grandmother whisked me back to Yorkshire, you see, so I escaped the worst of it. We were on the point of going to London when Robert's letter arrived, instructing me to return to Scotland to marry Duncan. I won't, of course—not that he will have me when he discovers I am no longer the chaste young woman he thinks I am.'

'How will you deal with it when you return to Drumgow?' Iain asked gently, already bending his head and brushing his lips over her cheek with the intention of making love to her again. 'What will you tell your brothers and Galbraith? That I took you against your will? That I raped you?'

'No, of course not.' She sighed, closing her eyes, content to let him lull her into a state of euphoria once more. 'Telling them the truth will not help to overcome the legacy of a bitter past. We cannot remain frozen in sectarian hatreds and suspicions forever. There has been enough strife between the Monroes and the McBrydes over the years without adding to it.' When he raised his head, she met his stare with an unwavering gaze. 'I wish no harm to come to you—or my kin.'

Iain looked at her with respect and dwelt on her answer

for a long moment, then queried, 'What loyalty do you owe me? I have deprived you of your freedom, subjected you to public embarrassment and humiliation, and worse—I have seduced you in the most dastardly manner, robbing you of your virtue.'

'I seem to recall it was by mutual consent,' Lorne generously reminded him.

He grinned wryly. 'That is extremely charitable of you, my sweet. You have a tender way of touching a man's heart, but I take full blame for what happened. With my vast experience of women I should have known you had never made love before. It isn't often I feel ashamed of my actions, but now I do. I have callously coerced you into surrendering your innocence. The sickening truth is that one day I took you as my hostage, and the next I lusted after you like a rutting beast, with no intention of using decent restraint. My campaign to have you in my bed began from that moment. It was inevitable and only a matter of time—made easier because I believed your maidenhood was no longer intact—and tonight I have achieved my disgusting goal.'

'And if you could undo what you have done—would you?'

'No,' he replied without any hesitation. 'But what of you? Do you regret what happened?'

'I should, shouldn't I? I should despise myself for it. Any self-respecting woman would.'

'And you don't?'

'No,' she whispered, feeling a little shy and self-conscious in admitting it. 'If I had told you I was a virgin, would you still have made love to me?'

He smiled with gentle charm as he pondered her expression. 'No,' he replied at length. 'I would have avoided you like a thousand plagues, but that would not have stopped me wanting you.' Now, her innocence only made her more desirable to Iain. He gazed down at her lovely, apprehensive face and intoxicating green eyes, unconsciously memorising her lovely features so that he would remember how she looked when she was no longer with him. Bending his head, he touched her lips with a soft kiss, feeling her body quicken beneath his, and in that moment he realised that sending her away, as he must, was going to be the hardest thing in his life.

Lorne lifted her trembling fingers and gently traced his cheek. 'I'm sorry I slapped you,' she whispered with genuine remorse.

'I deserved it,' he said gently.

'Will you return to your own chamber now?'

'Why?' he breathed, unable to believe the passion she contained, or the violence of his body's craving for her, as he felt a flame racing uncontrollably through his veins and he began to respond to her once more. 'The damage is done now, my love. Nothing can change it, so let us enjoy what is left of the night and allow me to savour the delights within my grasp. I have much to teach you, and I am sure you will prove to be an avid pupil.'

When he pulled her beneath him, Lorne's breath left her in a sudden gasp. She was aware once more of his naked chest and the hard feel of his lean, muscular body pressed to hers, while he was aware of her lithe form, of the warmth and the softness of her, as he inhaled the fragrant scent of her body and her rumpled hair that spilled across the pillows. There was no resistance in Lorne. She would soon be gone from Norwood, tomorrow or the next day, and then Iain's need of her would cease to exist. For a few hours more he belonged to her. Their time together was to be savoured, and all she could do was memorise it, remember it, so she could live on it for the rest of her life, for if she had thought to come out of this with her heart intact it was impossible now. It was already lost.

They stared at each other for a moment of suspended time,

and then slowly Iain lowered his mouth to hers, smothering her soft moan with lips both dominant and tender.

'What is this?' she whispered in a trembling breath when his lips left hers and traced a line to her breasts, unable to suppress a breathless moan when his mouth caressed a hard, pink crest, his tongue branding her with its fiery touch. 'Is it some mindless torture you've concocted for me to endure as your prisoner, my lord?'

'Nay, this is not torture, but love, my sweet. Don't be afraid,' he murmured huskily against her throat. 'This time I will be the most tender of lovers—and though tender I may be, denied I will not.'

Later, nestled in his arms, Lorne gloried in her lover's prowess as she breathed deeply the warm manly scent of him. She loved the quiet authority and strength in his firm features and his lazy smile. By nature he was a self-assured, dominant male, and she ought to resent him for kidnapping her and confining her to his castle. But after what they had done, lying in his arms sated and warm, her body still pulsating from his lovemaking, she felt protected and cherished, not afraid or threatened as a prisoner should.

Surprised at the discovery of a sensual appetite within herself that had been hiding for most of her life, with a deep sigh of contentment she closed her eyes. Iain's love making—along with Flora's herbal tea—was beginning to work. She was tired and went to sleep with Iain's arms around her.

But when the dawn light in the east tinged the sky a pale pink, when she awoke with a pleasant feeling of well being and contentment, he was gone. Only the familiar scent of his body lingered on the sheets, drugging her senses.

Blinking the lingering slumber out of her eyes and raising

herself on to an elbow, she was about to climb out of bed when she suddenly realised that she was naked beneath the sheets. She flushed as memories of the night past came rushing back. A host of conflicting emotions warred within her. To say that she was aghast at what she had done was an understatement. It seemed impossible to her now that not only had she allowed Iain to make love to her but that she had practically encouraged him to do so. She had thrown away her virtue without a thought. She was amazed at her abandon with her father's enemy— which should make him her enemy. But she could not see Iain Monroe in any other light than that of the man she loved.

A rosy hue crept into her cheeks when she remembered the incredibly wanton things they had done. Her body still tingled with their lovemaking. There wasn't an inch of her that he hadn't touched or tasted as he had aroused her body with such skilful tenderness and shattered every barrier of her reserve. Her breasts were swollen and sensitive, and between her thighs was tender from his ministrations.

The night had held a thousand unexceptionable and unexpected pleasures for them both, but she could not allow it to happen again. Iain had known full well what he was doing to her and that he was capable of annihilating her will, her mind and her soul, and now she would hunger for ever for that same devastating ecstasy. But she would not allow herself to become caught up in a romantic dream. Her emotions were torn asunder and she could find no solace in the depths of her thoughts. He had told her he would not marry her—not that she expected him to. Marriage between them would be unacceptable to either side, but she would have it no other way. Resolve about what she must do instilled itself in her heart.

Swinging her legs over the side of the bed, she draped her robe about her and paced the room as if looking for a way of escape. For the sake of sanity she had to get away from Castle

Norwood—from him, she decided desperately, even though it would break her heart to do so. It was no good idly waiting for fate to take a hand. Fate had never been an ally of hers, she thought bitterly. It was fate that she had been born a girl and it was fate that had taken her back to Drumgow where she had first met Iain. And it was fate that had taken a hand on the night she had left the inn and placed her in his hands.

The idea of going to Drumgow held no appeal. It loomed on the horizon of her mind like a terrifying spectre, waiting to devour her completely. Suddenly she was overwhelmed with bitterness and frustration because so many men had control over her life. Halting her pacing, she clenched her hands and raised her head high, staunchly deciding at that moment that it was time she took charge of her own life and started thinking for herself. Iain had made his intentions painfully clear. He would rid himself of her as soon as her father had been captured. She was to be callously discarded—used and shamed and sent back to her kin.

She had no alternative other than to go to Drumgow, but there she would do everything in her power to return to her grandmother. Only at Astley Priory would she be able to take up the threads of her broken life.

Turning her head towards the door when someone knocked lightly, she eyed Flora's breezy entrance uneasily.

'Good morning, Lorne. You're up early…' The smile died on her lips and her face turned ghost white when her eyes were drawn and became fixed on the dark bloodstain on the sheet—the damning proof of Lorne's indiscretion. The wind could be heard buffeting the walls of the great stronghold and a wagon rattling over the cobblestones in the yard below, and from the interior came domestic sounds of the castle stirring to life. Flora was hardly aware of any of it. She looked as if someone had bludgeoned her. Appalled by what had happened, inch by inch her eyes moved from the bed to Lorne's face and she stared, unable to speak because her tongue cleaved to the roof of her mouth.

At length she got out, 'Iain must have been mad. What could he have been thinking of? I thought he would have had the common decency not to seduce his captive. You do understand that nothing can come of it?'

Flora's words stung Lorne, but she gave no sign. She threw back her head and looked at the older woman with fire in her eyes and a challenge to the world. 'Yes, I do. There is too much against us for that to happen. But you don't understand. What happened has helped me decide something very important. I now have control over my own destiny. I no longer have to marry Duncan Galbraith, feeling crushed and beaten because I have no alternative—not that he will want me now that I am no longer chaste. I am no meek and helpless woman to be shunted around by circumstance, to feed the ambitions of my brothers and a man I loathe, and nor will I play the part of a victim in this house. I will not cower in corners while men manipulate my life. Now I can fight—and fight I will—until I am returned to England.'

'Have you any notion of what will happen should your brothers and Duncan Galbraith discover you have lain with Iain while his hostage?'

'Of course I have—but never fear. I won't disclose what has happened unless I am forced to do so. What I feel for Iain goes deeper than he will ever know, and I would like to think that somehow, someday, we could be together. But I am not a fool. I know he doesn't want me.' Her lips twisted bitterly. 'Don't think me remiss, Flora, for I know his mind on the matter. He has told me. He wanted only what any woman could give him. Although to be fair, he thought my virtue already lost, and I misled him into believing it was true.'

'I see.'

Lorne's look became sad. 'No, you don't, Flora. The irony of it is that I love Iain. More, I think, than I thought possible. I believe I always shall. I cannot fight it, you see. Feelings are not things to command. But I am proud—shamefully so—and I will not be content to live with him as his mistress. It is not to be considered.'

Flora was about to deliver a harsh rebuff until she caught sight of Lorne's face. It had softened, lowered its defenses, so that her underlip trembled and there was a misty glow in her eyes and a mute longing in her whole attitude. She sighed and moved closer to the younger woman.

'What you and Iain have done will not change anything. When your father is captured, Iain will send you to Drumgow and Duncan Galbraith as promised.'

Lorne lifted her chin as if to oppose any that would question her new-found courage, and Flora saw she was in full possession of herself and the light of battle was gleaming in her eyes. 'Maybe, but I will not marry him. The die is cast, Flora,' Lorne reminded her forcibly, her voice steady and cold, 'and there are certain things one cannot undo.'

'Aye—more's the pity—like what happened to Iain's brother that day in Kinlochalen all those years ago.'

'Iain blames me for that, too,' Lorne said quietly. 'Perhaps one day he will discover the truth of that dreadful day.'

'Loss of a loved one is common to all of us, and we have been given the means of overcoming it. But Iain can neither forgive nor forget the manner of his brother's death, and when he brought him home, it was as if he entombed a major portion of his heart with him.'

'I know that, Flora.' Drawing herself up, Lorne took a deep breath. Resolutely she met Flora's gaze directly. 'Now I must think about what happens next. No one here wants me in this house. They make it plain. Nor do I wish to reside here any longer. This is no time for senseless reflections. I must leave now while Iain is away from the castle. You have to help me, Flora.'

Flora nodded. 'Yes, after what has transpired I can see you must go. I will speak to John immediately. But I'm sorry, Lorne. How I wish things could have been different. You and Iain were meant to be together. I shudder to think how he will react when he finds you are no longer here.'

Flora accosted John as he was about to leave the dining hall. Taking one look at her face, he frowned and allowed her to take him aside. In lowered tones she quickly told him what had transpired between Lorne and Iain, confirming his fears. John became tight lipped, his face set. Iain's stupidity angered him beyond all understanding. The wench must leave here without delay, before Iain returned. John had seen the way he looked at her—and now, after what that foolish man had done, he might not want to let her go. A union between a Monroe and a McBryde was anathema to John, a travesty. Keeping her at Norwood would serve no purpose.

Chapter Eight

~~~~~~

Mounted on a sturdy, short-legged, shaggy Highland garron—
essential for the route they were to take, for they were admirable
for travelling over distance and rough ground, but not so fast—
Lorne looked at the silent John standing beside his wife, who
was watching her, her eyes deep and still and more than a little
sad. John nodded her on her way, understanding and accepting
why she must leave Norwood—which was more than Iain
would do when he returned and found her gone. Preoccupied
and with nothing more to say, Lorne rode towards Duncan and
they turned their mounts north-west for the Highlands.

Edgar McBryde had been captured by government soldiers
garrisoned at Fort William and was being taken to Inveraray—
the only town in the Western Highlands, stronghold of the
Campbells and the seat of the Crown's authority.

This information Iain gleaned from a party of redcoats he
met when he was five miles from Stirling. Immediately he and
his escort turned to make their way back to Norwood. He was
reluctant to tell Lorne his reason for returning so soon, and
yet eager to be with her once more.

As he rode he mused on the night past. He was amazed to think so mystical a woman could be made up of such simple, soft and warm human flesh. He regretted that his days with her were numbered and that when she'd gone his own future would ebb to nothing. Before he had bedded her he had made up his mind that she could never belong to him, and he accepted the fact as a permanent condition, but last night she had cast a lethal spell over his life that could never be broken. Just a few more days to hold her the way he had last night, to watch her, to hear her voice, but having been as close as it is possible for a man and woman to be, he only wanted more.

The closer he got to Norwood, the more he fought an inner battle with himself. The full reality of what he had done took over and his conscience chose that moment to reassert itself. He told himself that he'd been a fool in taking her to bed. He had been unfair to them both, and it was his own brand of cruel jealousy that could not bear to let her go to Galbraith.

She had told him Galbraith wouldn't want her now she was no longer virtuous, but he didn't believe that. Galbraith would marry her and make her life a living hell. Iain knew the McBryde brothers and Galbraith—he knew what violence they were capable of. Lorne would not be strong enough to withstand their collective wrath. They would break her down and, distraught, she would say more than she ought.

No matter how hard she protested to absolve him from blame, they wouldn't believe her. They would go hard on her, and by the time they were done her humiliation and disgrace would be complete. To have her virtue questioned by her insensitive and unfeeling brothers and Galbraith would be damning. Her position would be irredeemable.

Iain's jaw set in a hard line. He couldn't let her weather that alone. She hadn't been to Drumgow in seven years. There would be no one to befriend her and she would be branded an outcast—a slut. She couldn't endure the slights and slurs.

And so, deciding to ask her to remain with him despite being who she was, and wanting her whole existence to be dedicated to his need, his comfort, when he returned to Norwood and John told him she had gone, it was like a dagger thrust to his heart.

Rage exploded in a red mist before his eyes, and in that moment he was absolutely convinced that Lorne McBryde had committed the ultimate betrayal. Iain knew a fury such as no other he had felt before—fury about her deception and that she had left him, fury at his own gullibility, and fury at John for letting her go. After all John's efforts to hold her captive, Iain could not believe he could have done such a thing. John scathingly told Iain that he knew the wench had spent the night in his bed, and because of this he believed he'd had good reason to send her packing with Galbraith.

Over the days that followed he was in torment whenever he thought of her. He was coolly polite to those around him, wishing he could find a scapegoat to crush to ease the intensity of the fury and pain that refused to abate, that became like a deepening void that made each hour without her more unbearable than the last.

How well he had come to know her. He could still feel the fragile warmth of her body in his arms, in his senses, recall the delicate fragrance of her flesh, the taste of her on his lips, and see the luminous green eyes that had gazed into his with such soft, trusting candour. The memory was both a lifeline and a curse and he wished he'd never laid eyes on Lorne McBryde.

Without delay and with a large contingent of ferocious-looking Highlanders, Lorne and Duncan took the most direct available route to the Highlands, skirting lochs and following treacherous tracks through bogs and outlaw-infested woods. Tormented by weariness and cramped limbs, Lorne welcomed her discomfort, for it prevented her dwelling on thoughts of Iain, whom she loved with all her naïve and trusting heart. His loss was as fresh to her as the void inside her, that was as mortal as only death can be. She had no outlet for her emotions and the emptiness inside her was so total that it eclipsed everything. With that thought she slammed a door on his image, for she knew otherwise it would never let her rest again.

Entering the southern Highlands, they met up with her brothers at a commodious inn at the quiet village of Arrochar, situated at the head of Loch Long. The meeting was a medley of pain and remembrance, and for a moment Lorne was again that wild young girl at Drumgow. James and Robert, tall and robust, were happy to be reunited with their sister, but they were adamant that she would wed Duncan Galbraith. It was their father's wish. Despite Lorne's resolution to stand against them, she was helpless beneath the collective might of her family.

News came to them that a company of Argyll's dragoons had captured their father on Rannoch Moor. He was locked in the Tollbooth at Inveraray, and had been condemned to death. Refusing to abandon him to his fate, his rescue was a challenge not to be met with a force of Highlanders, but with cunning. It was Robert who suggested Lorne could be their accomplice in their ruse to free him.

Their father had been captured by a Captain Kilpatrick—a tough professional and soldier *par excellence*. Because of Edgar McBryde's notoriety and the possibility that those chieftains still willing to fight for him might stage a rescue, when reports of his capture filtered through to the glens, it was decided that Kilpatrick would remain in charge until after the execution.

Kilpatrick was one of the most notorious rake-hells ever
to come out of the Lowlands. He was a heavy drinker and
knew only one kind of behaviour with women. He had an eye
for a pretty face, a weakness that could prove useful. Lorne,
who would be known as Molly Blair, was to play the temptress, to use her body and eyes to beguile and ensnare him.
His nights were spent in the Tollbooth guarding his prisoner,
so it would be relatively easy for her to wheedle her way
inside and ply him with drink, into which she would slip a
strong narcotic, which would enable the brothers McBryde
to free their father.

But Kilpatrick was also capable of brutality and dealt
without mercy with anyone who dared to cross him. It was
agreed that he was not to be allowed too much liberty with
Lorne, and her brothers would be out of sight but close
enough to help should things not go to plan.

It was a prospect that would have daunted many women,
but there was no room for faint hearts. Lorne's thoughts turned
to Iain. She knew how enraged he would be by what she was
about to do and it almost tore her in two, but she would never
see him again and without him she no longer had anything to
live for. Her father's fate was like a leaden weight in her mind
and the sacrifice would be worth it if they succeeded in freeing
him from his prison. Whatever he was guilty of, he was still
her father. The bond of kinship was strong and she had no wish
to see him hang.

Lorne and her brothers set off alone for Inveraray. Duncan
should have been riding with them, but had decided against
it at the last minute, leaving instead for Kinlochalen, much
to Robert's fury. As a means of strengthening themselves
against the attack of rivals, generations earlier the McBrydes
and the Galbraiths had entered into a friendly coalition. It was
an alliance that had worked well over the years, but since the

deaths of Duncan's older brothers, making him Laird of Kinlochalen, Robert had become uneasy about his neighbour.

Duncan had plenty of bluster, but unlike his brothers he was too contemptibly weak and lacked backbone when it came to the fight. In a recent skirmish with a neighbouring clan, Duncan had seemed nervous and had kept to the edge of the fray.

The native courage that Highlanders had inherited from their Celtic ancestors was preserved unimpaired, but on rare occasions Robert had come upon those who had shown traits of cowardice. Their punishment by the clan chief was always severe and exemplary, often in the form of banishment from the bounds of the clan. Robert could not defend such behaviour, and he hoped he was wrong about Duncan, more so because he was to marry Lorne, but his gut feeling told him his suspicions were justified, and if this proved to be the case, then he could look elsewhere for a wife.

The plan to free Edgar McBryde was daring and desperate, and thankfully they succeeded, mostly due to Lorne. But how she had hated her part in it. She had almost recoiled from Kilpatrick's touch, but had forced herself not to shudder with revulsion. The feel of his mouth on hers and the smell of ale had revolted her and she'd almost gagged, a spasm of pure disgust wrenching through her when he thrust his tongue into her mouth and explored with bold familiarity. She had tried to disengage her mind from what he was doing to her, things no other man but Iain had done. Immediately she had cast such thoughts away. Iain Monroe was lost to her. What was the point of resurrecting his image?

Supporting their father, Lorne and her brothers left the snoring Captain Kilpatrick in the Tollbooth and, like shadows, slipped through the dark alleyways. It was imperative that they left Inveraray quickly, for when Kilpatrick came round and found his prisoner gone, all the gates of hell would burst open. Pride would come into it, for, having captured Edgar McBryde, he would not be thwarted and accept it.

James, Lorne and their father would ride east to the port at Leith, nigh on a hundred miles. Weakened as he was, Lorne thought it would be a miracle if their father survived such an arduous journey. From Leith they would take a ship for France.

Fearing for the safety of his wife, Robert was to ride to Drumgow to be with her. It was inevitable that the soldiers would go there. In the King's name they would arrest anyone with the ill blood of the McBrydes in their veins. But clever as Kilpatrick might be, he would trace no possible links. There were others loyal to the family who could have plotted to free Edgar McBryde. As for Lorne, every redcoat would have been issued with her description. If Kilpatrick captured her and delivered her into Argyll's hands, he would demand the full penalties of the law. For her own safety she must go with her father to France.

The sun was invisible when Captain Kilpatrick emerged from the Tollbooth to set off in pursuit of his prisoner. A rolling dark storm filled the western sky, clogging up the mountain passes and bubbling over the lofty crags like sea foam. The rising wind moaned as it went searching the crevices, and a distant rumble of thunder shook the ground.

Whatever Edgar McBryde had once been in the Highlands, he was still a broken man, a prisoner of the Crown, and he, Kilpatrick, had run him to ground. McBryde was still his charge, his responsibility, and his escape was not to be borne. Once again McBryde would have taken to the heather, free to follow the paths of the red deer. It was his duty to pursue and recapture the Highlander, but as Kilpatrick left Inveraray with a troop of dragoons, it became more than a matter of duty. It was also a matter of honour and pride. There was a rage in him, too, dark and violent, and he was determined to track his quarry down every path in order to lay hands on him.

Edgar McBryde's body slipped quietly beneath the icy waters of the North Sea with a small bundle of soil and heather from his beloved Highlands tucked close to his heart. At the limit of his endurance, he had boarded the ship, only to die after one day at sea. Bravely Lorne swallowed down the hard, choking lump in her throat. The blood tie that had bedevilled her for so long was there in her, though latent all these years.

Standing on the deck of the ship, she raised her eyes and looked towards the hazy English coastline in the far-off distance. The sky was hard and bright, and there was a cold clarity in the day she had not seen in a long time. Drawing her cloak tightly about her slender frame, only then did she speak to James, whose arm was about her waist.

'I have no wish to go to France. Ask the captain to put in at Whitby, will you, James? There are people I know in the town I can stay with. They are friends of our grandmother and will see I am taken to Astley Priory.'

James glanced at her sharply. 'I'm no at all certain that yer decision is for the best. I strongly advise ye to go to France until the trouble's died down.'

'I should be safe at Astley for the time being—until I have spoken to Grandmother. If she thinks it best that I go, then I shall.'

'Kilpatrick will know who ye are by now, that's for sure, and being the kind o' man he is, he wilna rest until he finds ye. Dinna think that when ye're at Astley he'll not reach ye. An investigation will have ensued following Father's escape, and yer true identity will have been uncovered. That alone is sufficient to warrant sending the King's men ta Astley ta ask questions. If it becomes known that ye are there, they'll be inside in a moment to seize ye.'

Lorne's frown faded to be replaced by a sad introspection. She wandered listlessly to the rail and stood gazing at the sea. They stood in companionable silence for quite some time, and at length she said. 'That's a chance I will take, James. I will not go to France.'

James's expression was one of deep concern. 'I wonder if ye have really considered the full depth of yer predicament. If ye wilna think of yerself, then consider what yer family—our grandmother—will have to suffer if ye're taken,' he argued fiercely.

'I have,' she replied firmly. 'I will not be a burden to my grandmother, and if she wants me to then I shall go away.'

James ground his teeth and jerked away from her, combing his fingers through his tousled hair in frustration. 'Dear Lord! We shouldna have involved ye in this. It was too much to ask of ye. We should have sent ye to Drumgow with Duncan.'

Lorne looked at him sharply. 'I'm glad you didn't. I'm glad I was able to play a part in freeing our father from that awful place—and to spare him the pain and indignity of being hanged,' she said quietly. 'Whatever happens now, I have no regrets—and I am free of Duncan Galbraith. Robert has released me from that, thank God.' She glanced up at her brother. 'What will you do now?'

James sighed, resigning himself to her decision. 'When I've delivered ye into our grandmother's safekeeping, I'll return to Drumgow. Robert may have need of me.'

Iain Monroe, who had savoured the moment of Edgar McBryde's capture for so long, uttered a terrible oath of outrage when news of his escape reached Castle Norwood, and that a lass by the name of Molly Blair with hair the colour of ripe corn had aided his escape, outwitting that tough professional soldier, Captain Kilpatrick. It was Lorne. Iain was convinced of it. No doubt her brothers had contrived the scheme and used her to achieve success. She had carried it off admirably, and he cursed her for it.

He lived from day to day in a silent, barely controlled private rage, rage at himself for having emotions he could not control. He cursed her and yet he missed her, and wondered at the cruelty of her abrupt removal from his life. But what was done was done. It was better this way. She was back where she belonged—until Kilpatrick got his hands on her, and then he didn't reckon much for that pretty neck of hers.

As his pride pulled him back to earth, Iain gave up trying to imagine what might have been had he arrived back at Norwood in time to prevent her from leaving. If he had linked her fate to his, her past and her McBryde blood would have mocked his foolish need to possess her. It would have haunted his mind like a still-living arena in which he could still see David's death.

Leaving Norwood, he rode south with his friend Hugh Glover, glad to put Scotland and the past few weeks behind him. But still he simmered, still he struggled to stem the tide of anger and frustration as he went through his days with ice-cold determination to cut her from his life as if she had never been, trying to hate her for having given birth to the instability in him.

But as a result of those few short weeks when she had been his captive, when no promises had been made or asked, he knew there would never be another woman like her for him, that not even distance would have any effect on the scorching fires of their emotions, and that was the cruellest irony of all.

* * *

Ever since Mrs Shelley had returned to Astley Priory with the dreadful news of Lorne's abduction by the Earl of Norwood and the reason for it, everyone had existed in a state of shock. Their proposed visit to London was cancelled. Lady Barton immediately sent a letter to her grandsons at Drumgow, insisting that she was to be kept informed of all that transpired. She also sent letters to influential ministers in his Majesty's government, demanding that something was done to ensure the immediate release of her granddaughter from the Earl of Norwood's Scottish stronghold, and that she was to be returned to her family. With that there was nothing much they could do but wait.

When she suddenly arrived on the doorstep with James, having travelled overland from Whitby on horses acquired from friends of Lady Barton's in that coastal town, there was profound relief, tears and laughter that she had returned safe and well. Looking at her with joyous, tear-brimmed eyes, Lady Barton took her hands lightly, then her grip strengthened and she drew her granddaughter into her arms in a rare show of emotion, giving Lorne the feeling of warmth, and a sense of belonging.

Lady Barton, her daughter Pauline and Agnes, who refused to let Lorne out of her sight for a moment now she was restored to them, listened without comment as James explained everything that had transpired in the Highlands, the death of his father and the reason for his appearance at Astley Priory with his sister. However, he considered it prudent not to mention one or two things. There were certain details that might offend and shock the delicate female ears listening attentively to what he had to say, and Lorne's seduction of Captain Kilpatrick was one of them.

It was with a heavy heart that Lorne said farewell to James

when the time came for him to return to Drumgow. There was just one thing she asked of him before they parted—that there were to be no reprisals against Iain Monroe—no retaliation.

James promised. They would have too much on saving their necks than to go seeking more trouble.

They embraced and Lorne watched him go. Motionless, she gazed at the doors through which he had gone, her hands held loosely below her waist, her gown falling in a circlet around her feet. The moment was one of extreme solemnity. A gnawing emptiness filled the centre of her entire being where her brothers had been—where Iain had been, swelling larger by the second—and nothing in the world would ever fill that gap.

Lorne's return to Astley Priory brought her relief, but little comfort. In a way it was more terrifying than anything she had known since leaving Norwood four weeks ago, because she now had time to think and to feel. She felt like a fox that has outrun the hounds and found temporary sanctuary in its earth, a respite, for she knew her torment would begin again when the King's men came to Astley Priory and questions were asked.

As yet she had not spoken of her imprisonment or Duncan Galbraith. She didn't want to talk about that just now, and she was glad everyone seemed to sense this, for they kept quiet about it. But when she could no longer ignore the changes in her healthy young body, or the exhaustion and the nausea that racked her body every morning—which in itself was a diagnosis—she knew questions of a different kind could not be avoided.

Initially, the revelation that a new life was growing within her, one in which Iain had equal share, brought her a feeling of fierce joy, a triumphant exultation, as if the child could wipe out all her unhappiness and the sins of the McBrydes. It gave her an amazing joy to think that Iain's blood was at work deep inside her. No matter what happened now, he was tied to her by flesh and blood, and not even the stigma attached to the word 'illegitimate' could destroy her happiness that she bore his child. But when a fresh wave of nausea swamped her, leaving her spent, this harsh reminder of her position struck her like a hammer blow.

She had a sudden vision of her father's proud face set against the misty Highland hills, and the younger features of her brothers and her forebears. She saw them as clearly as if they had risen out of the shadows, all those who had borne the name of McBryde, who had fought and suffered and perished to preserve intact their ancient name and honour. Surely her brothers would be justified in riding to Castle Norwood and tearing down that mighty stronghold stone by stone, and slaying its proud and powerful owner for what he had done, before turning their backs with fury on the sister who could not accept the sacrifices that family and honour demanded.

Observant of Lorne's pallor and the deep lilac circles beneath her eyes, and her melancholy mood, despite everyone's attempts to draw her out of it, Lady Barton was troubled. She had no idea what was wrong, but it must be something serious, something that went deeper than the trauma of her recent ordeal and the death of her father. On seeing her leave the house one morning to walk alone in the gardens, she followed, finding her seated on a bench hidden behind some conifers, staring at the black water of a lily pond. She glanced up at her briefly, then back to the water, her face set in unhappy lines.

Consternation grew in Lady Barton as she sat beside her. Taking Lorne's hand in hers, she gave it a little squeeze, looking with earnest eyes at the young woman and searching her face. 'What's wrong, Lorne? Please tell me what bothers you. You have been in such low spirits since your return to Astley. Is it what happened to you in Scotland? Your father's death, perhaps?'

Lorne shook her head slowly, a tear running down her cheek. 'No,' she whispered. 'It's nothing like that.'

'Lorne, listen to me. What concerns you concerns me. Now, tell me.'

Swallowing hard, Lorne looked directly into her grandmother's eyes, feeling an obligation to tell her the truth. 'I am with child.'

The silence that followed was thick between them.

Lady Barton's features tightened slightly, and although the words were softly spoken, they hit her with the blow of a pugilist. At length she said, 'I see. And who would the father be?'

'Iain. Iain Monroe.' At this revelation, Lady Barton's composure slipped, and Lorne was conscious of her dismay.

'I see. Did he—force himself on you?'

'No—he would never do that. I—was not unwilling, Grandmother,' she replied, having the grace to lower her eyes as she confessed quietly to the sin she had committed with Iain.

Lorne's innocent face betrayed a sensual and wanton longing she was completely unaware of, and her grandmother saw an intimacy beyond anything she had ever witnessed, that made her long to shatter that private, impure world Lorne had shared with Iain Monroe.

'So—you had a choice.'

The echo of her grandmother's sharp words lingered between them. At last Lorne raised her tear-bright eyes and looked at her, and she shivered at the unhappiness she saw. She was all too familiar with her grandmother's rigid moral principles and private code of honour, and she knew the disappointment and pain her confession had brought her.

'You are telling me that you gave your virginity to your

father's enemy, a man whose hatred for your family is renowned,' Lady Barton went on, her voice trembling with a quiet anger, 'who kidnapped you, abused you and imprisoned you, refusing to consider releasing you until some age-old feud had been settled and your father surrendered himself to the hangman. How could you do it?' She noted Lorne took her criticism with apparent meekness, lowering her eyes in acquiescence and flushing—not totally without shame. 'From what you have just told me, it's obvious to me he seduced you with solid gold charm,' she remarked with irony. 'The man is a Lowlander, so I assume he must be civilised—if an unprincipled libertine. His behaviour towards you was contemptible.'

'I don't know what to do. Will you help me?'

'How could I not? You unhappy girl—more foolish that wretched,' Lady Barton murmured, smiling softly. 'You are my granddaughter, the child of my heart. But I cannot condone what you have done. To do so would go against everything I believe to be right. Did you tell James about the child?'

'No. I—I've only recently become aware of my condition. I'm just so afraid that, if the King's men come and arrest me, my child will be born in prison. That is something too terrible to contemplate.'

Lady Barton reacted by standing up and looking down at her granddaughter's bent head, her face set in hard, determined lines. She knew it was no good waiting for fate to take a hand. She would have to deal with this affair herself.

'It won't come to that. We will take the initiative. I shall take you to London and seek advice from my good friend Elizabeth Billington and her husband—and maybe seek an audience with King William.'

Lorne jerked her head up, dumbfounded. 'You cannot mean that.'

'Yes, I do. And we will start first thing in the morning. I shall go and inform Pauline at once. I would like your condition to be kept between ourselves for the time being. Time enough later to tell Pauline and Agnes.'

As Lady Barton prepared to leave for London, when she thought of what the Earl of Norwood had done to Lorne, her anger was so intense, so great, that she no longer trusted herself to stay in speaking distance of her family. If she were a man and younger she would kill him for what he'd done. He had hurt and humiliated Lorne, shamed her, and that was not to be borne. Her granddaughter had told her he was an honourable man, the most honourable man she had ever met. Well, Lady Barton would see just how honourable this Scottish earl was after she had laid her case before King William.

King William scarcely understood the deep divisions between the Gaelic-speaking Highlanders and the English-speaking Lowlanders, but he knew the Highlands to be a hotbed of troublesome savages.

When the news leaked of the Earl of Norwood's abduction of Lady Barton's granddaughter, Lorne McBryde, it spread like wildfire through the Court. The King was most displeased with the Earl's behaviour, a displeasure that increased when his ministers informed him of Mistress McBryde's mysterious deliverance from her captivity, and that she had become directly involved in the escape of her outlawed father from the Tollbooth at Inveraray.

The day after William had granted an audience to Lady Barton and listened without comment to her complaints against the Earl of Norwood, and her impassioned plea that her granddaughter be exonerated from the crime of freeing her father from his prison—an outlaw who was now deceased, if Mistress McBryde was to be believed. On being informed that the Earl of Norwood was in London, the King sent for him. After much consideration, realising recent events in Scotland could be used to his own advantage and the realm's, he was determined to be as reasonable as possible, from common sense if not from compassion.

Despite being a popular and much sought-after figure at Court, there were those who were of a malicious nature with nothing better to do than vilify others. They laughed at how Scotland's powerful Earl of Norwood had been duped by a mere girl, who had outwitted him by escaping from his Scottish stronghold and played him for a fool when she had ridden to Inveraray, where, under the very nose of his military guard, she had freed her father from the Tollbooth and secreted him out of Scotland.

In his present mood, the wave of whispering that seemed to follow Iain wherever he went shattered something inside him, splintering his emotions from all rational control.

Despite his outrageous conduct of late, the King liked Iain Monroe and had always believed in his sincerity. His strength was his steadiness of principle and his loyalty to the Crown, and it was these virtues that persuaded him to take a lenient view of the abduction of Mistress McBryde to settle a personal feud between the Monroes and her warring family.

Iain listened calmly as the King chastised him for his kidnapping of Lorne McBryde. Wordlessly he stared at him, his expression almost comical in his disbelief as the King told him that Lady Barton demanded recompense for her granddaughter's ruined reputation and that he, Iain, should do the honourable thing and marry her. The King went on to say that for the good of the realm—in the hope that a union between a McBryde and a Monroe might go some way to quietening the conflict that existed between some of the marauding

Highland clans and settling their blood feuds—he saw marriage as a sensible solution.

It was important that Iain wed Mistress McBryde without delay, and if he did not comply then he would be called upon to answer the serious charge of abduction and imprisoned. If he agreed he would be pardoned, indemnified and fully acquitted of his crimes.

White-hot fury went pouring through Iain's veins like molten lava at the thought of wedding that deceitful, scheming bitch. Realising that he'd lost the battle to distance himself from Lorne for all time, the fury at having to capitulate in this humiliating way was ready to explode.

Iain bowed and went out, but once outside the door he did not move. For a full five minutes he continued to stand there, his dark head bent, his fists clenched, his mind locked in furious combat against the idea of marrying the woman whose image had scored its memory on his soul. That green-eyed witch had humiliated him and made him a laughing stock, and he damned her conniving heart.

At St James's Palace, Lorne was to meet Iain alone. Impeccably groomed, faultlessly arrayed in scarlet and black, he was half-turned from her, staring through the small panes of glass as if he displayed an utter contempt for the whole of mankind.

Lorne paused, her eyes riveting on his beloved face, on his thick black hair curling to his collar, loving every line of his form. An ache touched her heart, because everything about him was so achingly, wonderfully familiar. Her whole soul reached out to him through her eyes, which gazed and gazed at him.

She spoke softly, feeling the silence too hard to bear. 'Iain.'

His entire body tensed and his jaw clenched so tightly that a muscle began to throb in his cheek. Slowly he turned his head and looked straight at her, cold, dispassionate, and completely in control. His gaze snapped on her face and his expression hardened, his eyes turning an icy, metallic silver. In frigid silence Lorne waited for him to speak, desperately wanting to justify herself and bring back everything they had shared at Norwood. But she couldn't. There was no possible way of resurrecting that one night with this wholly contained, authoritative stranger.

His hostility was like a tangible force inside that small room. Wetting her lips, Lorne took a deep, steadying breath. 'All this is most unpleasant. I—I realise how difficult this must be for you—as it is for me,' she said quietly, in an attempt to diffuse his wrath. 'I also realise that you must despise me.'

'Correct,' he informed her icily, with no trace of pity or humanity in his glittering eyes. 'I am here because the King commanded me—for no other reason. He has decreed that we shall be wed—and there's not a damned thing I can do about it. He has some crazy notion that a union of this kind is a step in the right direction to bringing peace to the Highlands.'

'If that is what His Majesty believes, then he has no understanding of the character of the Highlanders.'

Iain looked at her sharply. 'And you have?'

'I have a better understanding than most. I know there will be no peace in the glens until a Stuart is restored to the throne—and that the majority of the clans strive towards that end. They would rise at a moment's notice should James Stuart across the water commission them to do so. A union between you and me will only succeed in exacerbating the bitterness that already exists between our families. We know that. It's a pity that the King doesn't.'

'I have made my feelings on the matter quite plain. The King is aware of my abhorrence of a marriage between us, but he remains deaf to my protestations. If I refuse, I shall be stripped of all my worldly goods and, I dare say, my head. His Majesty has granted us a pardon—but it comes with a high price.'

Lorne took a hesitant step towards him. 'Iain—I am so sorry.' Even as the words passed her lips she saw his face tighten with furious contempt.

'For what? Being a McBryde? Murdering my brother? Breaking my trust in you?'

Lorne's cheeks flamed at the injustice of his cruel remark, and his stubborn refusal to listen to the truth. She drew herself up to her full height, her tone edged with frost as she retorted, 'I did not murder your brother. Wouldn't it be sensible to let me tell you everything about what happened that day? I swear by my hopes of salvation to conceal nothing. Just give me one single chance.' She looked at him directly, and his imperious silver eyes looked right back. It was clear from the cold look he gave her that he was not prepared to listen. Even now, the words she said did not seem to pierce through the armour he had built around himself.

'Shut up,' he warned with deadly calm, his teeth gleaming in a savage grimace. 'I told you never to speak my brother's name to me again, and by God I meant it.'

She nodded, swallowing down her disappointment. 'I know you did,' she replied bitterly. 'But no matter what you believe, I did not break your trust. Bearing in mind that I was your prisoner at the time, when John Ferguson took it upon himself to release me, there was nothing I could do but leave Norwood. What would you have had me do? Oppose him?'

'No,' Iain conceded, turning away from her and concentrating his gaze on what was happening on the other side of the window once more, as if he could not stand the sight of her.

Iain was fighting her, Lorne knew, trying to shut her out, and he was succeeding. At that moment she would have said or done anything to reach him. She could not believe that this cold, remote stranger was the same tender, passionate man who had made love to her—that he could be doing this to her. 'Besides,' she murmured, 'what could I have achieved by staying? You had made it quite plain that there was no future for us together.'

'You're right. There wasn't,' he snapped. 'It was right that you left, and by all accounts it would appear that you coped adequately enough.'

He spoke sarcastically, with a kind of cold contempt in his voice. Anger welled up suddenly in Lorne's heart, flushing her cheeks and bringing a sparkle to her eyes. She took a step towards him.

'Will you kindly explain what you mean by that?'

He turned on her, accusing her roundly. 'Since you ask, I will, Lorne McBryde—or would you prefer me to call you Molly Blair?' he snapped, emphasising the words in a menacing voice. He had the satisfaction of seeing her wince on being reminded of the sordidness of her subterfuge at Inveraray.

'It is obvious to me that some misguided sense of honour caused you to feel duty bound to aid your father's escape, and you were condemned the minute you became intoxicated with that particular sentiment. But what the hell were those crazy brothers of yours and Galbraith thinking of to allow you to pit your wits against Kilpatrick—a man whose reputation as a womaniser is as renowned as the cruelties he bestows on his fellow man? Even men of his own class detest him with a brutish passion, and to the men under his command he is evil incarnate. Weren't your brothers men enough to do the job themselves without involving a woman—their own sister?'

'Goodness!' Lorne exclaimed. 'The gossip travels faster in the Highlands than at Court.'

Her apparent lack of contrition fuelled Iain's anger. 'Ha! So—you admit it then?'

She stared at him in puzzlement. 'I have nothing to admit—at least, nothing that signifies.'

Iain loomed over her, his eyes glinting down at her. 'You do not deny that your brothers and Galbraith put you up to it, and that they were directly involved in the plot to free your father?'

Lorne paled, realising too late the danger and that she had fallen into his trap and incriminated her brothers. 'I never said that,' she burst out in a quivering voice.

'No? After all this time I imagine your fertile imagination will have invented a splendid tale, calculated to appease those who seek the truth of what really happened at Inveraray and the people involved,' he said with biting scorn, his expression incensed and bleakly embittered. 'Do you deny playing the whore to lure Kilpatrick away from his prisoner? Were you so determined to free your father that you were prepared to wallow in Kilpatrick's bed to do it? Answer me, by God, or I'll make you speak.'

Lorne's heart quailed before the disgust and revulsion she could see in his murderous eyes. He was undoubtedly beside himself with fury, and there was a note in the hard, thickened voice that sent a thrill of fear down her spine. Having experienced Iain's tender lovemaking, the violence of Captain Kilpatrick's brutal passion she recalled with revulsion. He had treated her like the whore she had pretended to be. With a supreme effort of will she had perfected the technique of remaining coldly within herself, even though her skin had crawled at his pawing.

Courageously she stood her ground in front of Iain, giving

nothing away of her thoughts. Standing face to face, they were like two fighting cocks, staring at each other with the fascination of mortal enemies, each looking for the weakness in the other's armour so as to wound the most surely.

'How dare you accuse me so? How dare you criticise my behaviour? You, who forcibly abducted me and held me prisoner, humiliating me and compromising my reputation beyond recall, have no right.'

'There is one inaccuracy,' Iain stated with infuriating calm, a hard stubborn line having settled disquietingly between his black brows. 'I was not the one who kidnapped you.'

'Maybe not. It was your marauding relative who did that. But you condoned what he did—which is one and the same thing to me. And since you seem to be obsessed by my association with Captain Kilpatrick, my lord,' she said with biting sarcasm, 'nothing happened between us.'

Iain drew closer to her and she gasped in alarmed surprise as his fingers coiled around her wrist like a striking snake and crushed it. 'Are you telling me that your encounter with Kilpatrick did not impress you?'

'Not in the slightest.'

'Liar! What was he like? Were you as delighted and eager for his touch as you were for mine?' he jeered, wanting to put his hands around her slender throat and throttle her for defiling her body with another man, for betraying his trust in her. 'You grubby little whore!'

'Whore? No, I am not. But what are you, Iain Monroe? Tell me,' she cried, trembling with violent fury, 'if you can, for I doubt the word has been invented to describe what you are.'

Iain's nostrils flared and he jerked his head closer to hers with a violence to match her own. 'Did it not occur to you that there might have been other, worthier ways of freeing your father from captivity? Did he thank you for it when you succeeded—or were you too ashamed to tell him?'

Lorne recoiled as if she had been slapped. 'No more ashamed than I would have been had I divulged that I had already been sleeping with the enemy—a Monroe who had been holding me by force,' she hit back furiously, having to summon all her self-control to stop herself striking him.

Iain's eyes, burning with a sombre fire, were unrelenting. 'You witch,' he hissed. 'Were you so desperate to save the life of a marauding Highlander that you would lie with a complete stranger?'

Pain slashed across Lorne's features that he could think she would. 'The marauding Highlander you speak of was my father and the sacrifice was well worth it. It was never my intention to lie with Captain Kilpatrick—whatever you may suppose. You were the first man—and the only man—to set his seal on my flesh, and since we are to marry you will be the last.'

Iain's eyes glittered like shards of ice, and his jaw hardened. His fingers tightened viciously around her wrist. 'Think carefully before you make the mistake of referring to that night again. You'll regret it, I promise you.'

'At least listen to what I have to say.'

'Yes, I'll listen, but it doesn't take much imagination to guess what happened between you and Kilpatrick. Can you swear by all that is holy that you did not lie with him?'

Hideous recollections of the events of the night in Invera-ray flitted through Lorne's mind, dragging a groan of anguish from her lips, and, unable to find innocent cause for her obvious dismay except that of guilt, Iain glared at her accusingly.

'Iain—how can you ask me that?'

'Because I know the bastard. Answer me, damn you,' he

hissed, an array of emotions flitting across his face. The barbs of jealousy were sharp and pricked to agonising depths.

'Yes—yes, I can. I swear it.'

'And did the King speak the truth when he told me that Edgar McBryde is dead?'

'Yes, that is true.' Lorne trembled at the realisation of how much Iain must loathe her. She could see it in his eyes, staring out at her, but he could not loathe her as much as she loathed herself.

'Aye,' Iain seethed, observing her reaction. ''Tis wise that you learn to fear me. Since there's not a damned thing I can do about preventing a union between us, if I should ever find out you lied to me about Kilpatrick and that your father is still alive, I swear I will wring your neck.'

Despite the *frisson* of alarm his silken voice caused her, Lorne lifted her chin. 'If you have finished, will you let go of me? You are hurting me—and I know you would like to hurt me more—but you would gain nothing by it. The King compels us to marry, and since the entire world believes you not only to have abducted me but ravished me, it seems I have no choice open to me but to marry you—although I know how your pride will suffer when you sully your ancient line with the blood of a McBryde.'

Iain slowly released his grip. With a wry grimace she moved out of his way, rubbing her wrist where the links of the gold bracelet she wore had dug into her flesh. 'You are a cruel, blackhearted brute, Iain Monroe, and I hate you. You brought this situation on yourself when you made me your hostage. I no more want to be your wife than you are to have me.'

Iain stared at her beautiful face as if seeing her for the first time. It was one of those unique faces that makes everyone else look commonplace. She was wide eyed and vulnerable, and her golden tresses rippling round her shoulders shone in the dim light. He silently contemplated her eyes. They remained focused calmly on him, but their depths seemed to spread the longer he looked. Her irises were as complex as he remembered, touched by different shades of green, turquoise and peacock blue, and as exotic as the tropical oceans that lapped the sun-kissed shores of foreign lands.

She was lovely. By God, she was lovely, and he wanted her with a fierceness that almost shattered him. Even when they were not together there was something invisible and powerful flowing between them, drawing them together. Her gaze seemed to sap his will, throwing him off balance, but only for a moment before his iron control took over. He quickly recollected himself and gave her a hard look. She might look soft and fragile, but when he remembered how she had ridden away from Norwood and joined up with Galbraith and her brothers, becoming party to the scheming and plotting to free Edgar McBryde from his captivity and cheat the hangman, he knew her to be as strong as steel.

'It will be perfectly obvious to everyone that our marriage is no love match,' he stated with cynical indifference. 'I might even say it makes for a forced marriage, and neither of us will be spared the humiliation.'

'The humiliation will weigh more heavily on me, I think,' Lorne whispered, averting her eyes so he would not see the pain and the sudden glimmer of tears that clouded them. 'It would seem that the entire populace both here and in Scotland is aware of what transpired between us at Norwood. They will feed on it with malicious glee, and will not be content until I am shamed and brought to my knees by it. You are right, Iain,' she said flatly. 'Everyone will correctly conclude that ours is no love match.'

Each unhappy word she uttered pricked Iain's conscience,

making him feel like the heartless churl he was often accused of being, but he deliberately hardened his attitude. He was not ready to be touched yet. 'Where you are concerned, my feelings understandably cannot be defined,' he said with cynical indifference. 'In fact, the feelings you inspire in me, far from resembling those of a more tender nature, rather approach a feeling of anger and rage.'

Lorne swallowed down the hurt, shrugging her shoulders in a way she hoped was casual. 'Why should I care how you feel? I have already been subjected to gross indignities at your hands—made unhappy, even—but I have no intention of being so again, even if it is your aim to bind me to you, and in so doing inflict on me a lifetime of misery and scorn.'

Turning from him with as much dignity as she could muster, she moved towards the door. 'I don't think we have anything further to say to each other—but my grandmother would like to speak to you. I advise you not to give offence. She has a formidable temper, you see.' She paused and looked back at him. 'Having behaved in a manner ill suited to recommend you, you have given her every reason to dislike you. She considers your conduct towards me utterly deplorable and less than infamous, so it's up to you to vindicate yourself and placate her—although not even you will be able to persuade her you are entirely blameless. I hear you have acquired a certain reputation among the ladies of the Court, and that you have been credited with several resounding love affairs. Apparently you are capable of charming and melting the most reluctant and coldest heart, my lord. Now is your opportunity to test you skills to the full. I wish you luck.'

The conversation between Lady Barton and the Earl of Norwood was conducted in a polite and civilised manner. Meeting a pair of cool grey eyes, Lady Barton came straight to the point and left Iain Monroe in no doubt of her displeasure over his treatment of Lorne. He was impeccably calm and she was vaguely intimidated by his aura of command. She listened to what he had to say, measuring his response to her questions and judging it for the truth. It was clear that Lorne had not told him about the child, which annoyed her, but she would not betray her confidence.

When she got up to leave she knew there would be many obstacles to be overcome between Lorne and the Earl of Norwood, but she was confident that none of them were insurmountable. She smiled quietly to herself, feeling easier about Lorne's future than she had in a long time, and she was satisfied that she would be well taken care of.

She had not been long in Iain Monroe's company, but it had been long enough for her to form an opinion that the man loved her granddaughter with an intensity that would astound him if he could but recognise it—if his mind wasn't busy thinking of the reasons why he shouldn't.

Chapter Nine

It was Lorne's wedding day, but it was not as she had expected it to be. The mirror showed her looking graceful in a simple dress of ivory satin, its square-cut bodice hugging her firm breasts before tapering to a narrow waist. The skirt fell softly to her feet, and the sleeves were long and fitted and terminated in points over the backs of her slender hands. She sighed sadly on seeing her image, for neither rest nor Lady Billington's potions could dispel the worried look in her eyes. Mercifully her morning discomfort had passed, but it had left her pale, and mauve shadows ringed her eyes.

Lady Billington, who knew little of the facts surrounding Lorne's abduction, was delighted with the news that Lorne was to wed the Earl of Norwood. She pronounced him to be a handsome, fine figure of a man, who was esteemed and valued among his own connections. Although she was puzzled, since his name had been linked with that of Maria Fraser, and it was rumoured among court circles that he was on the point of offering for her. Maria Fraser was the daughter of a nobleman whose ancestors had come south on King James the First's accession to the English throne.

Lorne had been devastated by what Lady Billington had told her and there was no room in her heart, her mind or her vision, but this one vast disappointment. It was as if a ghost had stepped out from the dark shadows of the night to shatter all her hopes and dreams. She wondered if this other woman loved Iain as much as she did, and if so she could imagine the torment she would feel when she was told he was to wed another.

'Smile, my dear. A bride should look happy on her wedding day,' chirruped Lady Billington, happy over the occasion, but saddened that it wasn't to be the large, grand affair she would have liked.

'I know,' Lorne acknowledged as Agnes put the finishing touches to her hair, which she had brushed until it gleamed like molten gold, and tumbled to below her waist. It was drawn off her face and held with diamond and pearl clips at the crown. 'But I can't help feeling apprehensive.'

Hearing the emotion that clogged her throat, Agnes embraced her. Initially Agnes had received the news that Lorne was to wed the Earl of Norwood with disbelief and horror. She had listened with disappointment as with a good many tears and hesitation Lorne had acquainted her cousin of the meeting with the Earl and quietly disclosed that she was to have his child, but when Lorne had told her how deeply she loved the Earl—indeed, was there not the proof of it shining in her eyes?—then she was happy for her.

Agnes handed her cousin a small prayer book and watched as she turned and walked towards their grandmother, accepting the imminence of her fate without protest.

A fitful grey light struggled through the windows and lit St James's Church in Piccadilly where the marriage ceremony was to be held according to the Protestant rite. With one hand on Lord Billington's arm and the other clutching her prayer book, through a mist Lorne saw the black-clad priest ahead of her, facing her. A gold crucifix stood on the handsomely adorned altar, and she tried to combat her mounting alarm by focusing her eyes on that single object hallowed on account of its religious association, and hoping to gain strength from its holiness.

Apart from Lady Billington, her grandmother, Aunt Pauline and Agnes, no other guests were present.

Attired in stark black, Iain presented a daunting figure. Standing to one side with Hugh, he turned and saw his bride enter, and he couldn't define the mixed emotions he felt as he watched her move gracefully down the nave. A ray of light fell on her, giving her an almost ethereal beauty that belonged to another world and stole his breath. She was pale, slender and utterly breathtaking. He remembered how she had felt to hold, loving and warm, and his heart ached. When she stood by his side her eyes touched on him, but she turned her head and stared blindly at the priest.

They stood before the altar, the priest's words echoing in the quiet church. Lorne watched in fascination as Iain took her hand in a substantial grasp, and she was surprised to feel his hand was as cold as her own as he slipped the wedding band on her finger. In an assured voice she heard him plight his troth from somewhere far away, undertaking to love, comfort, honour and keep her in sickness and in health, and, forsaking all others, to keep himself only unto her, so long as they both shall live. When he fell silent, she felt an emotion almost too great to be borne.

Feeling his silver-grey eyes burning down on her like the heat of a flame, she undertook to obey and serve him, the responses linking her with the man still grasping her hand—Iain Monroe, Earl of Norwood, sworn enemy of her kin—father of her unborn child. At the moment of acceptance when she uttered the final 'I will', her fate was sealed.

They knelt, heads bowed as the priest uttered the solemn blessing, and then it was over and he pronounced them man and wife in the eyes of God. Iain put out his hand to help her rise and together, with the witnesses and the priest, they retired to the vestry to sign the register. It was with a trembling hand that Lorne wrote her new name for the first time—Lorne Monroe, Countess of Norwood. So far she had kept her eyes lowered, but now she glanced up to find Iain staring down at her, his face wiped clean of any expression. Formalities over, they left the vestry and walked down the aisle side by side, surprised to see the King at the back of the church.

Lorne immediately sank into a low curtsy.

Taking her hand, the King raised her to her feet, moved by the way she was gazing at him with her entrancing bright green eyes, and he agreed with the assertions that Lorne McBryde was indeed an exceedingly beautiful young woman. 'I have come to wish you well and much happiness.'

'Thank you, Sire. We are deeply honoured,' she murmured.

He studied her serene face. When he spoke his smile was kindly, lighting his hazel eyes. 'Be a good wife to the Earl, and forget the circumstances that brought you together. Let the past be laid to rest.'

'I will try, Sire,' she whispered.

The King glanced up at the bridegroom and raised an eyebrow, the corners of his lips turning up in the ghost of a smile. 'You haven't kissed your bride, Monroe. It is custom. Not like you to be so remiss.'

Iain stiffened, his jaw tightening. Clearly he didn't like being reminded of his duty, not even by his sovereign, but he could feel the collective eyes of all those present anticipating his next move. 'That can be amended, Sire.'

Sweeping Lorne into his arms Iain kissed her slowly, deliberately, feeling her lips open under his own. In that instant he felt the suppleness of her body, her breasts pressed against his black velvet coat, and when he felt her surrender, a melting sweetness flowed through his veins. When he finally raised his head her eyes lifted to his, and the gentle yielding he saw in their green depths almost melted the ice encasing his heart. He wanted to pull her back into his arms, but instead he looked away and stepped back.

'Are there to be celebrations among the courtiers?' asked the King.

'No, Sire. Just a private wedding breakfast at Billington House with my wife's family,' Iain informed him. He would have preferred to forgo any kind of festivity to mark his marriage, but Lady Barton had insisted on it. 'Considering the circumstances that have brought about this union, I hardly think celebrations on the scale you suggest to be appropriate.'

'Aye, well, perhaps you're right. But I sincerely hope—in all our interests—that your union will be a success and you do not neglect your conjugal duties. Who knows what the future holds north of the border? History may owe you a debt of gratitude.'

With a slight inclination of his head and a well-satisfied smile that his wishes had been obeyed, the King and his liveried escort left the church.

Iain turned towards Lorne who, along with all the other ladies, had sunk into a curtsy. During the conversation she had remained impassive, but the King's final words had brought a wave of crimson to her cheeks. Livid that the King had felt he must remind him of his conjugal duty, taking her hand, he raised her to her feet. 'Shall we go?'

Assisting his wife out of the carriage and entering Billington House, Iain stifled his annoyance when he found the house packed to capacity. Apart from Hugh, Iain had invited no one. All the people close to him were in Scotland, and would have had no stomach to be present at this particular wedding.

Iain stayed by Lorne's side throughout, each putting on a convincing performance of accepting well-meant congratulations and participating in the light-hearted conversation while they sipped their sparkling wine, but he did not address her directly or even glance at her. Despite the lavishness of the table, a sombre tone prevailed over the wedding breakfast.

Afterwards, when Iain left Lorne's side to converse with Lord Billington, Hugh came to speak to her. She was glad he at least showed some semblance of courtesy and friendliness.

Hugh had been looking forward to meeting this young woman he had met in very different circumstances. In Scotland he had taken in every detail of her appearance, and she was just as lovely as he remembered. He envied Iain his wedding night, although he fully understood why his friend had reluctantly agreed to make her his wife.

'May I say that I am happy to meet you again in less traumatic circumstances,' Hugh said amiably, inclining his fair head politely. 'You look enchanting. Iain is a lucky man.'

'Thank you, Sir Hugh, but I think Iain is feeling anything but lucky on finding himself wed to the daughter of his sworn enemy.' Lorne smiled engagingly into his bright blue eyes, thinking how handsome he was and how fine he looked in his gold jacket, cream breeches and white lace cravat. 'I do remember you, and I too am glad the situation is somewhat altered. Although I confess to being extremely apprehensive about going to Norwood. I shall feel like a trespasser. Everyone will hate me even more than they did before after what I've done—depriving them of seeing Edgar McBryde hanged. Nor am I looking forward to meeting John Ferguson once more. When he sees what Iain has done, he will no doubt refuse to set foot over the threshold of Castle Norwood ever again, and cut Iain from his life completely.'

Hugh chuckled at her words. 'Come now, John is not as bad as you would imagine, or Iain would not be so close to him. No doubt he'll rant and rave for a while, but when he cools down he will see Iain had no alternative but to obey the King's order. Besides, let us not forget that he has brought this upon his own head. He was the one that abducted you in the first place. If he'd gone about his business in the normal way, none of us would be here today.'

'I suppose you're right. I—understand that Iain is staying with you, Sir Hugh.'

'Yes. My house is in Kensington. Iain is reluctant to buy a property in town. He says it would be an unnecessary burden as well as an expense he can do without. He's not a frequent visitor to London, so I suppose you can understand that. So—I always place my house at his disposal whenever he feels inclined to travel south. Of course, you will be staying there tonight—and since I value my friendship with Iain, I intend making myself scarce.'

Lorne's eyes widened with bewilderment, then grew huge with understanding. A crimson flush mantled her cheeks. 'But—not on my account, surely.'

'Tonight is your wedding night,' he said firmly, but with a roguish grin, 'and I would not wish to intrude.'

'Oh—but—you wouldn't be, I mean—'

'Yes, I would.' He chuckled.

'But—we can't possibly turn you out of your own house.'

'Believe me, Countess, there are no shortage of beds at Court.'

Not so naïve as to mistake his meaning, Lorne's flush deepened, and she thought it prudent not to say any more on the subject.

Taking two glasses of wine from the salver of a passing footman, Hugh handed one to her, and, after drinking deeply of his own, he looked at her with quizzical puzzlement. 'So—you are not a Catholic like the rest of the McBrydes,' he said, thinking back to the ceremony. 'Why is that?'

She shrugged, sipping her wine. 'When my father sent me to live with my grandmother, she insisted that I be brought up in her faith and adhere to the Protestant religion.'

He raised his eyebrows. 'And your father and brothers were not disturbed by this?'

'No, not at the time. Although I think my father came to regret it afterwards.' She glanced towards her husband, who was still in conversation with Lord Billington. 'Iain will no doubt bless the fact that I am not a Catholic. The last thing he would want beneath his roof is a wife who might by sympathetic to the Jacobite cause. It would be just one more reason for him to resent me,' she blurted out, and then looked quite stricken for speaking without thinking.

'Iain wouldn't do that,' Hugh said quietly, 'but I know how you must be feeling right now.' He understood just how hard it would be for her to adjust to life in Scotland, surrounded by people hostile towards her because of who she was. She raised grateful green eyes to his and smiled tremulously, and in that moment Hugh thought Iain was a fool for antagonising this beautiful young wife of his. 'He is tolerant of all faiths—Christian and non-Christian. He is of the opinion that a man's religion is his own concern and God's. And I must point out that he has Roman Catholic friends—I, for one,' he informed her with a twinkle in his eye.

Lorne looked at him in amazement. 'You?'

'Yes, me.' He laughed. 'And let me assure you that I am quite happy with King William sitting on the throne and have no Jacobite tendencies. I have no wish to see James restored, who in my opinion was both foolish and arrogant, and I sincerely hope he remains in exile for the rest of his days.' He paused when Agnes came to speak to Lorne. Having already been introduced to her by Lady Barton, Hugh was quite enchanted by this young woman, with her delicate, heart-shaped face and auburn hair.

'Have you been introduced to my cousin Agnes, Sir Hugh?' Lorne asked, looking from one to the other, observing how Sir Hugh's eyes were frankly admiring Agnes's upturned face, his good white teeth flashing in his handsome face, and not missing her cousin's awestruck expression as she met his gaze.

'I have had that pleasure,' Hugh replied, bowing over Agnes's hand and gently brushing it with his lips, positively enchanted when a maidenly blush rose in her cheeks. He grinned when he saw Iain bearing down on them. 'I see your husband coming this way, so if you will excuse us, Countess, I shall whisk your cousin away to partake of a glass of punch and become better acquainted with her in private.'

Lorne watched Iain walk purposefully towards her. He looked like a predator ready to strike out at its prey.

'I would like to leave. It has been a long day and we have been here long enough.'

Lorne looked at him in alarm. 'So soon? But—can't we stay a while longer?'

Iain leaned forward and said in an ominously calm tone close to her ear, 'I said now, Lorne. Mark well what I say, the matter is not open to discussion.'

Fear of being alone with him was dire enough to make Lorne say anything that would delay their leaving—and she did genuinely want to stay, for this might be the last time she would have her family about her for a long time—but somewhere in the tumult of her mind, it dimly occurred to her that Iain might want to be alone with her. Raising her chin and squaring her shoulders, she nodded.

'Very well. I am ready.'

Iain looked down into her lovely pale face and he had to stifle a spurt of admiration for her courage, and when he gazed into her glorious eyes his stomach clenched at the thought of being alone with her and making love to her.

'Come, let us say our farewells.' Politely he offered her his arm and she placed her trembling hand on it.

The first person Lorne saw when she entered Sir Hugh Glover's grand, spacious house in Kensington was Archie Grogan. His cheerful, freckled face had not lost its habitual good-humoured expression. Genuinely pleased to see her, he beamed a welcome and bowed with the respect her station commanded.

'Archie! How glad I am to see you!' Lorne exclaimed brightly.

Iain's manservant stared at her with nothing short of worship. He was as surprised and shocked as everyone else by his master's marriage to Lorne McBryde, but unlike everyone else, Archie welcomed it. 'And you, my lady. Please let me know if there's anything I can do for you.'

'You're my servant, not a lady's maid,' Iain growled. 'Show my wife to her room.' He turned to look at his wife. 'I will be up shortly.'

Without a word Lorne accompanied Archie up the elaborately carved, wide oak staircase to a landing and a warren of bedrooms. Entering one of them, she thanked him and closed the door, leaning her back against it and feeling the tension begin to ease from her tightly strung body. She was glad of this respite before Iain would come to bed. However, she cherished the hope that a night spent in each other's arms would rekindle the depth of passion they had shared at Norwood. She would have to think of some way to tell him about the baby. She hoped he would be overjoyed—but she was dreadfully afraid that he might not be.

With a fire burning in the hearth the room was lovely and warm. It was large and tastefully furnished, and dominated by a huge four-poster bed. Jenny paused in her task of turning down the covers and smiled at her.

Coming from a poor background in the village of Astley, Jenny was fifteen years of age when she had started work as a lady's maid at the Priory. Two years older than Lorne and her devoted slave, she was known for her discretion and never indulged in idle gossip, which was one of the reasons why Lady Barton had insisted that she take care of Lorne in her new life.

When Lorne sank into a chair beside the fire, Jenny went to her, concerned when she saw the strain on her ashen face. 'You look pale. Are you all right?'

Lorne nodded slowly, grateful for Jenny's presence. She faced the night with trepidation. Everything had happened so quickly. 'It's not as though I'm ignorant as to what's going to happen,' she murmured on a wry note. Jenny knew about the baby—indeed, it would be hard to keep it from her since she was the one who cared for her every morning when the sickness came. 'I'm glad to have you with me, Jenny—both now and in the future.'

A while later, clad in her cream silk-and-lace nightdress, Lorne sat at the dressing table while Jenny brushed the shimmering length of her hair. When she'd finished she placed the brush down and smiled at her mistress in the mirror.

'There now, you look lovely. I think I'd better go before your husband comes.'

Panic possessed Lorne and she spun round. 'No, Jenny. Please stay with me a while longer.'

'Well—just for a few minutes.'

The minutes stretched into hours and still Iain didn't come. Pacing the room until her knees trembled, Lorne waited for him in a state of feverish anticipation, exhausted and her nerves exacerbated. When she could stand it no longer, she sent Jenny down to the kitchen on the pretext of fetching her a cup of milk. Perhaps she could find out what was keeping him. Jenny returned with the news that Sir Hugh had returned and the two of them sat drinking in the parlour.

Lorne's lips tightened ominously and anger began to mix with all her other rioting emotions. Sir Hugh had told her he would not be staying at the house tonight, so what had brought him back? And how dare Iain keep her in suspense like this? This was their wedding night, and for him to sit drinking into the early hours with his friend was intolerable. Was he doing it with malicious intent—to punish her even more than he had already?

Jenny sighed in a gesture of helplessness at Lorne's incredulous expression. 'Perhaps it would be best if I put you to bed before he comes,' she suggested hesitantly.

'If he can be bothered to come at all,' Lorne blurted out angrily. When she saw Jenny looking at her unhappily, she relented. 'It's all right, Jenny. I'll stay up a while longer. You go to bed. I realise you must be tired. Whatever is keeping my husband so long has certainly more allure than I have. I have a good mind to go to bed and lock my door,' she pronounced bitterly, which seemed to offer a little balm to her wounded feelings and her pride, which was suffering badly.

'An action you would live to regret,' a masculine voiced drawled from the doorway.

Immediately the two women spun round. Iain was leaning against the wood surround in a misleadingly indolent manner, his arms crossed over his chest. His face was grim and impassive, and his eyes were cold, with a compelling arrogance. Lorne's heart slammed into her ribs when she saw him, for despite his stern appearance he looked remarkably impressive standing there, with his white shirt half-open to reveal the strong muscles of his neck, and his black hair tumbling over his brow. Motionless, she let her eyes feast on him, feeling the same wonderful, bone-melting excitement stirring inside her that she did whenever she looked at him. But this moment of weakness was not to last.

Momentarily the lovely young woman in the revealing nightdress arrested Iain's eyes, the mere sight of her bringing all his desire for her into focus, but they went on to settle on Jenny as he strode inside. 'Leave us,' he said flatly.

His tone, cutting and rude, brought a protest bubbling to Lorne's lips. 'Iain—I think—'

'Please leave us,' Iain repeated on a softer note, indicating the door with a nod, which Jenny completely understood.

Warned by something in Iain's eyes, Lorne looked at Jenny. 'It's all right, Jenny. Do as my husband says. Goodnight.' When she was alone with her husband, she turned on him. She might have lost her heart to this Scottish laird, but she had certainly not parted with her temper when she had left Norwood. 'Iain Monroe!' she exclaimed hotly. 'How dare you dismiss my maid so rudely? Jenny has been with my grandmother a long time. I will not have you upsetting her.'

'Madam!' he said mildly, his voice belying the scorching breath in his chest, the blood running hot through his veins, the pounding of his heart, for she was alone with him now—

his wife, and he could do with her just as he pleased. 'As his Majesty went out of his way to remind me, I am under an obligation to fulfil my conjugal duty. May I remind you that the same applies to you, too, my sweet,' he murmured, advancing on her, his lips smiling about his white teeth, 'and I can assure you that tonight you will have no need of a maid.'

'Don't call me that,' she cried, surprising them both.

'What?'

'Your sweet. The endearment is empty and meaningless. I am not your sweet.' It reminded her of Norwood and that night, and the lingering memory of their pleasure always weakened her.

Iain shrugged, as if he couldn't care less. 'As you wish.' Unable to tear his eyes away from so much loveliness so temptingly displayed before him, his body throbbed with the need to possess her. She was his torment. He couldn't look at her and not want to touch her, he couldn't be near her and not want her, and he had wanted her for so long that it seemed he had been denied her for ever. It was almost more than he could stand. 'You really are quite extraordinary, my dear wife—stubborn and so quick to anger. But come,' he said, sitting down and beginning to pull off his boots, 'enough of these tragic airs and get into bed.'

'I am past the age of being sent to bed—and when I do I prefer to go alone.'

Tossing his boots aside, Iain stood up and quickly removed his shirt. Lorne watched him, a blush spreading across her cheeks, and a tremor of alarm quaked through her at the sight of his nakedness and the mat of black hair curling on his broad chest. In the candles' glow, the light cast bold shadows on his face. His skin was sleek, the heavy muscles of his arms and shoulders rippling as he moved. He was quite splendid, she realised, as splendid as she remembered, and her look became one of reluctant admiration, doing much to damage her resistance.

He didn't say a word. His fathomless silver eyes gleamed as he looked at her intently, and he still had that infuriating habit of hiding his thoughts behind an inscrutable mask. With a pounding heart, Lorne backed away when he moved towards her. His thick black hair curled about his face, and his mouth was slightly curved in a mocking smile—it was the assured smile of a willing conquest. Stubbornly refusing to surrender to the call of her blood, her soft lips tightened and her eyes blazed her rebellion.

'Don't you touch me. You can go to the devil for all I care and find some other bed to sleep in. I am not someone to be used when the fancy takes you. My grievances are many and valid. From the moment we met in church you have gone out of your way to hurt and humiliate me, and if that wasn't enough, you then keep me waiting half the night while you sit drinking with your friend, and then calmly walk into my bedchamber and expect me to meekly do your bidding? The insult is too great to be borne.'

'And is this what this display of temper is all about? Are you complaining?' he asked, with an infuriating, mocking smile, his eyes gleaming cruelly.

'I would not give you the satisfaction,' she fumed, his airy tone whipping up her anger by the second. He might at least show some contrition. But no. He was as calmly at ease as ever, and he even had the audacity to mock her.

'Would you like me to explain?' he asked with growing impatience, his eyes focused upon her slender form moulded so revealingly beneath the cream nightdress, and the hard peaks of her breasts uptilted and beckoning.

'It seems a little late for that,' she retorted, in what she meant to be a cool, disdainful tone. Unfortunately her voice wavered when a lump of nameless emotion constricted her throat. She became frozen as her husband's eyes travelled over every inch of her in a long, lecherous perusal that took her breath away. She was unnerved by the unleashed sensuality she saw in his expression, which was like a flame to her senses. When his gaze finally came to rest on her lips she found her voice once more. 'I told you not to touch me—and I meant it. Like a fool I gave myself to you once before. I shall not do so again until *I* am ready. Don't you dare lay a finger on me.'

Almost before the words were uttered, his eyes had flamed and he had moved closer. 'Is that a threat?'

Immediately Lorne saw her error. Unwittingly she had made it sound like a challenge. His breath was low and uneven as he advanced towards her. Alarmed, she retreated a step, wondering if she could make it to the door and escape.

Iain read her intention and his eyes narrowed. 'Don't even think about it. You aren't going anywhere.'

'Why don't you go away?' she whispered, feeling the anger draining out of her, leaving her with tears close to the surface. She bit her lip to hold them back.

'Nay, madam. Your antics in Scotland made me a laughing stock. I will not compound it by letting it be known that my wife showed me the door on our wedding night.'

They stood facing one another, intensely aware of each other—how could they not be? It was warm, the light soft, the atmosphere charged with tension and something else each of them recognised, having experienced it once before and not so very long ago. Lorne was scared. She wanted Iain so much it hurt, but his high-handed manner and his arrogant assumption that he could do with her as he pleased made her stand against him.

Iain moved without conscious thought. He was finished with talking, and it was neither passion nor affection that drove him on, but a determination to possess. Placing his arms around her rigid form, he swung her up into his arms, marvelling at her lightness, her softness, and the subtle fragrance emanating from her body.

Lorne cried out in protest. 'Let go of me you—you loathsome beast.'

One brow lifted and he looked sourly amused. 'You certainly know how to flatter a man,' he drawled. 'And I may be what you accuse me of being, and more. I can also be ugly when crossed, Lorne. I advise you in future to remember it.' His soft voice was a threat of revenge for the agonies he had suffered since their parting.

Carrying her to the bed, he dropped her unceremoniously on to the quilt. Beside herself with rage, Lorne erupted in a storm of anger, and, far from compliant, she thrashed out frantically, writhing and clawing at him, wanting to strike out at him and hurt him with all the anger inside her, unwilling to give him total power over her. In her heart she was already his, but still she fought him with a boundless fury. She was supple and slippery as an eel, but her hair was proving to be a problem, coiling round her like silken ropes.

Swearing beneath his breath, Iain took hold of her wrists and pinned them above her head. But then he hesitated, never having forced himself upon a female. There was something distasteful in the thought. He wanted to tell her that he forgave her rash actions with Kilpatrick, to tell her he wanted their marriage to work, that he wanted her to be happy and to assure her he would never do her harm, but when he saw her soft lips and felt her flesh warm and firm beneath him, his moment of hesitation passed.

'Let me go,' she hissed. 'I don't want to sleep with you.'

Plunging his hands into her hair, he forced her head back to meet his gaze, burning with furious triumph. 'I don't intend to sleep,' he said evenly, amazed by the savagery in her eyes. 'At least, not yet.'

'You know what I mean. I don't want to go to bed with you.'

Silver eyes gleamed down at her and he drew a deep breath, keeping his temper under tight rein. 'I don't recall asking your preference on the matter,' he said, his voice dangerously low. 'You are my wife.'

'Aye, your wife—forced on you by circumstance. But you will not force yourself on me. If I choose to reject you, I will.'

'You can try. But just in case you didn't understand the proceedings in church, you promised to obey and serve me.'

'Serve you? Never.' Her lip curled scornfully. 'I do not serve.'

Iain's eyes were merciless as he grasped her chin and forced her to look at him. 'Do not deny me, Lorne. I warn you, I will not allow it. You will subject yourself to me. If I want you, I will have you. I will own you, possess you, body and soul,' he said through clenched teeth, enunciating each word so she was left in no doubt of his determination, 'and be damned to your maidenly protestations.'

Falling silent, he stared down at her, and then he smiled, almost tenderly. She was lovely, like a delicate flower, and feeling the warmth of her, he felt a rare peace when he looked into her eyes. 'Come,' he said, brushing her cheek with his lips. 'Why this outraged modesty? 'Tis not the first time you've shared my bed.'

Mesmerised, Lorne gazed up at him, his warm breath on her face and his husky voice caressing her. She could feel herself beginning to melt. 'Do you think I could ever forget that?'

'I sincerely hope not,' he murmured, proceeding to assault her lips with his own.

In one last bid to defy him, Lorne tried to wriggle away, squirming beneath him, but it deterred him not at all from his inevitable path; in fact, her movements only succeeded in inflaming his desire. With all the skill of an experienced soldier, he began his siege, and the fortifications of her secure stronghold began to fall to him—the invader. He was a man in full possession of his strength, and he crushed her beneath his weight.

The candles' light showed Lorne her husband's face close to her own. It was grim, his mouth a tight, determined line. Then his lips closed on hers, capturing them even as she tried to draw away from him, but he moved her beneath him to make her more accommodating.

'Be still,' he ordered huskily. 'Cease your struggles. You'll wear yourself out for no purpose. No matter what has gone before, or what our future together holds, I ask you to forget all that and remember that this is our wedding night. You are my bride. Out of the shambles of our lives, let us have this one good thing to remember. We owe it to ourselves, do we not?' Pinning her to the bed, he slid his hands beneath her and held her hips firmly, keeping her immobile, holding her helpless under him.

Lorne lay there, taut and trembling, deeply moved by what he had said. It was more, much more, than she had dared hope for. She closed her eyes so as not to see his face, but she heard him breathing hard, felt his warm breath on her cheek. And then he was kissing her once more, his lips firm with sexual dominance, and she felt all the old demons waking inside her, clamouring for release, creating wild, primitive sensations racing along her raw nerve endings.

'Oh, no,' she gasped, when she felt his hands exploring her body. 'Iain, I beg of you—'

'Beg what, my love?' he murmured hoarsely, noting how her beauty was intensified by the way she was looking at him—her ardour and eagerness. 'To stop—to go on?'

Lorne no longer had any idea what she wanted. Her thoughts were irrational, and the feelings slipping through her body made her melt inside. She shivered even though she was not cold, and she could not have moved even had she wanted to—and of that she was no longer sure. She would never remember how it happened, but suddenly they were both naked, and she didn't even notice that she pressed against him and slipped her arms around his neck, tangling her fingers in his hair and drawing his head down to hers.

And then the miracle happened. His proud heat slid into her and they were joined as one. Iain's need for her became raw hunger, his body craving hers with a violence he could not believe, and as a result he did not love her tenderly that first time. Filling her again and again with masterly precision, straining to come closer still, he was no longer met with any resistance as he forced the beautiful, writhing creature beneath him to the edge of total surrender.

Lorne gave herself as never before. She forgot everything and allowed herself to be carried away ecstatically by this vastly superior power, expressing her love with every fibre of her being. And when it was over he began again, but gently now. The most tender of lovers, Iain led her along paths of sheer, exciting, incredible torment, as bitter-sweet as it was ecstatic, and she became lost in incoherent yearnings as their passion became all consuming.

Filled with a joy that effaced anything else, with a pulse that still throbbed deep within her, Lorne slept, exhausted, content in the knowledge that her body, heart and soul, belonged to no one but Iain Monroe.

Lorne stirred from a deep, contented sleep to find her head resting peacefully in the curve of Iain's shoulder. With the heat of her naked body blending with the warmth of his, and glorying in the cosy comfort of the bed, she closed her eyes and nestled against his broad chest, wanting to enjoy their closeness while it lasted and contemplate the hours of the night when they had made love, and what a real marriage between them would mean. Her happiness was greater by far than anything she had previously experienced. She found herself even more deeply in love with Iain, and she was astounded when she remembered how her pride and prejudices had fought him last night in spite of her determination to make him love her, before she had finally surrendered to him.

Awake, Iain turned his head and inhaled the sweet fragrant hair that spilled about his shoulder. With his finger he lightly traced the shadow of a bruise on her collarbone, marring her skin, which was fragile and clear. 'You look as if you've been in the wars, my love.'

'You look a little rough around the edges yourself, my lord,' she whispered, placing her lips against a scratch on his chest that he had acquired during their struggle.

Iain chuckled softly. 'If you bed a vixen, you must expect damages,' he murmured, nuzzling the warm hollow of her neck. He remembered the many nights he had laid alone in his bed when he had been unable to banish Lorne from his mind, from his dreams, knowing she was the catalyst that set his blood aflame until his desire for her seethed. Ever since she had left Norwood he had been a man burning with a single need to possess one woman, and that woman was in his arms. Now, his passion sated, he could only marvel at the contentment he felt.

Later, when the grey light of dawn filtered through the cracks in the heavy drapes, and Iain stirred again, it was to find Lorne absent from the bed. Propping himself up on his elbows, he scanned the room, but it was empty. Frowning, puzzled as to where she could be, he swung his legs out of bed and pulled on his breeches. Combing his fingers through his rumpled hair before thrusting his arms into his shirt sleeves, he was about to cross to the door when he heard a sound coming from the adjoining dressing room. So, she was in there. With a smile he moved towards the closed door, but then he froze. The noises coming from within were of someone being violently sick.

Oddly enough, Iain's first fleeting thought was that she'd probably eaten something the previous day that had disagreed with her, but when he pushed the door open and he saw his wife's scantily clad form heaving over a bowl, he was now inclined to believe it was something of a different, more serious nature entirely. A feeling of inexpressible dread surged through his body, pounding in his brain, and he shook his head as if to deny what his intellect was already beginning to suspect.

Sensing his presence, Lorne stiffened and raised her head, wiping her mouth on a small cloth. Her insides were churning and her face was a study of misery. It was like wax, her green eyes huge, hollow and lifeless. 'Iain!' she gasped. 'I apologise if I woke you. I—you see—I—'

Iain raked his gaze over her trembling form with insulting thoroughness, narrow and assessing, seeing her belly already showing signs of swelling with the few ounces of humanity forming inside. When he raised his eyes to her face they glittered coldly. 'You are with child,' he stated, not even bothering to ask the question.

Lorne shrank, trembling beneath the blast of his gaze. Her mouth went dry and her heart began to beat with a terrifying dread as she sensed that her husband had seemingly withdrawn from her. His expression was one of controlled anger. It was as if the passion and tenderness they had shared had never existed. This was a stranger, a terrifying stranger, who filled her with fear. In answer to his question she nodded mutely, a look of humble pleading filling her eyes.

Iain's entire body stiffened and he stared at her with incredulity, before his face hardened into a mask of freezing rage. 'And when were you going to tell me?' he demanded in a fury. When she didn't reply he placed both his fists on the table and leaned forward slightly, pinning her with his hard gaze. 'I am awaiting your explanation—if you have one to offer.'

'I—I was waiting for the right moment.'

'The right moment? Confound it, Lorne! You've had all night to tell me.'

Lorne felt her heart contract with pain and unbidden tears filled her eyes. 'I meant to tell you—I swear I did.'

'And did you agree to marry me to get yourself a father for Kilpatrick's brat?' Iain asked with brutal force, violence emanating from every pore.

Stunned, Lorne's eyes widened, her soft lips parting in shocked disbelief. When it finally sank in that he believed she had lain with Captain Kilpatrick, that the child was his, tears of hurt and outrage sprang into her eyes. Drawing herself up with painful dignity, two high spots of indignation highlighted her pale cheeks. 'How dare you say that? Hasn't it occurred to you that the child just *might* be yours?' she retaliated furiously.

'Might? You bitch! You deceitful, conniving, bitch.'

Lorne checked herself abruptly, realising that in her distraught state it had come out all wrong. Iain had read into her words exactly what he wanted to read.

'No wonder your grandmother lost no time in presenting her case to the King. Unable to bear the disgrace of having her granddaughter present her with a bastard, to allay suspicion and to cover the shame, it would be more convenient if she were to take her Scottish kidnapper for a husband than none at all. What did she do—offer to wave the charge of abduction if I agreed to marriage?' he seethed. 'If you honestly think an old lady could frighten me witless into wedlock, then you are mistaken.'

'Then why did you agree to marry me?'

'Because between them, your esteemed grandmother and the King left me with no alternative. Did you tell her about Kilpatrick?'

'No.'

'And she believes the child is mine?'

'Of course she does—and no matter what you believe, the child is yours,' Lorne cried fiercely, scalding tears beginning to run unchecked down her ashen cheeks, the pain so great she could hardly speak. 'I have never lain with anyone else—which must have disappointed you when you first came to my bed, when you believed I was a woman who had already dragged herself through the beds of half the gentlemen in London.'

'A touching tale,' Iain scorned drily, wanting to thrust her trembling form further away from him, just as much as he wanted to gather her into his arms. 'Do you mean to say you expect me to believe this?'

'You must believe what you will, but I have never lied to you.'

'Then just once in our misbegotten lives together, tell me the truth. I should like to know precisely what it was that did happen between you and Kilpatrick in that damned Tollbooth.'

Lorne's heart contracted. She tried not to think of what had happened at Inveraray, of how she had seduced the odious Captain Kilpatrick. Thank God she'd managed to administer the narcotic to his wine and he'd passed out before he became too amorous. It had been a dreadful time, fraught with danger and fear. She still had nightmares about it, but she did not regret what she had done.

'Must we go through all that again? I have already told you the circumstances of our meeting.'

'You have,' Iain replied, beginning to pace the carpet with impatient strides in the small room. 'But your confidences did not extend to the most intriguing parts. You can understand why it is this that interests me.'

'It is hardly worth the telling,' she uttered, wiping her wet cheeks with the backs of her hands. 'Captain Kilpatrick was guarding my father. The plan was to distract him enough to secure his escape. That is more or less what happened.'

Iain threw her a scathing glance. 'More or less? I do not care for more or less. What else is there?'

'I—had with me a bottle of drugged wine. Captain Kilpatrick drank it and it quickly took effect.'

'An easy tale. And if the drug had not taken effect? What then?' he demanded harshly, continuing to pace up and down. 'How far were you prepared to go with Kilpatrick to get your father out of the Tollbooth? Would you have allowed him to ravish you?'

'No—no, I would not,' she gasped, deeply hurt that he could think this of her. 'Robert and James were close at hand at all times and would have stepped in to prevent that happening. They were stronger than Captain Kilpatrick.'

'If that is so, why did they use you? Why did they not simply storm the Tollbooth?'

'Because to use force would have attracted attention. The whole town was swarming with redcoats. To do what you suggest would have been suicidal. Robert believed that stealth and cunning would succeed over force. In that he was proved right.'

Iain gave her a mocking, contemptuous laugh. 'And was it worth the risk?'

'Yes, it was. At least, I think so. Although I confess that at the time I was scared to death,' she added touchingly.

'As long as you do not expect *me* to applaud what you have

done,' Iain snapped. He turned from her and strode into the bedroom. Pulling back the heavy curtains from the window, he stood looking out, his body taut, his face grim.

Sick and weak, Lorne followed him. Seizing her robe from a chair, she shrugged into it, forcing herself to keep calm.

'So, during the time you were alone with Kilpatrick, just what did you do together? Did he touch you? Did he?' Iain demanded at length, firing the questions at her.

Lorne gulped and nodded miserably.

He turned and threw her a glance loaded with suspicion. 'And more?'

Again she nodded. 'Yes—but I have told you not in the way—'

'Enough.' Iain's face was white, his expression one of contemptuous scorn. 'You have said enough. Damn you for a reckless, harebrained fool,' he exclaimed violently. 'You really can be very stupid at times. And tell me, where was Galbraith when you were flaunting your assets before Kilpatrick like a whore?'

Lorne's stomach clenched, knowing this particular issue could no longer be avoided. Although she knew, that at this particular moment, what she had to tell him about her old suitor would only serve to further infuriate this volatile husband of hers. 'Duncan wasn't there. He left us and returned to Kinlochalen. When Robert learned of my aversion to the betrothal, he agreed it would be a mistake for us to wed.'

Iain was surprised. 'As easily as that?'

'Yes. For reasons of his own, Robert no longer considered a union between us suitable.'

Iain looked at her hard before turning and moving away from her in angry silence. When he turned once more his voice was quiet, each word carefully enunciated, and the eyes that met hers were as cold and hard as steel.

'You have betrayed me in the vilest way possible. And last night—I salute you. That was an incredible, convincing performance from you,' he said, with deliberate cruelty.

Lorne's eyes widened in shocked disbelief that he could think that. 'It was not a performance, and I am heartily tired of being cross-questioned, Iain. Nor will I bear my child in shame while you accuse it of being a bastard. Why should you be so outraged to realise I am with child? You must have known there was a possibility of such a thing happening when we made love together.' When she looked at her husband's rigid form, seeing his hands clenching and unclenching as he tried to bring his fury under control, she wrapped her arms round her waist as if to protect the baby inside her from his wrath. 'I don't need this now, Iain. I can't stand it. Maybe this marriage is a mistake—'

'Aye, a mistake that cannot be set aside,' he growled.

Lorne stood erect, as if carved from stone. 'If that is indeed how you feel, then there is little hope for us.'

She was quivering visibly, struggling against nausea. Suddenly she looked so frail, so fragile. The light fell softly on her face, which was like a tragic mask. The pitiful sight found a chink in Iain's armour and for a moment he weakened and almost went to her, longing to snatch her into his arms and pretend for a little while longer that she was still his alluring, passionate young countess of the night. But he couldn't, because he couldn't dispel the tormenting image of her and Kilpatrick embracing while she was coldly planning how to dispose of him to aid her father's escape.

'I should have kept you with me and put you in irons in my deepest dungeon when I rode to Stirling that day. It has been my hell to pay since.'

Lorne glared at him through her tears. 'Then I won't be your hell any more. Am—am I to understand that you do not want this child?'

'Damn it, Lorne—do I have a choice? It's an encumbrance I can do without just now.'

The angry words hit Lorne like a blow, bringing another rush of tears to her eyes. Looking away, she stared blindly at the door, clenching her teeth to try to stem their flow.

When Iain glanced at her, he cursed softly, realising what he'd said. 'I didn't mean that,' he ground out, raking his fingers through his hair. 'I have no excuse to lash out at you.'

Lorne swallowed down her tears. 'It doesn't matter,' she whispered.

'Of course it matters.' Going to her, he placed his finger beneath her chin and tilted her face. 'Look at me,' he said when her eyes remained downcast. Slowly she raised them to his and his stomach clenched at the pain and sadness he saw staring out at him. 'I don't mean to put you through this—truly. It was a stupid, childish thing for me to say. Of course I want children. I like them well enough—I just never had time for them, so it will take some getting used to. Do you accept my apology?'

She nodded. 'Yes,' she whispered, even though his words still smote her heart. Suddenly the ordeal was proving too much for her. She felt ill. Her sorrow rose in her throat until she felt she would suffocate, and her brain became so clouded that she could no longer dwell on what they had been saying. Once again her head began to swim with nausea.

'Will you please go? I—I'm going to be sick.' Running back into the dressing room, she fell to her knees and vomited between her sobs into the bowl. She was drained and humiliated, broken and terrified by the fright that Iain didn't want her or their baby, and it was almost too much to endure.

In the other room Iain remained motionless, listening to the chaotic pounding of his heart. The fingers he combed through his hair were trembling slightly. Listening to the sounds coming from the dressing room he walked towards it, pausing in the doorway and looking down at the young woman on her knees, huddled over a bowl into which she had just been sick. She was drawing breath in deep gulps to stop herself fainting, and at that pitiful sight the demon anger and jealousy relaxed its grip at last. Going to her, he gently picked her up into his arms and carried her to the bed. Placing her on the rumpled sheets, he drew the quilt over her before tenderly wiping her face with a damp cloth.

Scarcely conscious, her eyes flickered open and she looked up at him.

'Forgive me,' he murmured, backing away from the bed. 'I'm a brute, I know, but I cannot bear the thought of another man touching you. I'll leave you now and fetch your maid to attend you. I'll also arrange for a physician to examine you.'

Lorne stared up at him. His mood had become unfathomable. There was no smile or softness on his face, only a seriousness. She wanted to say something to make him come to her, to reach out, but something in the expression of his eyes, seen for just a moment, made her remain silent. She searched their depths with eager tenderness, trying to find something there, something left of the passion they had so recently shared. But they only looked back, watching her without emotion. He was thinking of her with Captain Kilpatrick, she knew he was, and there was not a thing she could do about it.

Chapter Ten

～～～～～

Over the days that followed Iain became distant, a cold, forbidding man who looked at his wife with such disinterest that it made her shudder. She felt that old desolation, that emptiness, that hopeless longing for the man who dominated her life, his smile, his comforting arms, and the warmth of his love he now denied her.

News of their marriage caused a stir among the courtiers at St James's Palace, which hummed like a beehive. Gossip was malicious and speculative, for they were uninformed, the details known only to the King, Lady Barton, trusted family and friends, and the couple themselves. Selfish in their preoccupation, courtiers gathered in groups to bandy spiked compliments and insults tempered with a smile. They discussed the relationships of others and ruined reputations just as they discussed the latest outbreak of the plague, politics and the weather.

Lorne could almost hear the sibilant whisperings and at first all her outraged virtue seethed within her, but she refused to be intimidated and after a short time paid no attention to it. There was a sense of sordidness and disillusionment about it all, and secretly she would be relieved when her pregnancy was more advanced and it would be indelicate to parade herself in public.

Every night she dressed in her finest gowns to accompany Iain to the theatre or a Court function, where they were surrounded by all the pomp and circumstance of royalty. The gentlemen of the Court were eager to make themselves known to her, whereas she came under critical scrutiny from the ladies—the same ladies who sought the attention and admiration of her husband.

At times like this she would smile and pretend she was unmoved by his easy manner towards them and the women's fawning, but in reality she was profoundly upset and couldn't help experiencing an ungovernable jealousy at all the attention he attracted. She was never alone with her husband and she longed for some intimate communication between them. Iain was always polite. He was concerned for her health, complimented her on the way she looked and smiled when his eyes alighted on her. But he treated her like a stranger. And, God help her, she wanted him every night, and fell asleep dreaming of his naked body possessing her own. Where he slept, she really had no idea.

Vibrantly aware of the strained atmosphere between the newly-weds, Hugh silently and critically surveyed the situation and tried desperately to alleviate the tension, but all his attempts to draw them together yielded nothing but courteous, brief responses from his friend.

Almost four months into her pregnancy, mercifully Lorne's early morning discomfort left her. Suddenly she felt so well and with a lifting of her spirits she felt lighter—although there were times when her emotions seemed to veer all over the place. She was determined to increase her efforts to jolt Iain out of his cool reserve. She didn't care how she went

about it, what lengths she had to go to to make it happen—
even if it made him furious and made him lose control and
confront her, anything would be preferable to his polite indifference.

The English court maintained many activities at St James's
Palace. Tonight they were to attend a ball being held in honour
of some foreign dignitary, and Lorne was determined to look
her best. It would also be even more enjoyable because Aunt
Pauline—who had decided to stay on in London until Lorne
left for Norwood—would be there and she had consented to
let Agnes attend, which explained Hugh's high spirits. Having
had her fill of town, her grandmother had returned to Yorkshire shortly after the wedding.

Hugh came upon Lorne in the hall. His eyes filled with unconcealed admiration as he gave her a sweeping glance. Her
glorious hair cascaded in an abundance of golden curls,
framing her exquisite face, and her emerald-green gown with
its voluminous skirt matched the colour of her eyes. The
waistline was fashionably set slightly above her natural waist,
thus concealing any hint of her pregnancy. The front panel of
the cream silk underskirt, heavily decorated with gold braid,
was clearly meant to be seen and admired, and full sleeves,
decorated with the same gold braid as the underskirt, ended
at her elbows in a froth of lace.

However, with its scooped neckline and narrow, sloping
shoulders, it was the most revealing gown Hugh had ever seen
her wear, and he could imagine Iain's reaction when he saw
the tantalising swell of creamy flesh almost spilling out of the
boned bodice. He sensed what she was up to, and if she
wanted to shock his friend into noticing her, she was going
the right way about it.

'How do I look?' she asked, her face aglow as she pirou-
etted on her toes in front of him, the full skirt of her gown

billowing out around her slender ankles to reveal the fine lace petticoats beneath.

Hugh raised his eyebrows in silent acclaim and favoured her with a roguish grin. 'You look positively divine—and I congratulate you. I admire your strategy. I hope it works.'

Lorne sighed, clutching her painted fan in front of her. 'So do I, Hugh. Out of all the people I have met since knowing Iain, you are the only one who knows the complexities of our relationship. I think it's time to do something about it and to set things to rights. We can't go on like this. It is not in my nature to be meek and humble, and I am feeling so much better now and more able to take what life—or my husband— has to throw at me. Desperate needs call for desperate measures, don't you think?'

'I couldn't agree more. But take care. Iain is extremely difficult to manage when he's been provoked beyond what he deems reasonable, and my friend is beyond that unfortunate state. If you are to succeed, then I very much fear that the burden of doing so will fall on you.'

'I know,' she said, with a gleam of mischief dancing in her eyes, 'which is why tonight I've spent more time than ever over my appearance, and why I chose to wear this dress—the most daring and provocative in my wardrobe. I am prepared to give him whatever invitation is necessary to make him notice me. What do you think his reaction will be?'

'Explosive,' Hugh answered, laughing. 'He will definitely not approve. There is every chance that when he's unleashed some of his rage on you, he'll drag you upstairs and select something eminently more suitable for you to wear.'

'I'll risk it,' she replied with a smile.

'Then courage, little lady,' Hugh murmured, his eyes drawn to the tall figure that had appeared at the top of the stairs. 'Here comes your husband now.'

Lorne assumed a mild air as she watched Iain descend the stairs, but inside her heart was pounding. Tenderness and regret surged through her every time they were together, and the love she carried for him in her heart reinforced her courage to face him and do whatever was necessary to resolve matters between them.

He looked so splendid tonight that every female eye at the ball would be drawn to him like a magnet. His coat was fashioned of rust velvet, the tailoring flawless. He wore cream-coloured breeches, and white silk stockings moulded his muscular calves. His waistcoat was of gold satin embroidered with gold and silver thread, and his cravat was pristine white, secured with a sapphire-and-diamond stickpin. His black hair gleamed and was neatly tied in the nape by a thin band of black ribbon. With such a fine head of hair she was glad he declined the wearing of a wig, which was so much the fashion among both ladies and gentlemen in fashionable society.

When he reached the hall Iain cast his friend a casual glance before settling his gaze on the enchanting vision in a shimmering gown of emerald green. He froze, and then very slowly, very deliberately, he moved towards her. 'Good God!' he exclaimed when his eyes rested in a furious, censorious stare on the creamy expanse of two gorgeous, glowing orbs exposed above the bodice, and the glittering diamond pendant winking and nestling cheekily in the shady valley between. 'Change it,' he said, in a low, ominous voice. 'Go and take that dress off and find one more suitable.'

At close range, Lorne saw the burning rage that fairly sizzled in his grey eyes but, undeterred, she smiled brightly, managing to look sublimely innocent in the most seductively alluring gown Iain had ever seen her wear. 'Why, don't you like it?' she said brightly.

'You have others I like better. Go and change.'

'No,' she said firmly. 'I see no reason to.'

'Lorne, I asked you to change it,' Iain persisted implacably.

'You did not. You *ordered* me to change it—and I don't intend to,' Lorne replied with a defiant lift of her chin. 'I think this gown is perfectly suitable for the ball. Hugh, be so good as to pass me my cloak.'

'Anything to oblige,' Hugh chuckled, rushing to do her bidding while at the same time ignoring his friend's eyes boring into him, accusing him of complicity and treachery.

Iain levelled his gaze on his wife, his jaw clenched so tightly that a muscle began to throb in his cheek. 'Do not provoke me, Lorne.'

'Do you mean more than I have already?' she rejoined pertly, with a toss of her head and a vivacious smile, aware of the warning note in his voice, but refusing to let him intimidate her now she had come this far. 'I would think that is virtually impossible.'

'I trust you will remember your condition and behave accordingly.'

She gave him a pointed look. 'I am reminded of that every minute of every day, Iain. Unlike you, it is hardly something I am likely to forget, and when it becomes apparent I shall not embarrass you by flaunting myself in public. Thank you, Hugh,' she said sweetly, when he draped her velvet cloak on her shoulders. 'Now, shall we go? We don't want to arrive at the palace late, and I am so looking forward to enjoying the evening.'

'Then do so to its fullest, madam, since it will be your last,' her husband informed her coldly.

The gathering at St James's Palace was a study of lavish elegance, the room into which they entered a burst of brilliant, vibrant colour. The moment the Earl of Norwood and his wife arrived, Lorne commanded total attention, and a group of painted and bejewelled courtiers soon surrounded her, much to her husband's chagrin. She was no stranger to the company assembled and had become a popular figure, but tonight she looked different. Like a superbly crafted gem, she shone with a radiance that put every other woman present in the shade. There was an aura about her, an inner light that gave her more lustre than diamonds.

With his shoulder propped against a pillar, Iain sipped his wine, his dark brows drawn together in thoughtful concentration as he watched Lorne dancing the intricate, lively steps of a minuet with an exuberant young fop. Her movements were dainty and graceful, and she was looking at her partner with the most innocent expression on her face. Iain wasn't paying much attention to what was going on around him, and was unable to concentrate for any length of time on his companions' conversation.

It was a merry affair, and as the evening wore on, everyone became more lively and boisterous as more wine was consumed and most of the guests were no longer sober. For the first time in his life, as Iain watched Lorne take her place in a progressive country dance, where one's partners constantly changed, observing how her face positively glowed with whispered compliments, he experienced an acute feeling of jealousy, which caught him completely off guard. It was a feeling he found decidedly unpleasant, and the sooner they left London the easier he would feel.

Ever since their wedding night his tortured imaginings had caused him to exist in a state of righteous fury, and he didn't know how much longer he could stand living under the same roof as her and deny himself the pleasure of her body. The memory of what they had shared became more alive with each passing day. It touched him and lived inside him, was visual and tactile, had odour, texture and warmth. It had been perfect, and because he was powerless to banish the memory from his mind, he longed to savour its potency once more. Never had he seen Lorne look so provocatively lovely, so regal, glamorous and bewitching—and she belonged to him.

He argued with himself, asking himself why he was behaving like a churl towards her, why he was deliberately hurting her and keeping her at arm's length. Was it because she had damaged his male pride by leaving him so abruptly at Norwood? Was it because she had involved herself in that nefarious scheme to get her father out of the Tollbooth at Inveraray, and in so doing deprived John Ferguson and everyone else at Norwood of the satisfaction of seeing him hang? How could he condemn her for involving herself in her father's escape? Wouldn't he have done the same for his own father? Was he hurting her because she had become closely acquainted with Kilpatrick? Or was it the oldest reason of all— that she was a McBryde and he was still haunted by David's ghost and the part she had played in his death?

Whatever the reason, he was convinced of two things—she had not lain with Kilpatrick, and the child she was carrying was his. No one who was guilty could have feigned such outrage on being accused of carrying another man's child as she had done.

In Scotland, at the height of their lovemaking, she had cried out that she loved him. Did she still love him, or had he broken her spirit and driven a stake into her heart? But then he smiled, remembering how she had stood up to him as no other would dare to do, both tonight and in the past, and how she had openly defied him by refusing to change into something more suitable for the ball—a gown that exposed far more than was decent, and was for his eyes alone. No—her spirit was still intact, and God help him if he should ever destroy that.

Placing his empty glass on the salver of a passing footman, he pushed himself away from the pillar and drew himself up to his full height, telling himself that something must be done to heal the breach between them before it destroyed them both. Seeing Hugh on the periphery of the throng, he was about to go to him when a tall, dark-haired woman who had just entered the ballroom caught his attention. Their eyes locked, and with a faint smile he made his way towards her to present himself.

Breathless, her feet aching, her head spinning, Lorne declined the next aristocrat that tried to claim her. Excusing herself to Lady Billington and her Aunt Pauline, with whom her last partner had deposited her, she went to talk to Hugh, who was standing to one side with Agnes. She was also secretly hoping that her husband would ask her to partner him. All evening she had been aware of his tall figure watching her. He was not dancing, and was surrounded by several companions. There was a tension in his stance, and his expression was dark and brooding. He had made no attempt to ask her to dance, and when he was approached by gentlemen seeking his permission to partner her, he gave it easily enough and did not seem unduly concerned when she was whisked away.

'You look as though you're enjoying yourself,' Agnes commented, noticing Lorne's high colour and shining eyes.

'Very much, although I confess to feeling a little exhausted.' She looked around, searching the crowded room for the face she knew best, but she saw nothing of him just then. Perhaps he had gone into one of the gaming rooms, which were crowded with men and women obsessed with the turning cards and rolling dice. The King was across the ballroom surrounded by a ring of courtiers, but her husband was not one of them. 'Where's Iain?'

Hugh and Agnes exchanged significant glances. Following the direction of their gazes, Lorne was provided with the answer. The woman her husband was dancing with was quite tall, slender and graceful. Her features were delicate, her expression serene. The neckline of her gown was square cut and so modest in comparison to Lorne's own, that she suddenly felt like the commonest drab.

Unable to tear her eyes away from them, her heart wrenched. The dance was a stately procession so they were able to converse with ease. She saw them laugh simultaneously at something the lady said, and Lorne would never know what Iain was feeling at that moment. 'Who is she?' she asked, knowing the woman's identity before Hugh spoke her name.

'Her name is Maria Fraser,' Hugh divulged.

Lorne's throat constricted painfully. All the colour drained out of her face and neck as she continued to look at them, feeling a profound sorrow and despair. 'The woman Iain would have married if the King hadn't interfered,' she whispered.

'Nothing had been decided,' Hugh said quietly, wanting to spare her feelings.

Lorne swallowed, close to tears. Averting her eyes, all her hopes and dreams of the future suddenly dissolved around her. Why did she suddenly feel as though every eye in the room was upon her, glittering, watching, waiting, eyes set above mouths that were secretly smiling, covertly sneering? In all her anguish and self-consciousness, she wished passionately that she were anywhere else but here.

'It's all right, Hugh,' she said flatly. 'You can talk about her. Why haven't I seen her?'

'She's been in France with her family, and only returned to London yesterday.'

'She—she's very lovely.'

'So she is, but you put her—and every lady present—in the shade.'

Lorne smiled slightly, grateful for the compliment. 'Thank you, Hugh, but I can see why Iain is so taken with her—and that gown she is wearing is so exquisite it must have been made in Paris.'

Seeing the suffering Lorne was unable to hide, Agnes stood close to her and gripped her hand. 'It's all right, Lorne. Don't pay her any mind,' she advised. 'It means nothing.'

'No, of course it doesn't. I'm not concerned,' she whispered untruthfully, blinking back her tears and forcing a tremulous smile to her lips when she looked at Agnes, glad of the warm, comforting pressure of her hand. 'I never was very good at hiding my feelings from you, was I?'

'I know you too well. Besides, your face betrays you. It is the most expressive face I know.'

'Oh, Agnes! Look at him. How could he do this to me? Does he have to stand so close?' she said in a low, indignant voice that did not conceal the hurt she was feeling. 'Does he have to look at her in that way and hold her so? And am I imagining it or does she have a proprietorial manner towards him—one he doesn't seem to resent.'

'Yes, Lorne, you are imagining it and read too much into it. They are dancing together—just like all the other couples are doing. That is all.'

Just then Iain shifted his gaze momentarily and met her eyes across the room, and Lorne flushed to have been caught watching him. She looked away and focused her gaze on the other dancers, but she was unable to distract her thoughts from her husband and Maria Fraser.

The dance ended and Lorne watched Iain lift his partner's hand to his lips and kiss it, lingering longer than was seemly, she thought. She felt ill. 'I want to leave, Agnes. I can't bear it.'

'Yes, you can. Come, Lorne, this isn't like you. You're one of the strongest people I know. You can't leave just because your husband is dancing with another woman. Why, you've danced with half a dozen gentlemen and he hasn't complained.'

'Maria Fraser is not just any woman.'

'Maybe not, but Iain married you, didn't he? And you can't leave,' Agnes whispered, pleading with her. 'Look around you. Can't you see what everyone is thinking? If you leave now, it will cause a scene and provide the malicious gossips with enough fodder to feed on for weeks.'

'Agnes is right,' Hugh told her softly. 'For the love of God, Lorne, Maria Fraser means nothing to Iain. If it's any consolation, he hasn't been able to tear his eyes off you all night, and he looked fit to annihilate every one of those fops you were dancing with. He was ready to pounce should any one of them try to monopolise you. Don't forget that you wore that gown to deliberately provoke him, and you have succeeded. I can't ever remember seeing him so furious.'

A moment later, having returned his partner to her escort, Iain wended his way through the crowd, moving towards the three of them. Silently he regretted asking Maria to dance. He should not have done it, he realised that now, not with a room full of bystanders looking on, watching them together, including his wife. He was not oblivious to the portent of what they were seeing and thinking. Lorne must have known who she was, even though her name had never been uttered between them.

Iain looked at Hugh. 'At the risk of intruding on what appears to be a serious discussion the three of you are having,' he drawled, 'would you mind if I took my wife away? I think we should mingle.'

Iain slowly transferred his gaze to his wife's face, a half-smile on his mouth. He dipped his gaze to her bodice with a kind of insolence and then slowly returned to her face. One eyebrow lifted almost imperceptibly. That was the moment Lorne thought she was going to die. Never had she felt so exposed, so naked, and she bitterly regretted her decision to wear this particular gown, displaying herself so disgracefully for every man to look at, when all she had wanted was Iain's attention, and he hadn't even the courtesy to dance with her.

'Have you exhausted all you partners?' he inquired sardonically.

On the verge of crying with humiliation and hurt pride, with an effort Lorne looked at him and managed to keep her expression neutral. 'Quite the contrary,' she answered, proud that her voice scarcely trembled. The memory of Maria Fraser was still harsh in her mind. 'I am the one who is exhausted.'

'Then a little respite will do you good. Come. There are a few people here that I would like to introduce you to.' Politely offering her his arm, she placed her ungloved, trembling hand on it. 'And smile, my love. Try to look congenial, even if it kills you,' he said in an underbreath as they moved away, an artificial smile pinned to his lips. Arching an eyebrow, he looked sideways at her. 'Is something amiss?'

'No. Why do you ask?'

He shrugged. 'No reason.'

His muscles taut, his expression wary, Iain waited for his wife's reaction to him partnering Maria. She wouldn't look at him, he noted with chagrin, though he glimpsed that wounded look in her eyes. But if he expected her to take him to task, he was mistaken. Somehow her indifference stung him more than her anger would have. Finally he drew her aside.

'Come, let us stroll by ourselves where it's quiet.'

'But I thought you wanted to mingle.'

'We just have,' he replied drily.

As they left the throng, to the vast disappointment of anyone who was interested, it was clear that for the remainder of the ball the Earl of Norwood would decline to seek any other company except that of his wife.

Directly in her path Lorne could see Maria Fraser in conversation with a group of ladies. She froze, her control slipping as the floor began to rock and tremble beneath her feet. The mere thought of coming face to face with this woman was too much to be borne. Surely Iain didn't intend introducing them? Surely he would not be so cruel as to do that to her?

Sensing his wife's distress, Iain took her hand and linked it through his arm, steering her in another direction. He realised the subject of Maria could no longer be ignored.

'You have heard of Mistress Fraser?'

Lorne looked straight ahead. 'How could I not? She was the woman you would have married were it not for me.' It was said in a low, calm voice that made the directness of her conjecture all the more startling.

'We have known each other for a long time. Nothing was decided between us,' Iain told her, echoing Hugh's words in an eminently reasonable tone.

'She is very beautiful,' Lorne observed, not allowing him to escape so easily.

'I agree, she is that,' Iain replied. 'She is also kind and has a gentle nature. You would like her.'

'Yes, I'm sure I would.'

At Lorne's wry reply, Iain shot her a hard look, suddenly angry at having to defend himself. 'Whatever thoughts are occupying that head of yours, I will tell you that any connection between us was severed when I married you.'

Lorne was conscious of a nasty tug somewhere in the region of her heart. She did not like to hear her husband speak of another woman's beauty. A born fighter, there followed a natural urge to cross swords with him. 'I'm glad to hear it. And would you have ruined her life, as you have mine?' she accused bitterly.

Iain stiffened at the intended insult. 'If I am indeed guilty of doing so, I am sorry. But if you are miserable, then most of it is due to your own making.'

'And that is just the kind of arrogant reply I would expect from you,' Lorne snapped. 'You must have had strong feelings for her if you were considering asking her to be your wife.'

'I was—fond of her.'

'Do you still want her?'

Iain hadn't expected that question, but he answered it honestly. 'No.'

Lorne experience a surge of relief, but her expression remained fixed as they walked slowly along a gallery, where others seeking respite from the heat of the ballroom were sauntering.

Iain would not do Maria the dishonour of speaking ill of her, not even to Lorne. But secretly he confessed she was not entirely to his taste. Her passivity rendered her uninteresting. She was too refined, too rigid, her curves too modest— compared to his wife, who, in the fourth month of her pregnancy, positively bloomed in her gorgeous, emerald-green gown. Looking down at her, Iain found her lovely eyes regarding him steadily. She had such beautiful eyes, he thought, as she gave him a smile.

'You are behaving just like a jealous wife, my love,' he told her on a softer note.

Lorne looked at him with just the right degree of amused scorn. 'No more jealous than you were, when you were watching me dance—fit to annihilate every one of my partners, I recall Hugh saying.'

'Hugh says too much,' Iain retorted with a scowl. 'He would do well to concentrate on his own affair with Agnes than interfere in mine—lest your dear Aunt Pauline finds another suitor for her daughter and arranges a marriage not to her liking.'

'Aunt Pauline wouldn't do that. Despite what you say, it seemed to me and everyone present that you are still enamoured of Mistress Fraser. You certainly looked your fill and had plenty to laugh and talk about,' Lorne retorted crossly.

'You are hardly in a position to lecture me, when you have danced with half the gentlemen present.'

'Six, to be precise,' Lorne informed him with cold sarcasm, lifting her chin a notch. 'And there is one slight difference. I did not try to seduce any of the gentlemen I danced with.'

Her outburst stunned Iain. He felt like laughing out loud and shaking her. At the same time he was struck by the realisation that she was jealous and that there were tears in her eyes. Tired of sniping and bickering, his temper mollified and a smile of admiration broke across his features.

'What a little spitfire you are when you're angry,' he chuckled softly. 'Are you disappointed that I did not dance with you instead?'

Lorne looked at him incredulously, relieved to see his black scowl had disappeared and his face had relaxed into pleasanter lines. 'Dance with me! I could cheerfully murder you.'

'I would come back to haunt you, my sweet,' he threatened, a slow, roguish grin dawning across his handsome features, his silver gaze locking on hers. 'I swear I will be a thousand times more formidable when my body has been reduced to dust. You will see me everywhere. My ghost and my memory will give you no rest.'

Having lost the battle to remain aloof, Lorne was unable to repress her answering smile, and she could feel laughter bubble up in her chest. 'That's absolute rubbish. I don't believe in ghosts.'

'Then since you are clearly reluctant to let me haunt you, I shall just have to make sure that I remain alive to harass you in the flesh,' he teased.

Lorne bit back a teary smile at his quip, happy to let her anger melt because she loved him. 'Really, Iain, you confound me. First you castigate me for wearing a dress you don't like,' she berated him, taking away the sting with a smile, 'then you refuse to dance with me, and then I see you becoming reacquainted with my predecessor in the most touching manner, and after all that you want to haunt me when you are dead. Have you no mercy?'

The remnants of mirth gleaming in his eyes slowly dissolved as he laid his hand tenderly against her cheek. 'None,' he replied obligingly, 'and I happen to love that dress you're wearing. It becomes you more than I cared to admit when I first saw it.' He cast a glance of approval at her thrusting breasts. 'Unfortunately it displays more of you for other gentlemen to gawp at than I approve of, and makes you the very essence of temptation.' After studying her face for a moment with a heavy-lidded gaze, he finally said, 'Let's go home.'

'What! No more introductions? No more dancing?'

'I have a different kind of dance in mind—with its own steps and its own rhythm. I'm sure you'll like it.'

His voice was seductive and ever so persuasive, and his eyes gleamed. 'I think I will,' she smiled.

Lorne accepted Iain's help into the coach and they sat in silence as it rumbled and lurched over the cobblestones, with link boys carrying flares to light their way. The streets were silent, save for the trundle of carriages and the occasional drunk wending his way home.

In the dim light Iain looked across at his wife. Her pale features and deceptive hint of fragility held such powerful allure that it made him want to reach out and drag her into his arms. But he must control his moonstruck urges until they reached the house.

'I have decided that we shall leave London within the week,' he told her suddenly.

His words came quite out of the blue. Lorne froze and stared across at him. She could not believe it.

'Did you think we were to remain in London indefinitely? You know we have to go to Scotland sometime.'

'Yes—but—not yet—not so soon. Besides, it would be suicidal to embark on such a long journey at this particular time—with winter upon us. The roads will be a quagmire.'

'Which is why we will sail to Scotland. No doubt we will hit the winter gales and the sea will be a trifle rough, but we'll risk it.' He noted the worried frown that puckered her brow. 'Do you really wish to remain in London?'

'Not really. But the prospect of returning to Norwood—a house where I will find no welcome—terrifies me. I know what everyone's feelings will be about our marriage—about me—not least John Ferguson.'

'I agree he stands in need of being charmed, but he'll come round.'

'Still, I'm afraid of what awaits me there. I am not ignorant to the fact that, if I were not your wife, there would be few of your neighbours who would consent to meet me. There will be those who will despise me and speak ill of me behind my back because of who I am, but not speak openly of it because of their loyalty to you. In this respect, as you will have learned from your own past experiences, it is a failing common to both Highlanders and Lowlanders, being a matter of instinct, the distrust of one enemy for the other. I cannot see how it can be overcome. You must have thought of this.'

'I will not pretend that things will be easy at first, and that there must be tolerance on both sides, but you will have my support. In time you will earn their friendship and acceptance—and respect.'

'Yours is the only respect I care about,' she said quietly, meeting his gaze. 'Do I have that?'

Iain was unable to escape the soft bewitchment of those lovely, imploring eyes. 'Of course you do.'

'Still, all things considered, it's a pity you can't divorce me.'

'Is it? And why do you say that?'

'Because then it wouldn't matter what anyone thought. And—I don't want you to stay married to me if you don't want me—if you want someone else. I—I meant what I said. I thought Maria Fraser was beautiful, and I can't blame you for—for…'

'For what, Lorne? Loving her?'

She nodded, struggling to control the trembling that threatened to reduce her to tears. 'Yes.' Her answer was barely audible.

'You little fool,' Iain said, with a mixture of tender and touching desire. 'I have already told you what my feelings are towards her. She would make any man a perfect wife, but she means nothing to me.'

In the dim light Lorne looked at him, her eyes brimming with tears. 'I'm glad,' she whispered simply.

'So am I. You care about that, don't you?'

'Yes, I do care, and I'm not ashamed to admit it.'

'I'm sorry, Lorne. I should have told you about Maria and not let you find out from someone else.' He was not flippant, but serious and troubled.

'Yes, you should.' She smiled faintly. 'But if you don't love her, then it doesn't matter.'

'It's no good dwelling on regrets,' Iain went on quietly. 'In the past we have wronged each other—but what is done is done and we'll have to make the best of what we have. But we can't pretend it didn't happen. If we do there will be times when incidents occur that make us remember, reopening old wounds, and when it does it will affect us in different ways.'

Lorne listened to him, her heart lurching with unexpected dread. Yes, they had wronged each other, and she knew all too well the pain he would feel if she attempted to open one particular wound—the one concerning his brother David. She knew if she were to raise the subject it would make him angry again, and she wasn't entirely certain she wanted to spoil this moment of reconciliation, even though she believed that bringing the matter into the open and talking about it was the only way for them to move forward and put the past behind them.

'There is something I think I should tell you,' he said, 'something you should know. When I left you at Norwood to ride to Stirling, my conscience and I became embroiled in a battle royal. I had told myself that you and I could never belong together, but that one night changed everything.'

'The night I behaved like a shameless wanton,' she whispered.

His relentless gaze locked with hers. 'Shame? I felt no shame. We were lovers. I see no shame in that—and neither should you. Let us call it a gift from fate. We came together for the same reasons, and there was nothing sordid in what we did. We wanted each other—and I had no scruples to ignore that impulse. It's as simple as that.'

His deep voice coming to her in the semi-darkness made all Lorne's senses jolt almost as much as the steady way he was looking at her across the short distance that separated them. Her throat was thick, her mind stunned as she tried to believe that this was really happening. Wanting to hear the rest of what he had to say, she struggled desperately to ignore the sensual pull he was exerting on her.

'Before I arrived back at Norwood I had already decided to ask you to remain with me. I also knew your brothers and Galbraith would make your life hell at Drumgow. I couldn't let you weather that alone—nor could I bear the thought of you going to Galbraith and becoming his wife. The mere thought of him touching you almost drove me insane.'

Lorne gaped at him in astonishment, a peculiar warmth beginning to seep throughout her body. 'Iain, what are you saying—that you—you would have married me—a McBryde?'

'Perhaps—yes. I think I would have—in time,' he said honestly. 'But that was before I reached Norwood and found you gone—and before I learned of the part you had played in your father's escape. That was when my passion for you became doused by bitterness. I tried to hate you, telling myself you thoroughly deserved your fate. I did everything in my power to try to forget you.' His lips twisted with irony. 'Yes—I even contemplated marriage to someone else. But your grandmother and King William put paid to that.'

Lorne swallowed down the hard lump that had risen in her throat. 'How you must have despised me for placing you in that position.'

'I told you I tried to hate you, but I failed miserably.'

'But I know you didn't want to marry me then. You were so hostile towards me.'

'That's only because my hand was forced, and I couldn't see what a treasure I was getting. In five months' time we will have a child, Lorne—our child. What kind of example do you think we will present if we are to be for ever at each other's throats?'

'So—you accept that the child is yours? You do want it?' Renewed hope was beginning to stir in Lorne's breast.

Her question tore through Iain. 'What kind of man would be so unnatural as to not want his own child—his own flesh and blood? Of course I want it. I have an obligation towards both you and the child. I cannot dismiss responsibility. I confess that the thought that you might have used your body to aid your father's escape is acutely repugnant to me. But I believe you when you say that you did not let Kilpatrick make love to you. Any other kind of woman might have been so brazen as to lie about such a thing, and while you might be reckless and extremely foolish at times, I know you couldn't tell an untruth of such magnitude. Besides, you couldn't hide it from me. I would see it in your eyes.'

'Thank you,' she whispered.

'For what?'

'Believing me.'

'My pleasure. I never attempted to earn your regard and did nothing to prove myself worthy of you, but I am determined that will change. I intend to pursue you relentlessly and with every skill I possess—to court you with all the charm and gallantry I can muster. If you make it difficult for me, then it's no more than I deserve.'

'And when do you aim to begin this assault, my lord?' she asked, her cheeks starting to fill with colour as the heady words seeped into her brain.

A roguish grin spread over his face. 'Now.'

'But we will soon be at the house.'

'I know,' he said, 'but we can make a start.'

Lorne did not answer. Then, leaning forward, he stretched out his hands and brushed her cloak aside, and very gently placed his lips in the warm, pulsating hollow of her neck.

What followed when they reached the sanctuary of their room was to be held and cherished. There were no barriers, no pride, just sensations of body and mind. Nothing else mattered, not even tomorrow, when they each knew it might be hostile. They were both determined to leave the past behind, to move on with their lives together, and for Lorne the vision of their future stretching endlessly ahead was as golden as the sun rising over the Scottish hills. But the dark shadow of David's death was still there and always would be, until she had Iain's absolution.

Chapter Eleven

Freezing temperatures frosted the landscape around Edinburgh in a bedazzling array of crystals that glittered beneath the early morning sun, that same sun that peeped through a chink in the curtains like a voyeur, where Lorne nestled in her husband's arms. Stirring from a sleep-contented stupor, she snuggled closer to her male companion and placed her head peacefully in the curve of his shoulder. A fire had been lit and crackled in the hearth, dispelling the chill from the room.

Disturbed, Iain half-opened his eyes and looked down at the golden head beneath his chin. Placing an arm about her, he pulled her closer still, bestowing a good-morning kiss on the top of her head. His mind went back to the memory of their lovemaking the night before, and a satisfied smile curved his lips. He found himself much enamoured of his lovely young wife, with her easy, natural femininity that never failed to stir his ardour.

They lay quiet for a while, flesh against flesh, each aware of the other's warmth and smell. Iain was the first to break the silence.

'Another night aboard that damned ship and I'd have been

forced to think of a way to possess you,' he murmured, planting another kiss on the top of her head. 'You, my love, are adorable.'

Lorne tipped her head back to look at him. 'Will you continue to look at me when I've grown fat with child?'

'I will place you before me at all times so that I can feast my eyes on your beauty. Do you doubt what I say?'

'I believe you,' was her answer, whispered a little unsteadily.

Iain's mouth savoured hers for one blissful moment, and when he raised his head again he released a long sigh and set her away from him. 'As much as I would rather spend a while longer with you, madam, I have things to do.'

'You are not leaving me?' Lorne objected.

'I'm afraid I must. I have to see if John has arrived in Edinburgh. If so, we must leave for Norwood before the weather worsens.'

Lorne followed him across the bed and wrapped an arm around his waist. 'John Ferguson can wait a while,' she breathed, adjusting her body to fit his own. 'The hour is still early.'

Iain's arms enfolded her when she began pressing tantalising little kisses as light as butterfly wings on his lips and chest. Looking down at her, he raised a brow in mock amusement. 'There is always tonight.'

'I know, but I can't wait that long.'

He grinned down at her. 'Shameless hussy.' He chuckled softly. 'I see you have no intention of going back to sleep.'

'None whatsoever. It's much like you said. Another night aboard that ship and I'd have been compelled to come looking for you, too,' she murmured, the cramped conditions on board the vessel bringing them to Scotland having forced her to share a cabin with Jenny. 'We have to make up the time we lost, and there's no time like the present.' Raising her head, she looked up at him, her eyes dark and slumberous, her lips soft and slightly parted. 'Can't I persuade you to stay for just a little while?'

A smile twitched Iain's lips, despite his effort to control it. 'I have every faith in your ability to do so.'

'And I can convince you that we're not meant to separate for at least half an hour?'

'You have cleverly set aside all my arguments,' he replied softly, lowering his mouth to touch the spot below her chin where a pulse gently throbbed. 'I can do nothing more than surrender to your demands.'

A soft expression of warmth and tenderness shone in her eyes. 'I knew you would see things my way,' she whispered, turning her head and ardently placing her lips on his once more.

Lorne was alone in the house when John Ferguson arrived. Her heart was pounding as she met his hard, domineering gaze and felt the power of him. He was still at war with her, a war that was intense and personal.

'I scarcely expected us to meet again,' he said coldly, 'or under such circumstances. I feared this, and would have prevented it, if I could. Like everyone else I've heard of your exploits before ye left Scotland. Now we have ye back in our midst, can we expect a visit from your marauding brothers?'

'I cannot answer that. I am certain they're as opposed to my marriage to Iain as you are.' The smile that touched Lorne's lips was one of irony. 'If I had hoped for a welcome, I can see one is not forthcoming. I also see that nothing is changed. You have not changed.'

'Nay, nor will it. Should any harm come to Iain by your hand or your brothers', you will rue the day ye married him.'

'And I give you warning, John Ferguson. Do not oppose me too much. I know Iain has told you that I carry his child, so I have far more to scheme and fight for than ever before. You could find me a more certain foe than either of my brothers,' she declared coldly. 'I can fight if need be—and as you have learned from my exploits at Inveraray and in my dealings with one Captain Kilpatrick, I succeed.'

'Ye are very sure of yerself.'

Lorne deliberately gentled her tone. If she wanted to improve her relationship with John, which she must strive to do if there was to be any kind of peace at Norwood, she must cast off her pride and pander to his sensibilities. 'I swear that as I live and breathe I will never do anything to hurt Iain, and if I do it will be unintentional.'

'As his wife and mistress of Norwood I shall treat ye with the courtesy which is yer due,' John conceded grudgingly.

'Thank you,' Lorne answered, satisfied to see a responsive glint in his eyes. 'Returning to the house where I was a prisoner does not come easy to me. I desire no more than Iain and our child and to live at Norwood in peace. Because of what happened to his brother in Kinlochalen, I am still not secure in his heart, but with what I do have I am content. Since it was a royal command, Iain and I had no choice but to wed. I was not asked and certainly did not seek it. I have learned—and so should you—that where circumstances cannot be changed they are best accepted with fair grace.'

Despite himself, John rose to that. For Iain's sake, to save him from the consequences of becoming enamoured of Lorne McBryde, he had been the one to send her away—and he had suffered Ian's wrath because of it. The distress of mind this had brought Iain had deeply affected and changed him, and made John regret his action. And now he was most anxious not to let Iain's marriage destroy the close relationship that had developed between them over the years, and it was for this reason that he must accept this situation.

* * *

It was bitterly cold when the Earl of Norwood's cavalcade left Edinburgh. The roads were icy and often dangerous. For Lorne to undertake such a gruelling journey in her pregnant state gave Iain cause for concern and he remained close by at all times in order to keep a watchful eye on her.

As her horse picked its way carefully along the route, Lorne was surprised at how exhilarated she felt to be back in Scotland. She remembered how swiftly she had fallen under the enchantment of the Lowlands and the magnificent Highlands, the very air and the sense of freedom when she had ridden from Inveraray over the wild expanse of landscape with her father and James.

Tears sprang to her eyes at the recollection of her father and brothers. The memory of them conjured their short time together as a family. She had a fierce longing to see Robert and James again, to beg their forgiveness for what they would see as her betrayal by marrying Iain.

When the turrets of Norwood were sighted, snow had begun to fall, cocooning them in a silent white world. Norwood seemed becalmed—like a ship that has lost its mast after a storm. The ride through the gates and into the courtyard was unsettling for Lorne. Men stopped what they were doing and gave their attention to the weary cavalcade, their eyes finally coming to rest on the woman who rode closest to the laird.

Acutely aware of an underlying tension, Lorne looked straight ahead. She felt the eyes of every groom, stable hand and lackey converge on her from every corner of the courtyard, felt their hostility, and she could well imagine their thoughts.

When their horses came to a halt, Iain dismounted and gently lifted Lorne from the saddle, his gaze locking on hers with concern. 'Welcome home,' he murmured, for her ears alone.

Home! Yes, she thought, with little interest just then. Whether she liked it or not, this place was to be her home for the rest of her days. Flora was waiting to greet them, and it gave Lorne a good deal of pleasure to see her again.

Lowering her eyes, Flora made a deep curtsy. 'Welcome to Norwood, Countess.'

Lorne smiled and reached out her hands to her, drawing the woman who smelled of herbs and rose water closer, feeling the flesh of her hands chilled in her grasp. 'Please call me Lorne, as you did when I was here before. Your friendship meant a lot to me then, Flora, and I'm going to need it in the days ahead.'

Flora stiffened slightly at her touch, her blue-grey eyes wary, but after a moment she gently squeezed her hands and smiled. 'You have it. When John sent you away he hoped to change things, but anyone with sight could see how things were between you and the Earl, so I'm not really surprised to see you back.'

Castle Norwood might present a grim outer face to the world, but inside it was one of domesticated comfort. It was inevitable that Lorne would remember the last time she had entered through the iron-studded oak doors, when Iain had drafted in a large contingent of men to guard her and protect the castle from her father and marauding brothers. How long ago that seemed to her now, when in reality it was little more than four months ago.

Feeling the tiredness of the journey, she was impatient to seek her bedchamber. She stood straight and erect, as if carved from stone. Her whole soul seemed to speak through her large eyes, which gazed at the large group of gathered servants.

Iain's eye swept over each and every one of them, sensing their thoughts—their antipathy. Determined to put down all opposition to his marriage, his deep voice rang out in the ancient hall, loud and commanding.

'I would have you meet my wife, Lady Lorne Monroe, Countess of Norwood,' he pronounced. 'It is my wish that you give her welcome, and treat her with due respect as befits my lady. She is no stranger to Norwood, so most of you will be acquainted with her. You know who she is and you are all familiar with recent events,' he went on, recalling their fury at Edgar McBryde's escape, and how they would snatch at any opportunity to work off some of their fury and frustration on the woman who had played a major part in that escape.

'But it is over. Edgar McBryde is dead. The King has stressed his desire for peace and a political union between England and Scotland. This union of a McBryde and a Monroe in marriage is just a small but significant step in achieving that. But it will never be accomplished while the old rivalries and feuding continue. It will be hard, I know, and patience and tolerance is required on both sides. However, if I can put the past behind me, then so can you. If you wish to remain in my employ, you will have to learn to accept Lorne McBryde as my wife, my Countess and mistress of Norwood. If these conditions seem too hard to you, you may leave Norwood. I expect you to give my wife the same loyalty as you do me, and it is your duty to honour her and obey her wishes as if they were mine.'

A collective sigh seemed to rise from them as one by one they began to disperse. Lorne watched them go, realising that their loyalty came out of their love for Iain. When he had begun to speak, at that moment he seemed to grow in stature and his eyes blazed out at the people in the hall. Abruptly she was reminded that this handsome husband of hers possessed a striking magnetism that was capable of taking over the hearts and minds of all those he came into contact with, whose orders were carried out without question or argument.

With something akin to reverence Lorne gazed at him with a profound gratitude shining from her eyes. 'That, my lord, was some speech.'

Iain looked down at her, his expression grave. 'It had to be said.' Suddenly he turned to Flora. 'Be so good as to take Lorne to her room, will you, Flora? It's been a long ride and I know that she's exhausted. See that she rests.'

Observing Lorne's strained, pale features, Flora laid a hand on her arm. 'Come. You look as though you could do with a little care and comfort.'

Flora opened the chamber door and stood aside for the new mistress to enter ahead of her. It was the first time Lorne had been inside Iain's apartments and she was impressed by their comfort. Heavy curtains at the windows shut out the snow-shrouded world, and the well-stoked fire to ward off the chill was a welcome sight. After removing her heavy cloak and placing it on the luxurious quilt of the high curtained bed, she went towards the hearth, holding out her hands to the warmth.

'Well, Flora—who would have thought it,' Lorne said flatly.

Seeing no point in answering the obvious, Flora came to stand beside her. 'Fate certainly has a strange way of changing things. I know Norwood holds many bitter memories for you, but I sincerely hope you will be happy living here.'

'I'm glad you're here, Flora. I always thought of you as my companion and my friend. My days as a prisoner were greatly improved thanks to you. I shall always be grateful to you for that.'

'You do not owe me thanks. I merely did what my conscience dictated—and because I liked you. And for what it's worth, I missed you when you'd gone.'

'I'd like to put everything that happened behind me and look forward to the future, and with the child coming there is something to build a new life for, but how can I when I feel like an infiltrator at Norwood?'

'I won't pretend it's going to be easy for you, but you must try. I'm glad Iain has taken a wife at last. It means I can relinquish my duties here. It will be good to spend more time at home with my husband.' Seeing the worried look enter Lorne's eyes she smiled, understanding what was going through her mind. 'Don't worry. I assure you that I have no intention of deserting you. I know just how daunting the mere thought of running this place must be for you. But with Mrs Lockwood and me to show you how, you'll have everyone eating out of your hand and Norwood running like clockwork in no time at all.'

When Iain finally came to bed he found Lorne in her night attire standing in front of the fire. Without taking his eyes off her still form, without haste he removed his jacket and unfastened his shirt. Concerned when she did not acknowledge his presence, he crossed towards her, sliding his arms about her waist, feeling the now familiar swell of their child.

He stood there, holding her, very still, savouring the feeling. It was a good one, exquisite, one of unbearable joy, one that was becoming achingly familiar the more he was with her. It was deep and strong and quiet. It was peace. Carried away by the touch and the scent of the slender form pressed close to him, he placed a kiss on the top of her shining head and sighed.

'What are you doing?' he murmured at length.

'Thinking,' she answered softly, leaning against the hard rack of his chest. 'Or I was.'

'Then I shouldn't have interrupted you. It's been a long day,' he whispered, drawing her hair aside and tenderly kissing her ear. 'Come to bed.'

'Yes, I will,' she replied, feeling him rest his chin atop her head.

'Are you all right?'

Sliding her arms over his still about her waist, she felt the warmth of his breathing on the side of her face. 'A little tired, perhaps.'

'Would you like to tell me what you were thinking about?'

'I don't think you would like to hear my thoughts.'

'Let me be the judge of that. Try me.'

Lorne sighed. 'I was thinking that it is wrong for me to be here. That I might have committed a sin in marrying you. I was also thinking that I should not have let my grandmother and the King manipulate me or you into marriage.'

'Dear me, these are serious thoughts indeed. Are you saying you regret marrying me?'

'No—I'm not saying that. But—I will confess to being confused at the time.'

'And are you still?'

'No.'

'And do you feel it is wrong being my wife—that it can be no true marriage made under such duress?'

'No, I'm not saying that either.'

'Then—do you believe it is wicked to want me as much as I want you?' Iain murmured, placing his lips on her neck where a pulse gently throbbed.

Lorne closed her eyes and trembled at the delicious sensations shooting through her as his lips gently teased. 'No,' she murmured softly.

'And what of our child? Is that wrong, too?'

'No. The child is one good thing to come out of all that has happened, and for that reason alone it is right that we are together. But our marriage will cause a furore of talk among both the affluent and lesser mortals in and around Norwood.

Your friends and fellow nobles will be scandalised,' she said softly, trailing her fingers long his forearm.

Iain smiled as she voiced her concern. 'Don't worry, my sweet. It will die down soon enough. I am confident you will win them over. When you feel up to it and the weather improves, we will give a ball and invite them all—and they'll come—out of curiosity, if nothing else.' He chuckled softly. 'Those who haven't met you will respond to your beauty and charm and natural breeding. You'll see. Like me, my love, they will find you enchanting and welcome you into their ranks with open arms.'

Lorne had her doubts about that, but she wasn't going to argue.

Clasped together and bathed in warmth, they fell silent, neither of them moving, but Iain sensed that something continued to trouble her. Gently, he turned her round to face him, searching her face for some clue to what she was feeling, but her features were blank.

'What is it, Lorne? Why so melancholy? There is something else, something you're not telling me. I sense it.'

Knowing Iain would not let the matter drop, that he would insist on an answer, she whispered, 'You'll be angry if I tell you.'

'Since when has that stopped you from speaking your mind? Come, tell me.'

Lulled by the warmth and quietness of the room and Iain's amiable mood, raising her eyes she looked at him steadily. 'I—I would like to go to Drumgow?' she said, asking the question she had been too afraid to voice.

Immediately the mood was shattered. The words hung in the air between them like a threatening blade. Iain's arms dropped to his sides and he took a step back.

'No,' he uttered with quiet, controlled anger and absolute finality.

Lorne quailed as she beheld the square set of his broad shoulders, the hardness of his taut jaw and the ice-cold glitter in his eyes. He seemed to emanate the restrained power and unyielding authority she often feared in him. Her mouth went dry and her heart began to beat with a terrifying dread as she sensed he had withdrawn from her, as if those moments of closeness had never been.

'I would prefer it if you do not persist in this foolish determination to confront your brothers.' Since the day of their wedding Iain had gathered and organised his thoughts to this end, knowing Lorne would be drawn back to Drumgow eventually, but he had not expected it to be so soon. Not since the night of the ball had he encountered resistance from this soft and graceful creature with her deceptive air of fragility. But no matter how hard she tried to persuade him, he would not allow her to go to Drumgow.

'Do my wishes count for nothing?'

'In this case nothing at all. Do not suppose that because I married you I will ever go to Drumgow. Like all their arrogant, savage breed, your brothers are still men of too much pride and small judgement, whose most conspicuous talent has always been for violence, and I, for one, would make an end to them.'

Lorne put her hands over her ears. 'Be silent, Iain. I will not listen to this.'

'Yes, you will—you and ultimately anyone else who cares to listen.'

'But you are wrong about them. They can be—'

'Don't defend them to me,' Iain snapped scathingly. 'Are you telling me they have been unjustly maligned? Forgive me if I do not share your new-found faith in your brothers. Have you forgotten that I have less reason to like them? You may cherish a certain nostalgia for Drumgow and Kinlochalen—although how this can be after all that has occurred there in the past defeats me. My own memories are by far less alluring, I do assure you.'

Lorne listened to what he said with understandable dismay. She shrank before the hard, stubborn line that had settled between her beloved's black brows. 'I know,' she whispered.

'Your brothers remain blinkered in their ways,' Iain went on angrily, 'unable to see good as an alternative to evil, or intelligence and common sense as an alternative to thick-headed stupidity. They are lethal, abrasive Highlanders who antagonise everyone with whom they come into contact.'

'Is it so wrong to try to forgive the past?' Lorne dared to ask.

'Not in principle. Practice is a different matter.'

Lorne wished she'd kept silent about her desire to go to Drumgow. Tonight was their first night as man and wife at Norwood, and it was terribly important to her not to ruin it. The worst of it was that for all his curses and spleen, she understood Ian's hatred of her brothers, and she couldn't really blame him.

'I merely expressed a wish to see my brothers,' she murmured. 'Their silence is unendurable.'

'The fact that they have not contacted you is entirely their doing. They clearly feel no compulsion to rush to your side. Ask yourself how angry they must be feeling, as they lurk in their Highland castle—as well as humbled and humiliated— which is in the nature of things. Their enemy, like a common thief, ensnared their sister, stole her virtue and such affection I have no right to, and then married her—and all with the King's blessing—a man who is also their enemy. There can be no question of you going to Drumgow. Do you forget that you are no longer a McBryde?'

Lorne's head came up and her cheeks flamed as though he had struck her. 'Whatever name I am known by now, nothing can alter who I am. No one can take that away from me. I may be your wife, Iain, but my family is still my own.'

His eyes glittered like ice. 'You may visit Drumgow as often as you like within the confines of your imagination, but I will not allow you to travel such distance in midwinter, putting yourself and our child at risk. Is that clear enough?'

'Yes,' she mumbled. He folded his arms across his chest and regarded her with a terrifying firmness. Lorne gave a hopeless sigh and her eyes dimmed with tears. 'Do you have to be so hard—so unforgiving?'

'Unforgiving, yes—but not hard, Lorne. Sensible. I'll be damned and in hell before I set foot inside Drumgow—and if you are hoping to persuade me to allow you to undertake the journey alone, forget it.'

'So you don't care that you will disappoint the King. You never did mean to try to heal the breach, did you, Iain?' She turned away, tears clogging her throat. 'You can be as thick-headed and as stubborn as my brothers.'

Iain stepped close. 'Knowing ours would be a marriage that would heal no wounds, I never did intend trying. I thought you knew that. I found it ran against my conscience. Besides, your brothers have given me no cause to be magnanimous.'

'Oh—stop it,' Lorne cried, with a grimace of pain. Feeling something snap inside her, she turned away, covering her face with her hands. 'Stop it this instant.'

Iain did stop. Seeing her shoulders shaking, he gently turned her round to face him. The sight of her tears drained the last of his anger away. Filled with remorse, he felt a melting inside of him, and a desire to hold her gently and beg her forgiveness. His arms went round her, clasping her tight. Bending his head, he kissed her wet cheek. 'I didn't mean to make you cry. I do not wish to cause you such unhappiness.'

'I'm in no mood to fight with you,' she murmured.

'I have no wish to fight, either,' he said softly, his voice like a caress. 'How quick you are to weep, my love—a weakness due to your condition, I think.'

'I am just as quick to laugh, my lord, as well you know.'

'Aye, and I thank God for it.'

Lorne leaned back in his arms and looked up at him, her expression serious. 'I shouldn't have asked you to let me go to Drumgow. I know how angry any talk of my brothers makes you, but please try to understand how much their silence concerns me.' Iain's lazy smile was so unexpected and so contagious that Lorne's heart warmed.

'I would assume the reason you suddenly want to see them is to secure their blessing. Is that correct?'

She nodded. Struggling with herself, she managed a smile, a weary and infinitely sad smile, but one full of gentleness.

'In which case, knowing that you are capable of doing something rash to spite me, let me offer you a solution to your predicament which is quite simple and might appeal to you. Write to them if you wish,' he suggested quietly, watching the reactions play across Lorne's expressive face. 'I have no objection to that. I will see that the letter is taken to Drumgow.'

'You would allow me to do that?'

'I'm not the callous brute you might think. I don't expect you to break with your brothers completely.' The joy that flared in his wife's green eyes was almost blinding. Iain felt something dark, heavy and formless stir and rise up in his heart and fly away.

Slipping her hands beneath his shirt and encircling his waist, Lorne buried her face against his naked flesh, her breasts measuring the steady rise and fall of his chest as he breathed. The contact was like an exquisite explosion somewhere deep inside her. Unseen hands caressed her hair, exploring the length and texture, before coming to rest at either side of her face, the long, firm fingers touching the nape of her neck, thumbs sliding with sensuous slowness across her cheeks. Lowering his head, Iain kissed her long and deep before she rested her face on his chest once more, closing her eyes and inhaling the manly smell of him.

'I love you,' she whispered.

'I know you do.'

Iain stooped and picked her up, holding her as if she weighed no more than a feather. Carrying her to bed, he set her down and lay beside her, his embrace unbreakable as his lips claimed hers. That night he made love to her with painstaking gentleness, kissing and caressing her like a virtuoso playing a fine and beautiful instrument, in an effort to dispel any fears she might have that his invasion might harm the child. It was long into the night before their bodies finally succumbed to the lethargic aftermath of repeated consummation.

When Lorne lay with her head on her husband's chest and felt the slowly cooling furnace of his body, she knew how complete their passion had been, for there was nothing left within her that she could give him, and what he had given her defied the telling, because words were simply inadequate and not enough to define—but how she yearned for him to tell her that he loved her as deeply as she loved him.

The dark closed around the bed and the woman who had lost her heart. And the man sleeping beside her knew he held the key.

For better or worse Norwood was Lorne's home and she was its mistress, and there would be many responsibilities thrust upon her. With a hard-headed realism she knew what had to be done. The fears she'd harboured about her reception at Norwood were slowly allayed during the weeks that followed as she set to proving herself. As she began to make decisions and take more and more tasks upon herself, things settled down, and when she was in her fifth month of preg-

nancy, apart from John's quiet antipathy towards her, her
small world was irrevocably won, much to her husband's admiration and satisfaction.

Her nights spent in Ian's arms, as naked and unashamed
they proudly bestowed the beauty of their bodies on each
other, were a timeless enchantment.

Iain was dismissive of Robert and James McBryde, of
what their reaction would be to the news that their sister had
wed their most bitter enemy, but when a missive, short and
to the point, arrived at Castle Norwood, the issue could no
longer be evaded. Robert and James would be in Stirling two
weeks hence. If their sister was well enough to travel, they
would meet her there.

Iain was seriously concerned about allowing Lorne to
embark on such a perilous journey so far into her pregnancy,
which would have to be undertaken on horseback, but he reluctantly agreed to it.

Fortunately the weather was reasonably fair when the
Monroe retinue left Norwood, but when they eventually
reached Stirling, situated between the Lowlands and the
Highlands and fortified behind the massive, whinstone
boulders of the town walls and with its castle towering on top
of a frowning rock, they were being buffeted by an icy March
wind that penetrated their clothes and chilled them to the
marrow. The house where they were to reside for their short
stay in the old town was impressive and spacious.

The following morning, after confirming that the McBryde
brothers had arrived in Stirling, with her husband, John and
Archie, Lorne walked the short distance to the tavern. The air
inside was thick with ale, food and sweat, and the greasy
smell of tallow candles.

A room had been allotted to the two Highlanders to entertain their guests. Lorne and Iain entered alone. Robert, his weatherbeaten face surly and suspicious, looked at Iain Monroe. It may have been the flash of light from the open door or it may have been the silence that suddenly descended on the room, a silence that could be felt—almost like something physical—but, whatever it was, it sent a cold shiver down the Highlander's spine.

Robert recalled the last time he had been in the presence of this man—the day the lad, David Monroe, had been killed and Iain Monroe had ridden into Kinlochalen at the head of his men. He also recalled this Lowlander's unforgettable, unforgivable outpourings that day, and he silently cursed him anew.

Their eyes met and locked, cold and unyielding, the dislike and distrust of each other clearly as great as they had ever been.

Robert was the first to speak, addressing his sister. 'I canna tell ye how it angers me to see ye yield so readily to Monroe and the King's will.'

The sudden vehemence of Robert's words brought a shudder to Lorne's spine. His coldness, his lack of the most elementary politeness, disappointed and hurt her deeply.

Robert's gaze shifted back to Iain. 'I will speak to my sister alone.'

Without shifting his eyes from Robert's, Iain nodded. 'You lay a finger on my wife,' he warned, his tone low and deadly, 'and I'll carve you into so many pieces you'll be fit for nothing but fish bait. With all the excuses I have to kill you now, 'twould be folly to add another.'

'Please—stop this—both of you,' Lorne begged, throwing Iain a look of anguish. 'We are not here to settle old scores. It's all right, Iain,' she said, placing a hand on his arm. 'Do as Robert asks. Please wait outside.'

Raising Lorne's hand, Iain placed a reassuring kiss on her fingers, and from Robert's face he could see pure madness flame in his eyes at this simple, open gesture of affection. The balance of peace was extremely delicate, so delicate that Iain conceded to Lorne's request and moved back to the door. However, he had no intention of leaving the room and his wife altogether, so he remained in the shadows in case his near presence precipitated a crisis. With his shoulder propped against the wall and his arms folded, the orange glow from the fire gave his face a satanic look. His features remained impassive, his reserve hiding the steel core within him, but each man present was aware of it and wary.

Standing beside his brother, James, whose affection for his sister had deepened during the many days they had been together when they had escaped from Inveraray with their father, stepped forward and took her hand. His eyes passed warmly over her strained features.

'Lorne—how are ye, lass?'

'I am well, thank you, James,' she replied, her lips trembling in a smile as she gave him a look of gratitude, relieved that one of her brothers could give her a kind word.

Robert scowled at his brother. 'That'll do, James,' he said, his voice holding a ring of authority that had James releasing Lorne's hand and stepping back a pace. Robert's eyes passed over his sister, imagining her swollen abdomen concealed beneath the folds of her cloak. His expression was stern and pitiless.

It was a few minutes before Robert had finished his speech, designed to demonstrate his severe displeasure at her conduct and her lack of restraint, and carelessness of her reputation while she had been Iain's captive.

'Why did ye conceal what had transpired between you and Monroe when we met at Arrochar?'

'I saw no reason to tell you. When I left Norwood I truly believed I would never see Iain again. I entered into this most solemn contract with all my mind, my heart and soul, loving Iain more than I believed it was possible to love another human being—far, far more than he will ever love me, I think,' she declared proudly, her head thrown back and her eyes blazing with defiance, daring her brother to challenge her words. 'Rightly or wrongly there it is, and how can you censure me for seeking to make better a situation that for me might have been infinitely worse?

'Iain is the father of the child I carry. How it came about is not important any more. I know you disapprove and I accept that. What I cannot accept are the reasons why you disapprove. You make poor excuses for despising Iain's behaviour towards me—and other misdemeanours I know nothing about, I shouldn't wonder, when your own conduct wouldn't bear too close scrutiny.'

'Enough.'

Robert shouted the word, the force of it bringing Iain to a rigid stance at the back of the room and a murderous glint to enter his eyes, while his hand closed convulsively round the hilt of his dagger. Despite his apparent nonchalance, he was watching the scene across the room closely and listening intently. His jaw was rigid and a muscle twitched dangerously in the side of his neck. It took a physical effort for him to maintain his calm and stop himself going to his wife. Even though he knew she would be going through hell inside, unless her brother became violent towards her he had to let her get this meeting over with in her own way.

'Robert,' Lorne said hoarsely, moving a step closer, feeling as if the world were turning upside down. 'What is happening to us? We are brother and sister. Why are we fighting like enemies?'

'Ye have only ta say the word that ye'll leave Monroe and return with us to Drumgow ta bring us together.'

Lorne stared at him in shocked disbelief, a bitter taste of anger and disappointment filling her mouth. So that was it. That was the reason he had agreed to meet her. Finally she murmured. 'You ask this of me, knowing I am to bear his child? Must I remind you of the conditions the King laid down—that there must be no reprisals?'

'If ye leave Monroe of yer own accord, it will not be seen as reparation. You are not a Catholic and were not married by Catholic rite—divorce is possible, though 'twill be fraught with complications.'

All the blood drained from Lorne's face and she looked at him aghast. 'Divorce? Never! I will not even consider it. I will not prejudice either my own honour or that of my child. Catholic or Protestant, my marriage vows are equally as sacred to me. Without Iain I have no future,' she added in tones of finality. 'I cannot—will not—agree to do what you ask. It would be like tearing out my heart. I am Iain's wife. My place is with him.'

Robert stared down at her cold eyed. 'And that is yer final word?'

'No other is possible.' Taking a step back she said, 'Since there seems no purpose in prolonging this discussion, I will leave you now.'

She realised that her hope to be drawn unconditionally back into the McBryde fold was irremediably lost, and for a reason she was powerless to prevail against—her deep and abiding love for her husband. Her chin was up and she was breathing quickly, with defiance and pride, not with fear or remorse. She had an exultant moment of triumph as she straightened her shoulders and turned her back on her brothers.

Only then did she see Iain. Her heart almost burst with gratitude. She might have known he would not have left her to face Robert alone. Knowing he must have heard every word she had said, as she walked away from her brothers towards this incredible man, the world crumpled and all that existed for her was him. Clasping her hands in front of her, she took her place by his side in an act of obeisance.

Iain gazed down at her, pride bursting inside him at how she had handled the situation. He had been mesmerised as he had listened to the sweet sound of her voice, caught somewhere between torment and tenderness as she had made her astonishing admission. It was the most achingly poignant moment of his life, and the shattering emotions he felt made his chest ache.

Lorne loved him despite all he had done to her. She had just stood by him when her brothers had branded him evil, wanted him when he'd incarcerated her in his fortress against her will, and forgiven him his crimes against her. She had become his wife and filled his life with purpose, with laughter and joy, and was soon to be delivered of their child—and he loved her for it. Yes, he did.

'Thank you,' was all he said.

Tipping her head back, she gazed up at him. 'You're welcome. Take me home, Iain. There's nothing more to be said.'

'I will. But first, I wish to have a word with your brothers— in private. Wait with John and Archie in the other room.'

'You give me your word that you will not anger them further? Promise me you will be tactful and not incite them to violence.'

Tact and diplomacy were tools Iain would need in handling this affair with her brothers. 'Trust me,' he murmured gently.

Obediently Lorne opened the door, turning and looking back at her brothers. 'Deep in my heart I knew you would not forgive me. You are still governed and too steeped in the ways of the past to do that. But no matter what you think of me, I shall always remain your loyal, loving sister.'

Iain narrowed the distance between himself and the two men with the stealth of a predator. The tension and hostility in the room was palpable. Iain stopped three yards from them, emanating a wrath so forceful Robert took a step back.

'We have nothing more ta say to each other, Monroe,' Robert growled.

'I have plenty to say to you, McBryde,' Iain returned, moving in closer to gain a more dominating position, his face hard and set, eyes narrowed and as cold as steel.

'Be warned, Monroe. If ye have any sense, ye'll leave us.'

Iain's lips curled with scorn. 'Do you think I care for your threats?'

'You made a serious error when ye took our sister. You made an even more serious one when ye seduced her.'

'I accept that. But it is in the past and better left dead. What you ask of your sister is contemptible. Did you really think she would go with you? Did you really think I would allow her to? As for divorce—you can forget it. Lorne is under my protection now. You no longer have a say in her future.'

'It canna be no true marriage, made under duress. Lorne is as much yer prisoner now as she was before.'

'Correction. She is my wife. My feelings where she is concerned are my own affair—to be shared with her, but what I will say is that I will not break faith with her, and she has nothing to fear from me.'

Iain spoke with such quiet conviction that Robert grudgingly believed him.

'If you have any feeling for your sister at all, you will not persist with this, but wish her well. Is your hatred of me so great that you cannot put it aside for her sake—to accept her offer of love and conciliation?' A brief moment's pause ensued, a moment in which Iain searched the Highlander's stony profile for some hint of softening. Seeing nothing but the stubborn thrust of his square jaw and the glint of determination in his eyes, he turned and strode towards the door, the heels of his boots ringing sharp on the stone flags. He turned and looked back. 'Since his Majesty was anxious to join your sister and I in marriage in order to bring some kind of peace between our two families, if he should hear of this he will not be lenient.'

'His Majesty may indulge in vain dreams,' Robert countered with scorn. 'I concede 'tis a noble effort on his part. But with no due respect, Monroe, the King would be wise ta realise that there is not the slightest chance of peace between us.'

With a shrug Iain turned away. 'Speak to me not of respect, McBryde, in any form. You know not the meaning of the word.'

Chapter Twelve

Past all rational thought, not until Lorne was alone with Iain in their bedchamber did she give vent to her feelings. She went into his arms that opened wide to her, then closed around her with stunning force. His hand cradled her head against his chest as she wept bitter tears of loss and regret, and not until she was all cried out did he take her face between his strong hands and say 'I love you.'

She gazed at him, unbelieving. 'You do? You love me?'

'Yes—love.' He smiled and bent to rest his cheek for a moment against her sweet-smelling hair. 'I know you've waited for me to say that, but because of who you are, and everything that has happened, I couldn't say it. I believed I hadn't the right to love you. I was afraid—afraid that all the souls of my ancestors would rise up and condemn me for it. But I do love you, Lorne,' he murmured, again looking into her brilliant eyes, without strife, but quiet and deep. 'You have become as much a part of my flesh as my heart. You are a warm, courageous, remarkable young woman. I love you so much. You are my life. I want nothing but you.'

'And I love you,' she whispered, unable to stem the

torrent of tears pouring from her eyes—tears of immense joy.

'I know you do, my darling,' he murmured, tenderly wiping the tears from her cheeks with his thumbs. 'I see it shining in your eyes every time you look at me.'

An icy wind blew over Stirling the following morning when Lorne left the house with Jenny to visit the market. They were accompanied by Archie, who was to keep an eye out for any offending cutpurse. Lorne was in a melancholy mood as she wondered if her brothers had left for Drumgow, and had little enthusiasm for any of the items on display on the many stalls. Leaving the throng, they were drawn beneath a low, dark opening into a narrow wynd, where there were several thriving shops and a tavern. Unfortunately Jenny slipped on the icy cobbles and fell heavily, emitting a cry of pain as her head hit the metal ring of an empty hogshead, just one of many stacked against the wall of the tavern.

Lorne fell to her knees beside her. 'Goodness, Jenny! How badly are you hurt?' she cried.

Jenny clutched her head. 'It—it's my head,' she gasped, a trickle of blood oozing through her fingers from a cut on her temple.

Lorne immediately dispatched a concerned-looking Archie back to the house to fetch Iain and any other help that was available. In an attempt to make Jenny more comfortable while they waited, she placed one of the packages beneath her head to act as a pillow, her concern deepening when her maid didn't open her eyes. She seemed almost dead, so still was she.

Curious onlookers, who had gathered to gape, began to move away and the wynd became quiet. After a few minutes a tall man shrouded in a caped cloak emerged from the tavern, uttering a low curse on finding his progress obstructed by a kneeling Lorne and her prostrate companion. Impatiently he stepped briskly around them, and then stopped dead.

At first Lorne didn't look at him. 'I'm so sorry,' she apologised sincerely, speaking to his feet. 'My friend has slipped on the ice. She's hurt her head.'

Totally ignoring the injured woman, the man's eyes were fixed on Lorne.

When he neither moved nor spoke, she looked up at him. The ripples of shock spread from the epicentre of her stomach to every part of her body. Very slowly she drew herself up, staring at him in disbelief, for the man was none other than that hard-bitten warrior, Captain Kilpatrick. In spite of the lines of fatigue that marred his handsome face, she would have recognised those cruel, carved features anywhere. His eyes were like cold, blue steel. The memory of their encounter at Inveraray was enough to make her want to take to her heels, and she would have, were it not for Jenny.

'Captain Kilpatrick!' she gasped.

Captain Kilpatrick arched one brow, cool and reserved. Ever since their last encounter, hatred for this woman had nestled like a tiger in his heart. His actions of that night at Inveraray, combined with his failure to recapture Edgar McBryde, had so angered the Earl of Argyll that he had been brought before a military court. He had exposed himself to the criticism and odium of his superiors, and by the time they had done with him his military career was in ruins. The indignity of being driven away, as a dog is kicked aside when it embarrasses its master, was almost too great to endure.

'Well, well! Our paths seem destined to cross, do they not, Molly Blair—or should I call you Lorne McBryde?'

Lorne went numb as he stared at her, that hateful, cocksure smile she clearly remembered fixed in place. He swayed a little. She smelled liquor on him. She tried to compose her features, but the fluttering sensation in the pit of her stomach persisted. He was drunk and dangerous.

'I am after your blood, Lorne McBryde. You committed a crime against the Crown, proving yourself a traitor in my eyes—although were you to hang, you would not rank high on the list of martyrs,' he sneered. 'The same could be said of your father, had he not escaped the Gallows Tree. I swore that when I caught up with you I would tear the life out of you with my bare hands, and by God I meant it.'

Lorne shrank back, aware of Jenny gasping and pulling at her skirts, having come to and been frightened by what was happening, but somehow she couldn't look away from the man who was threatening her. She gasped when he stepped closer, his arms encircling her and preventing flight. Even as she drew breath to scream, he clamped his hand over her mouth, dragging her into a dark alley leading off into a small court. It was in one of the houses opening on to it that he rented rooms. Hauling a struggling Lorne up a steep flight of dangerous, icy steps to one of the upper storeys, he shoved her inside.

Iain, John and Archie arrived in the alley with a litter to convey Jenny back to the house. When Iain saw the young woman lying in an unconscious state on the cobbles, he dropped to one knee beside her, looking around for his wife. He shook Jenny none too gently in an attempt to rouse her. 'Jenny—answer me. Where is Lorne?' He breathed a sigh of relief when her eyes flickered open.

'Oh, sir—something terrible has happened to her—I just know it. She—she's gone…' Jenny's voice died away and her eyes fluttered closed as once again darkness engulfed her, but Iain's shaking brought her back momentarily. 'A—a man came—and—and he took her away,' she whispered, trying to fight the darkness, but feeling herself losing the battle. 'I know nothing beyond that. You—you must go after her before he does her harm.'

Iain's brain refused to function as his senses told him something was badly wrong. 'Gone? Gone where? And who was this man?' But it was useless. When Iain raised her, her head fell back. She was like a rag doll in his arms. He looked at John. 'We'd best get her back to the house. She must be tended at once. Archie, send for the physician. Tell him it's urgent.'

It wasn't until Jenny was lying on her bed that Iain turned to John, his face hard, his eyes blazing with a savagery that John hadn't seen in a long time. 'It's those damned brothers of hers who have taken her—I'd stake my life on it.'

Immediately they left for the tavern, finding Lorne's brothers in the yard. They were on the point of leaving Stirling.

Robert paused in the act of mounting his horse, his face almost comical in its disbelief as he stared at his most bitter enemy, who was striding purposefully towards him. 'Monroe! I thought we'd said all there was to say. Have ye come to bid us farewell?' he remarked with biting sarcasm.

'You know damn well why I'm here.'

Robert's expression was one of honest puzzlement. 'I do?'

Quickly Iain looked at James, and back to Robert. He shook his head as though to clear it, trying to ignore the cold feeling of dread that was beginning to uncurl in the pit of his stomach and spread its tentacles throughout his body. 'You mean to tell me that you don't have Lorne—that you haven't taken her?'

Concern flared in both brothers' eyes. It was James that spoke, his voice strained.

'What are ye saying?'

'You don't know?' Iain spat accusingly, refusing to believe they might not have taken her.

'No,' Robert answered. 'If we did, we wouldna ask. Tell us, Monroe, and be quick about it.'

'She has been abducted. Naturally, I had every reason to believe you had taken her.'

Robert's eyes flamed. 'Lorne has made her decision. James and I have decided ta leave her to her fate. We were about to leave for Drumgow, but this changes things.'

Momentarily distracted, the sound of clattering hooves from the other side of the courtyard turned all their heads. The newcomer was a young man. Soaked and muddy, it was clear he had ridden far. Recognising Robert and James, he dismounted, and with long strides he came across to them. Iain looked at him with steely eyes. Of medium height, markedly upright in bearing, and with a serious countenance, he bore no likeness whatsoever in looks or physique to his older brother, Duncan Galbraith.

Robert acknowledged him with a blank face and a brief nod. 'Rory! I didna expect ta see ye here in Stirling.'

'I'm on my way back to Edinburgh from Kinlochalen.'

Though he had no fondness for Duncan Galbraith, Robert's opinion of his younger brother's devotion to family and duty was high. He turned to Iain. 'This is Rory Galbraith,' he offered.

Quickly the studious young man looked at Iain. If he thought it strange to find the three of them together, he gave no sign of it. His manner was civil but still, wary and noticeably more courtly than the McBrydes. He nodded briefly. 'Your servant, sir.'

Iain ignored him, for it was at that moment that James, impatient to learn what had befallen his sister, stepped forward.

'Ye were about to tell us about Lorne, Monroe. Get on with it.'

Quickly Iain told them what he knew. 'We must find her,' James said, clearly worried as to what could have befallen his sister.

'I'll come with you,' Rory told them, already passing the reins of his horse to a hovering stable lad.

'If we return to the house, her maid might have recovered consciousness and be able to throw some light on who might have taken her,' John suggested, trying his best to ignore his Highland companions. As much as he would like to see all three of them consigned to hell, he could not deny that, if they were to find Lorne unharmed, their help would be beneficial.

It was a relief to find Jenny lying in bed with her eyes open.

'Jenny, it is imperative that you try to remember what happened,' Iain said, trying to stifle his impatience as he looked down at the pale young woman with her head bandaged. 'Did you recognise the man who took her?'

'No, but she called him Captain Kilpatrick. I'm almost certain that's what his name was.'

Iain's eyes sprang to vivid life, and his face became contorted as he absorbed the name, one single, appalling thought lancing through his brain like an arrow through flesh. Kilpatrick had Lorne! The implications of this were too terrible to contemplate. He straightened slowly, his jaw clenched. 'My God!' His voice vibrated about the room, hurtling violently against the walls as his formidable rage began to grow, but he quickly pulled himself together, fear for his wife overcoming all other emotions. 'Where did he take her, Jenny?' he demanded, gripping her shoulders. 'For God's sake, tell me.'

'They disappeared into an alley—close to where you found me.'

Even as she uttered the words Iain was already running down the stairs to the men waiting below.

Within seconds he had left the house, with the others close on his heels.

Entering the alley and passing into the small court where Jenny had seen Lorne disappear with her abductor, with his heart pounding, Iain paused to take stock of his surroundings. There was no way out, so Kilpatrick had to be behind one of the doors facing into the court—but which one? It was Lorne's scream coming from the upper storey that had him bounding up the long flight of slippery steps to the source of that noise, sharply instructing her brothers to wait in the alley. Reluctantly they obeyed, but all their senses were attuned to what was happening above, their bodies tensed, ready to go bounding up the steps after him at any second.

Bursting in through the door, Iain stopped, taking in the flurry of his wife's petticoats as she strained beneath the straddling Kilpatrick at a glance.

Immediately alert by the opening of the door, Kilpatrick's loss of control had not weakened the instincts bred during years of soldiering. His lust for ravishing the woman beneath him was overlaid by the ingrained habits of survival. Dragging Lorne with him, with the agility of a panther he sprang to his feet, looking towards the door.

With superb control, sword in hand, Iain took in his surroundings, the sight that met his eyes sending cold, merciless fury charging through every pore in his body. His eyes were deadly, his face as if carved from marble, hard and ice cold, his utter contempt for Kilpatrick manifest in the lift of his arrogant head and the curl of his lip.

'Take your hands off my wife, damn you.'

At the sight of her husband Lorne almost collapsed with relief. Her nightmare was almost at an end.

Kilpatrick gaped, his eyes fixed on the man who filled the doorway in awful recognition. The two men had met on occasion during their military years, but they had no particular liking for each other and had spent little time in each other's company.

'Your wife?' His eyes went from one to the other, as though confronted by twin spectres. When realisation of what he had done sank in, pure madness flamed in his eyes. He became once more insane with hate and a lust for revenge. Still holding Lorne's wrist, he jerked her brutally towards him, spinning her round so that she stood in front of him, facing her husband, tightening his iron-thewed arms as she kicked and struggled in an attempt to free herself.

'Your *wife* and I have unfinished business, Monroe. All my life I have been a soldier first and foremost, and this bitch's scheming finished me at Inveraray,' he hissed, his lips drawn back over his teeth in a savage snarl. 'So, you see, I have an account to settle with her.'

'Any account to be settled will be settled by me. Now release her,' Iain commanded, his voice cold and lethal and his eyes as penetrating as dagger thrusts.

Kilpatrick had neither the means to hand nor the clarity of mind to challenge him. Against all expectations he threw his captive from him and glared at his adversary. Respectful of the threatening blade, he kept his distance.

'It appears, Kilpatrick,' Iain mocked, 'that my arrival has cheated you out of the pleasure of ravishing my wife. It would also appear that your passions for her have quite upset your reason.'

'She was not your wife when she whored herself at Inveraray—and she gave a fair impression of being one,' he sneered. 'In fact, her performance was so convincing that I suspect she has experience of that not-so-noble profession.'

'And you would do well to consider what you say. I have excuses enough to kill you—it is vain to add another by bandying insults about her. This lady is my wife, rightful mistress of Norwood, and she is carrying my child. As for you, I won't mind killing you.' He took Lorne's trembling hand and drew her towards him, seeing the strain of her ordeal showing on her face. 'Are you all right?'

She nodded, swallowing hard.

'Then go below,' he ordered her. 'There you will find John Ferguson and your brothers.'

Sick with worry and despair, Lorne protested, 'No—not unless you come, too.'

'This is a matter between me and Kilpatrick.' There was a tensing of the muscles of Iain's lean jaw and a feral gleam in his eyes when he looked once more at Kilpatrick. 'You will answer for your attack on my wife. I see I find you at a disadvantage and that you do not carry your sword. Get it and prepare to defend yourself. We will settle this here and now.'

Kilpatrick feared no man and was renowned for his swordsmanship, but Iain Monroe held a deadlier blade than most. Monroe's reputation with both pistol and sword was an enviable and well-known fact. Kilpatrick's face was drawn and waxen white, and the hiss that he emitted was more venomous and more fearful than any snake. 'Aye, and it's unlikely that you will emerge from this encounter alive. I'll see you in hell before I'm finished with you.'

Lorne gripped Iain's arm in alarm. 'Iain,' she cried. 'Please—you cannot do this.'

Iain gave her an exasperated glare. 'Stay out of this,' he ordered harshly. 'It is no longer your affair.' He shoved her out of the door, telling her to hold on to the wooden rail and to tread with care on the slippery steps.

Refusing to accept defeat, a guttural sound rumbled from deep in Kilpatrick's chest and crimson hate filled his sight. He launched himself across the distance that separated him from the other man. Unable to avoid the forceful assault, Iain lunged out with his fist when his sword clattered to the floor. The two men grappled ferociously, becoming locked in a frenzied thrashing of mortal combat, strained in a battle of pure strength, hammering each other with blows that would have broken the bones of lesser men. In physique and strength Kilpatrick was an equal match for Iain, and the insane fury, combined with the fear that he was about to be thwarted yet again, only added to that strength. But then Iain's fist landed beneath his jaw with a sickening crunch, jerking his head back.

Picking her way carefully down the steps, when Lorne saw her brothers she begged them to assist Iain. Vaguely she wondered what they were doing there, but she was too distressed and worried about Iain to clutter her mind with further complications.

Robert didn't need any prompting. For a man so large he moved with incredible speed, taking the steps two at a time. On entering the room and seeing Kilpatrick stagger to his feet, surrendering to a rage that was about to become out of control, he behaved as he always did—with savage violence. Roughly he flung Iain aside.

'Leave it,' he hissed. 'Kilpatrick's mine.'

Finding himself unexpectedly confronted by this rage-filled Highlander, recognising him and having further cause to fear for his life, Kilpatrick backed away.

'What is it, Kilpatrick?' Robert taunted, his fists bunched. 'Don't you have the guts to fight—unless it's an old, ailing man hiding on the moor or a defenceless pregnant woman?'

He became like an enraged bull. Reaching out, he grasped Kilpatrick's shirt at the neck and hauled him forward, shaking him like a dog. 'Looks like the tables have turned, eh?' he growled, and with a forward jerk of his head he butted the already beaten and weakened man in the face, watched in grinning satisfaction as he sank to his knees, clutching his busted nose.

Realising that if he was to survive he would have to help himself, with a bellow of rage Kilpatrick launched himself in a soaring leap at the Highlander with a flailing of arms, only to find himself rendered incapable when Robert's massive fist struck him squarely in the groin. Reeling backwards, he stumbled out of the open door on to the icy step. Slipping and losing his balance, he fell heavily against the wooden balustrade, which splintered and cracked beneath his weight. Unable to regain his footing, with a look of absolute astonishment registering in his eyes, he fell backwards. There was a moment's shocked silence when he seemed to pause and clutch at the empty air, before plummeting to the yard three storeys below, his head hitting the cobblestones with a nauseating thud.

Iain and Robert came down the steps and bent over Kilpatrick's limp form, which was lying grotesquely with blood pouring from his head.

'Seems I've done for him,' Robert said to Iain.

'Aye, but he's not worth hanging for.'

Robert eyed him questioningly.

'He fell,' Iain said. 'The broken rail speaks for itself.' His lips twisted with irony. 'But worry not, McBryde. This will be added to your other crimes and, in time, like the rest of us you'll have to answer to the Almighty.' His expression became hard when he looked down at Kilpatrick, and when he next spoke—almost as if he were speaking to himself—his voice was low and filled with loathing. 'If you hadn't killed him, I would have.'

Taking a last look at the dead man and seeing that his eyes were already glazed over, Iain turned and looked at his wife standing beside Rory. Her face was deathly pale and she was shaking like a leaf, her hands clutching her torn cloak at her throat. Taking her in his arms, Iain felt a surge of deep compassion as she huddled against his breast like a child.

'Don't be frightened. It's over. Kilpatrick is dead, my love.'

Lorne could hardly hear him as she clung to him convulsively. The terror of the short time she had been Kilpatrick's prisoner seemed to have eaten into her. She opened her lips to speak, but they were trembling too much for her to utter a word.

Suddenly she burst into tears and Iain sighed with relief. She was safe now that the terror and spectre of Kilpatrick was drawing away from her, and he rocked her as tenderly as he would a babe. 'Weep, weep, my love, if it helps,' he murmured gently, his lips against her hair. 'He can't hurt you now.'

All the rancour seemed to have disappeared from the McBryde brothers' faces. It had happened the moment they learned of Lorne's disappearance, when the three of them had been brought together by mutual concern. They moved closer, feeling oddly helpless and clumsy when confronted by this outpouring of their sister's terror. Her husband's face was white, and for a moment they felt a remarkable kinship with him. Kinship and sympathy, too, and they understood the agony he must have gone through when he'd realised she was missing.

The first thing Lorne did on reaching the house was to go and see Jenny.

Her eyes were closed, but she was not asleep. When she saw her mistress bending over her, she gasped and clutched her hand. 'Oh, Miss Lorne! Thank God! I was so worried about you when that man took you away.'

Lorne smiled down at her and gently took her hand. 'He didn't hurt me. It's thanks to you Iain found me before he could do me any harm. But don't you worry your head about that. You took a nasty knock when you fell, so try to sleep.'

Lorne returned to the others. However, before she entered the room, she heard heated words being exchanged, and she was sure it was Rory's voice that was raised in anger. Pushing open the door, she went inside. Her brothers were standing together by the hearth, while her extremely irate husband was striding up and down with his hands clasped behind his back and with no hint of softness in the marble severity of his face. He was clearly furious at something Rory must have said, and when Rory spoke she knew what it was that had so angered him. In her absence, one of her brothers or Rory had mentioned that fateful day in Kinlochalen when Iain's brother had died. She felt her heart contract, for the moment she had dreaded had come.

'I remember the circumstances of my meeting with your brother all too well,' Rory said forcefully, undaunted by the Earl of Norwood's wrath.

Moving further into the room, Lorne shrank with horror and put her hands to her face. 'For pity's sake, Rory—say no more,' she cried.

Rory turned to look at her in surprise. 'Why not? Your husband talks of all Highlanders as barbarians. He has the misguided opinion that we're all the same—that we steal each other's cattle and kill our neighbours and burn their homes indiscriminately.' His voice suddenly changed as he added, quite calmly, as though making a simple statement of fact, 'It is time he learned there are some of us who are not so vicious, that we don't all bear grudges, and that there are people who are farmers, innkeepers and blacksmiths— ordinary, simple folk, who wish to go about their business and be left in peace.'

'I know, but please—please stop,' she begged. 'We don't speak of what happened—Iain won't—'

'What? Listen? No, Lorne,' Rory said firmly, knowing that what he had to say would open up many painful wounds in all those present, but he plunged recklessly on through this madcap folly with all the gift of youth.

'Out of stubbornness, perhaps, despite being his wife, your husband still harbours the belief that you are the irre-concilable enemy of his family and of the person he once held most dear—his brother. It is clear to me that the mis-understanding of the day he died has grown to such an extent that the time has come to put the record straight.' Disregarding the Earl's icy, murderous expression, Rory boldly stood his ground as the older man bore down on him, eyeing him relentlessly, a look of indescribable disgust twisting his face.

'I haven't lost my memory of that day, Galbraith, and I would thank you to keep your mouth shut.'

Tears sprang to Lorne's eyes. Iain's scorn was more that she could stand. 'Please, Rory,' she pleaded softly, her eyes appealing to him in humble supplication. 'Say no more. This is not the time for memories or regrets.'

'I will not be silent, Lorne—not when I can see how this thing is still tearing you apart. It has to be said—and by my reckoning, it is long over due.' A gleam of anger and deter-mination lit up his eyes and, unafraid, he moved to stand close to the towering, glowering presence of the Earl of Norwood. 'I, more than anyone else, know what happened on the day your brother died. I was there, and for the short time Lorne knew him she was devoted to him.'